Praise for the Davis W[...]

DOUBLE [...] (#4)

"Seriously funny, wicke[...]

"As impressive as the a[...]
the details concerning [...]
The author never fail[...]
action, and intrigue she loads [...] this immensely fun series."

— *Kings River Life Magazine*

"Davis has made her Way in this delightfully entertaining tour de force. The author's descriptive and creative narrative pulled me in immediately in this fun-filled and action-packed drama that quickly became a page-turner as I could not put this book down until the last sentence was read."

— *Dru's Book Musings*

DOUBLE STRIKE (#3)

"*Double Strike* is special—funny, unique, and I love Davis."

— Janet Evanovich

"Fasten your seat belts: Davis Way, the superspy of Southern casino gambling, is back (after *Double Dip*) for her third wild caper."

— *Publishers Weekly*

"It reads fast, gives you lots of sunny moments and if you are a part of the current social media movement, this will appeal to you even more. I know #ItDoesForMe."

— *Mystery Sequels*

DOUBLE DIP (#2)

"A smart, snappy writer who hits your funny bone!"

– Janet Evanovich

"Archer's bright and silly humor makes this a pleasure to read. Fans of Janet Evanovich's Stephanie Plum will absolutely adore Davis Way and her many mishaps."

– *RT Book Reviews*

"Slot tournament season at the Bellissimo Resort and Casino in Biloxi, Miss., provides the backdrop for Archer's enjoyable sequel to *Double Whammy*...Credible characters and plenty of Gulf Coast local color help make this a winner."

– *Publishers Weekly*

"Hilarious, action-packed, with a touch of home-sweet-home and a ton of glitz and glam. I'm booking my next vacation at the Bellissimo!"

– Susan M. Boyer,
USA Today Bestselling Author of *Lowcountry Bordello*

DOUBLE WHAMMY (#1)

"Funny & wonderful & human. It gets the Stephanie Plum seal of approval."

– Janet Evanovich

"Filled with humor and fresh, endearing characters. It's that rarest of books: a beautifully written page-turner. It's a winner!"

– Michael Lee West,
Author of *Gone With a Handsomer Man*

"Archer navigates a satisfyingly complex plot and injects plenty of humor as she goes....a winning hand for fans of Janet Evanovich."

– *Library Journal*

DOUBLE KNOT

**The Davis Way Crime Caper Series
by Gretchen Archer**

DOUBLE KNOT

A DAVIS WAY CRIME CAPER

Gretchen Archer

HENERY PRESS

DOUBLE KNOT
A Davis Way Crime Caper
Part of the Henery Press Mystery Collection

First Edition | April 2016

Henery Press
www.henerypress.com

Trade Paperback ISBN-13: 978-1-63511-029-6
Digital epub ISBN-13: 978-1-63511-030-2
Kindle ISBN-13: 978-1-63511-031-9
Hardcover Paperback ISBN-13: 978-1-63511-032-6

Printed in the United States of America

For my sister; she's the best.
Not for my brother; he knows why.
(Our Madame Alexander dolls? Ring a bell?)

ACKNOWLEDGMENTS

Thank you, always, Deke Castleman. You too, Stephany Evans. Thanks Laura Henley, Claire McKinney, Larissa Ackerman, Tiffany Yates Martin. And we wouldn't be here if not for the efforts of Art Molinares and Kendel Lynn. Thank you, Art. Thank you, Kendel.

ONE

Probability anchored a half mile out into the Mississippi Sound just west of Cat Island at midnight on the last Friday in March. From the shore, from barges, and from the roof of the Bellissimo Resort and Casino in Biloxi, crews from ABC, CBS, NBC, Fox News, BBCA, Travel Channel, MSNBC, CNN, and Yahoo! News lit up the bandwidths broadcasting the event.

It was as if a spaceship had landed.

A masterpiece in naval architecture, the ship was 380 feet long, eighty feet wide, had ten decks, seventeen restaurants, and a submarine. For underwater excursions. Sophisticated and sleek, whispering magnificence, *Probability* was the largest and most lavish private yacht ever built and came with a cool half-billion-dollar price tag. It was a floating island of luxury and opulence. It glowed.

Commissioned by a conglomerate of three privately-held casinos, the ship was designed in Kuwait City, Kuwait, constructed in Puttgarden, Germany, and registered in the Bahamas. The officers and crew were mostly European. Onboard amenities included all those restaurants, plus an ice bar, a molecular bar, and an oxygen bar, a driving range, a fine art gallery (twenty-four Picassos), a Tiffany & Co. showroom, and a casino. Deck Eight was a casino. *Probability*, more than anything else and in spite of everything else, was a floating casino. And it would be my home for the next seven nights.

My name is Davis Way Cole. I'm thirty-four years old and almost six months pregnant with twins. Double duty. Cruising with me were my OB/GYN, a neonatologist, and my pregnancy assistant. Who was also a certified multiple-birth neonatal nurse.

Can you say overboard?

My pregnancy had been easy, math notwithstanding, as there were two of them and only one of me. I was perfectly healthy, I'd had an uneventful pregnancy, I felt great, and I was six weeks away from restricted travel. Still, to hear my husband tell it, I was leaving to be air dropped in the middle of the Siberian tundra, where I would probably go into labor and give premature birth to his children five thousand miles from him and five hundred miles from a hospital.

"Your vitamins."

"I know, Bradley. I won't forget."

"And be careful in the sun," he said. "It won't feel as hot as it is. Try to wear a hat or stay in the shade."

"Hat. Shade."

"And sunscreen."

"Sunscreen."

"Have fun," he said, "but quiet fun. Get as much rest as you can. Try to relax."

"Bradley, *you* need to relax."

He hadn't had the easiest of times since we found out. He was very close to taking a deep breath when ten weeks in, the tech heard *two* little heartbeats. Fifteen minutes later it was confirmed by ultrasound—twins—at which point, the sonographer had to lead Bradley to a chair.

"No, Mr. Cole, you stay right there. Keep your head between your knees until you're not wobbly. We don't need two patients."

"My wife!" Bradley yelled at the floor. "She's *three* patients! Three!"

Now he's a textbook prenatal expert, as in there wasn't a *What to Expect* in print he hadn't memorized. The more he highlighted, paragraph after paragraph in thick yellow Sharpie, the more he worried. His pregnancy jitters completely negated mine. Which is to say if it weren't for constantly reassuring him everything would be all right, I might be anxious too, but calming him down somehow kept me calm. I reminded him every day, with many days to go, I wasn't the first woman to give birth. There were seven billion people in the world. And they all got here the same way.

"Yes, but of those seven billion, how many are twins?"

I kept meaning to look it up.

The level of Bradley's anxiety had reached a crescendo, all centered around this week. The week we'd be apart. "What is it, Bradley?" I'd asked a hundred times. "Just tell me." "I don't know," he'd say. "I honestly don't know." Which was a switch; it was usually me who had the funny feelings. The best I could come up with was geography. How physically far apart we'd be. I woke the night before the cruise to find him staring at the ceiling. He said he couldn't put his finger on exactly what had him awake at two in the morning, and I honestly think he was lying there imagining me falling off the ship.

My balance was a little off. But not that off.

The Bellissimo Resort and Casino in Biloxi, Mississippi owned one-third of the super yacht my husband would rather me not spend week twenty-four of my pregnancy on. Bradley and I both worked for the Bellissimo; he was the chief operating officer and I was the Super Secret Spy. Well, I had been the Super Secret Spy, lead spy on a team of three. The more pregnant I got, the less spying I did. This trip would be my last official time on the clock before the babies were born. And Bradley's worry aside, a Caribbean cruise on a luxury liner wasn't a bad way to kick off maternity leave. It wasn't like I'd be roughing it. Picasso and all. But when we stepped out on our balcony Saturday morning and got our first good look at *Probability* on the water, the sheer mass of it taking up half of the horizon behind the Bellissimo, the father of my twins looked a little seasick.

"It'll be okay, Bradley," I said. "It's just a week."

"On *that*." He tipped his coffee cup.

I squinted in the early sun. "It is big."

"Too big," Bradley said. "Way too big."

As way too big as *Probability* was, you'd think the Bellissimo would stuff it with thousands of gamblers, right?

Wrong.

Probability accommodated fifty guests. Fifty very wealthy guests. I would be traveling with one-tenth of the Forbes 500, a few I'd heard of, most I hadn't, and I'd be working. I was on special assignment.

I came to the Bellissimo three and a half years ago, joining an elite undercover team whose job it was to sniff out bad guys, both in the casino and all too often, in our own ranks. The Bellissimo is the largest casino property in the United States outside of Las Vegas, with gross gaming revenues of $700 million and a staff of 4,000. The 4,000 mostly counted the $700 million, and believe it or not, they weren't all honest. Some of them wanted to keep a little of the $700 million for themselves. Half of my job was to keep that from happening. The other half of my job was Bianca Casimiro Sanders.

Bianca, almost ten years older than me, was married to the owner of the Bellissimo, Richard Sanders. And she was preggers too. One of those September babies, unexpected in every single solitary way a baby could be unexpected, a shock all the way around. She was two weeks from giving birth and I still couldn't believe it.

Bianca and I looked like we swam our first laps in the exact same gene pool. To see us side by side, you'd think she was my older sister. Because we looked so much alike, lucky me, I was her celebrity double. I made appearances for her, sat on charity boards for her, and since she'd been pregnant, I'd done everything but inhale and exhale for her. She hadn't lifted a finger in eight and a half months except to dial my number.

In a way, she didn't get that I was pregnant too.

In another way, she did.

Bianca Sanders's pregnancy made headlines. "Whoa, Baby! The Bellissimo's Bianca Sanders: Fab, Fortyish, and in a Family Way!" The press all but packed Bianca's bags and moved her to Hollywood to join the ranks of celebrities who waited until well into their forties to have children, and every mention of her was accompanied with photographic evidence of Bianca wearing it superbly well. Except the photographs weren't of her—they were of me. And that's why I was leaving my husband and my home to go on a cruise. At six months pregnant with twins, I was on a modeling assignment. Bianca had me cruising around the Caribbean for one final documentation of how great she looked and felt just days before giving birth. But the pictures wouldn't be of her, they would be of me, because the truth was she wasn't wearing it well at *all*. And she was wearing it worse by the minute. As easy as my pregnancy has been, she's gone out of her way to make hers as difficult as possible. Granted, she had legendary morning sickness—I'll give her that. But she traded one set of problems for another when she turned that corner and began feeling better in a very deep dish way. At forty-three years old, Bianca had her first slice of pepperoni pizza and now Papa John was her new best friend.

At four months along, Bianca woke up one morning after an extra-large double-pepperoni double-cheese stuffed-crust party for one, stepped on the scale, fainted, and took to her bedchambers. Since then she'd managed to gain forty additional pounds, her feet looked like balloons, and she refused to get out of the bed. She insisted her self-imposed bedrest was the only thing keeping her alive, and the baby's health was also singularly dependent on her absolute confinement. If you ask me, there wasn't a thing wrong with her except for the fact she was scared to death someone would see her other than her husband, me, or Jorge.

Jorge was her Papa John's delivery guy.

The woman would not get out of the bed and she was driving me batty.

I'm not sure if I was more excited about the big ship, the calypso blue of the Caribbean, or getting away from Bianca for a few days. Not that I hadn't grown genuinely fond of Bianca through the years—maybe that was my pregnancy talking—and I did want to be here when Ondine was born.

Yes, Ondine.

Bianca was naming her daughter Ondine. Ondine Eugenie Casimiro Sanders.

Ondine.

For the next seven days, I would be on a half-billion-dollar superyacht posing as the woman naming a child Ondine.

So in addition to my medical staff, also traveling with me was a photography crew of ten: four photographers, three hair and makeup people, two stylists, and one wardrobe girl. I met with one of the stylists earlier this week to go over the Armani Collezioni details one last time. She, believe it or not, was pregnant too, must be something in the water, and I asked if her husband was anxious about her cruising the Caribbean with fifty billionaires. She said, "Are you kidding me? He can't wait to get rid of me for a week." Her husband was celebrating and mine was hoping Saturday afternoon would never come.

It did.

At two o'clock, Bradley looked at his watch. "It's almost time."

The bellman brigade would be here any minute to load the huge trunks, cavernous suitcases, and rolling wardrobe going with me. Ten percent was what I'd packed and the other ninety was what Bianca was sending for the maternity shoots. Sitting to the left of the Louis Vuitton showroom at our front door was a lonely brown leather duffel, matching hanging bag, and a briefcase stuffed full of Labor and Delivery textbooks that weren't cruising. They were going with Bradley, because he was traveling today too. For the next five days, he'd be keynote-speaking at the Global Gaming Expo in Macau, China. Since the day we met and certainly since we married, we'd never been this far away from each other for this length of time.

He inventoried our luggage one last time, then turned to me.

These would be our last moments alone.

"Davis." He ran a hand through his blonde hair; he shifted his weight. "You're beautiful." He swallowed. "And I love you more than life."

"Bradley—" I opened my mouth to call the whole thing off when a knock on the door interrupted. Several knocks, in fact. Sharp insistent knocks. With one last kiss to the top of my head, I could feel his heart beating against my cheek, Bradley, jaw set, opened the door. It wasn't the maritime moving company.

"Davis, what in the world are you blubbering about? And you look like a botanical garden. Surely to goodness you're not planning on wearing that. For one thing, you'll catch pneumonia. For another, it's too bright and busy." A crooked finger pointed down the hall. "Go change out of that right now."

That was a really cute Chanel floral sundress covered in bright pink and mint green rhododendrons, a cropped three-quarter-sleeve pink sweater, and Kate Spade Melanie heels in fuchsia with a matching shoulder-strap bag. It was a perfect mommy-to-be ensemble for embarking on a luxury liner with fifty billionaires, a crew of four hundred, a medical team, a glamor squad, and my mother.

"Caroline." He kissed her cheek.

"Hello, Bradley, dear." She squeezed his arm, then turned to me. "Davis. Change clothes. Right this minute."

Right that minute, my phone rang in the shoulder-strap bag somewhere just behind me. Bradley had it out of my purse and in my hand before I could get past the babies. It was my pregnancy buddy, calling to wish me bon voyage.

"Bianca?"

"David, get up here. I need to discuss my birth plan with you."

*   *   *

My birth plan was simple: get the babies out of me.

Bianca's, on the other hand, had kept a staff of twenty hopping for months with the only end in sight being the actual birth of the baby, because she wouldn't stop changing her mind. Last week she fired the caterers and hired a new crew out of Charleston, South Carolina. "After all," Bianca said, "I'm giving birth to a Southern

Belle." (We'll see about that.) (And childbirth caterers? Have you ever?) Before it was over, I fully expected her to change her mind about physically birthing the baby and tell me to do it for her.

"I'll be right there, Bianca."

"You don't have time to go anywhere," my mother said. "You need to change clothes or you'll be late."

"It'll be fine." Bradley put an arm around Mother's shoulders and pointed her toward a set of royal blue club chairs beneath an abstract oil painting the size of a garage door. "The ship won't leave without her. Have I told you how nice you look, Caroline? Very sporty."

"Sporty?"

"Sophisticated," he said. "I meant sophisticated."

Mother, who's never been in a canoe that I know of, much less on a cruise ship, was dressed as Mrs. Fleet Admiral in Christmas red double-knit pants with a navy blue cotton blouse buttoned up to her chin. Over the blouse, she wore a crisp white linen jacket with gold piping and big gold anchor buttons. On her feet were red Easy Spirit crisscross sandals with a wide wedge heel. The only things she needed were stars, stripes, and a marching band behind her playing "Anchors Aweigh."

"Very stylish," my husband said.

My mother blushed. Shaking my head, I crossed the room the other way for the elevator in the closet.

Bradley and I lived on the 29th floor of the Bellissimo in more than ten thousand square feet of the casino manager's residence. We'd recently redecorated, and by redecorated, I mean we stripped it down to the bare bones and put it back together in a contemporary way with lots of windows, cherry wood floors, beamed ceilings, clean lines and open spaces. Included in the remodel was a (Jack and Jill nursery!) private elevator that only passed between our home and the one above us. Where Richard and Bianca Sanders lived.

I pushed the up button. This would get me out of changing clothes. Except it didn't.

"David, you look like a pregnant twelve-year-old."

"How are you today, Bianca?" I lowered myself into a gray slipper chair at her bedside, my sundress blooming around the babies. The chair had no arms, so it would be up to me to hoist myself out of it when the time came.

"I'm miserable, David. Perfectly and completely miserable. You realize my very life and that of Ondine's is gravely jeopardized. How dare you ask how I am. How would you be, David, if you didn't know if you'd live to see tomorrow?"

Tomorrow, Bianca, I'd be in the middle of the Caribbean Sea.

Last week, she finally got her wish and was diagnosed with an actual complication of pregnancy, this one not imagined and no laughing matter—gestational diabetes. Who knew pizza had so much sugar? She was on the lowest of the low end of the diabetes scale, and her team of doctors said she could enjoy safe blood glucose levels immediately, within the hour, if she'd just get out of the bed and stop with the Papa John's.

Thus the misery.

"I need to sit up, David."

It was like two sumo wrestlers trying to help each other off the floor. I got behind her, then counted down. "Three, two—"

Mission accomplished, and we were both out of breath.

Bianca fanned her puffy face with both hands. "What time do you sail, David?"

(It's Davis.) "At seven."

"Good. You have plenty of time to change clothes."

"The Vera Wang jumpsuit."

"Exactly." Now she was fanning herself with the top half of the bed sheet. Her breasts were enormous. And by enormous, I mean freakishly large. "Wear it to the party. Make a very good impression for me. I mean it, David."

I sneaked a peek at my watch. If I didn't get on the ship soon, I wouldn't make an impression at all. I waited. And waited. I didn't want to sit down again for fear of having to get up again. "Did you need me, Bianca?"

She let the sheet go and it floated around Ondine. "It's my birth plan, David. I need to go over it with you again."

We'd been over her birth plan exactly one million times. A suite of labor, delivery, and if needed, surgical rooms had been constructed and completed to her birth team's specifications at Biloxi Regional Medical Center on Renyoir Street. Every possible scenario for getting Bianca to the hospital, three-tenths of a mile from the Bellissimo (honestly, she could waddle there if she had to), had been accounted for, and Bianca's transfer team had been at the ready for weeks. If she told me she felt a twinge in her pinkie finger this very second, I could push one button on my phone and have her at the hospital in five minutes, four of those hauling her out of the bed.

"Everything's ready, Bianca. Your transport team is on standby, they're doing two drills a day, and I promise you, everyone's ready."

"It's not that." She smoothed the sheet. "It's the people. I've decided there are too many people attending Ondie's birth."

I could have told her that. I did tell her that. Months ago. When she added the nannies (nursery, lactation, day, night, and an on-call—one baby, five nannies) to the roster so they could bond with Ondine at birth, I gently suggested it was too many people for such a deeply personal event. She told me I could scurry off alone and have my babies behind a bush like a woodland creature, but don't tell her a videographer and someone on hand to touch up her hair and lip gloss were too much. In addition to the videographer, the lip gloss lady, the nannies, the doctors, the nurses, her labor coach, her husband, and her teenage son (ewwww), Bianca wanted her *dogs* in the labor and delivery suite. Gianna and Ghita, her Yorkshire terriers, who were getting a little gray in the snout, were also on the guest list for Ondine's birth.

"It will be one physician instead of four. Two nurses instead of six. Richard will be there, of course, and you. Everyone else is out and you're in." She made direct eye contact with me, something she didn't do often. "I need you there."

My phone buzzed with a text from Bradley. *Davis, it's time.*

"Bianca." I stood. "I can't be in two places at once." A theme that had been peeking into the window of my heart since the day we learned I was carrying twins. "What if you go into labor while I'm on the cruise ship having my picture taken?"

"Work it out, David, and change clothes."

* * *

I grew up in Pine Apple, Alabama, a little spot in the road below Montgomery, where not much happened. I moved to Biloxi and took a position with the Bellissimo almost four years ago, and since then I've been incarcerated, poisoned, and had my hair set on fire, and all that's in addition to learning enough Chinese to get through countless high-roller dinners impersonating Bianca Sanders. I loved my job, I made six figures, I missed it already, and I could honestly say I'd given it my all and I'd hang up my spy hat next week with no regrets. But when it comes to Bianca Sanders, I wondered who in the world would fill my size six shoes.

TWO

Jessica DeLuna wanted my job.

She had a job of her own; she was Miss *Probability*.

Jessica and her husband Maximillian were contracted—not by me—to fill *Probability* with rich people. They were loosely, or tightly, I'm not exactly sure, connected to DeLuna-Elima Securities in New Orleans, a bank loosely, or tightly, depends on how you look at it, connected to the Knot on Your Life slot machines in *Probability*'s casino.

The deal went down over Virginia striped bass.

The husband, Max, handled a bazillion-dollar trust for the Fillauer Estate, old New Orleans money. A year ago, about when project *Probability* went into full swing—timing is everything—Jess and Max accompanied the controlling-interest playboy son to the Bellissimo on the occasion of his twenty-first birthday so they could be there to intervene if young Richie Rich Fillauer went a little casino crazy. The Fillauer kid took first in a $500,000 blackjack tournament without touching the trust and the DeLunas were so impressed they didn't leave.

Richard and Bianca Sanders, and by Richard and Bianca Sanders I mean Richard Sanders and the person who sits through boring dinners pretending she's Bianca Sanders—and that would be me—had young Fillauer over to celebrate his big blackjack win. He asked if his financial advisor and wife could tag along. It was the first time I met the DeLunas and I hoped it would be the last.

That didn't happen.

Over jumbo lump crab and shrimp, Mr. Sanders told our guests about the next big thing on the Bellissimo horizon— *Probability*. Max DeLuna was delighted. He wanted to hear more. Between creamy asparagus bisque and baby wedge salads we slipped out to the Sanders' library to marvel at the scale model of the fabulous ship. It was when the Virginian bass was served and the amenities and events aboard the maiden voyage were discussed in detail that DeLuna proposed he reach out to his upper-crust clients and gauge their interest levels in booking ($1,000,000 spots) one of the fifty luxurious suites for this once-in-a-lifetime opportunity. Mr. Sanders, in a moment of vanilla bourbon cheesecake madness, hired DeLuna *and* the wife as *Probability's* host and hostess—no background checks, no salary negotiations, no corner office disputes.

I almost choked on my white chocolate meringue.

First, as anyone in the gaming industry would tell you, never spontaneously hire casino management. Next, isn't it curious, and by curious I mean a flaming red flag, that a successful banker would accept an impromptu job over fish? What's wrong with the job he has? And why the wife too? What was she supposed to do? Lastly, and most important, I wouldn't have sanctioned the hiring of these two to fold napkins, if for no other reason than the fact that Mr. and Mrs. DeLuna didn't speak to each other or make eye contact one time in five courses. There's a story there, a story better not played out on a half-billion-dollar ship in the middle of the sea. Regardless, and without a thought to policy, procedure, or marital discord, Mr. Sanders put them on the payroll.

It's (his casino) not like I could kick him under the table.

From that moment on, Max DeLuna worked offsite doing who knows what. I'd barely seen him since the Virginian bass. Jessica, on the other hand, got a big office right down the hall from my husband. She'd done an impressive job, if an impressive job can be measured by how many times she weaseled her way into my husband's office for no good reason. That, plus the fact that the ship was, indeed, full of ridiculously wealthy people.

I was hoping to avoid the DeLunas for the duration of the cruise.

That didn't happen either.

Hers was the first face I saw the second I stepped onto *Probability*.

"So! You're here!"

Barely. I had one foot on the gangplank and the other on the teak deck when Jess popped up.

She stared past me. "You're alone? All by yourself?" She clutched her heart. "No one to see you off?"

She was looking for Bradley. I swear the woman was after my job *and* my husband. Every time the subject came up, and it was usually-to-always me bringing it up, Bradley somehow worked the words "wildly fluctuating progesterone and estrogen levels" into the conversation.

"There's something not right with the DeLunas, Bradley. And whatever it is, it has nothing to do with me being pregnant."

"You need to get to know her," he'd say.

"Oh, really?"

"Give her a chance, Davis. She'll grow on you."

"Are you saying she's grown on you?"

He pulled me close. "Oh, my pregnant Davis."

Jessica met me, real me, early on. Not something a Super Secret Spy usually sanctions—it's hard to stay super secret if everyone knows who you are—but in her case, I was ready and willing to make an exception. Her job, as it turned out, was to staff and stock the fifty suites to the whims of the fifty guests' every imagined desire, and word had come down from the Bianca Sanders Maternity Ward that if Jessica sent one more intrusive questionnaire, Bianca would get out of the bed and kill her. At some point, Jessica would have to be told the guest in the Sanders Suite wasn't Bianca. Instead, it would be me. Send the foie gras surveys to me. I was all for telling her the truth, thinking it would get her out of my husband's office. Which is where we were when we swore her to secrecy.

"So, wait." Jess looked up from the confidentiality agreement. "When I see Bianca Sanders I'm really seeing *you*?"

"Correct." I smiled.

"That night at dinner it was *you*?"

"Yes."

"You two are *married*?"

"Right again." I tucked into my husband a little closer. "We are."

And here we were. On *Probability*.

"Well, you look just adorable," she said. "Like a little flower mommy."

Next to her, I felt like I was wearing little flower mommy wallpaper. Enough to cover a very large wall. She was barely dressed in head-to-toe cream satin, a cropped sleeveless top over a long pencil skirt, and the skirt was slit. All the way up one of her long brown legs. Jessica was runway tall and stick thin, with long silky black hair, Maleficent cheekbones, and ink-black almond-shaped eyes. To offset all the thin, she had DDD breasts; to offset all the exotic islander dark, she dressed in shades of white—vanilla, antique, and smoke. The package of Jessica was very dramatic and she was well aware of her effect. Let's put it this way: If the whole room wasn't looking at her, she wasn't happy. And since we weren't in a room at all, Jessica spun me around, hooked an arm through mine, and chattered me to a more populated venue like we were BFFs. Which was part of her grand scheme to rip my job and husband out from under me. This constantly being nice to me.

She nicely told me my medical crew had just arrived and my photography crew had already checked into their staterooms on Deck Two, the level housing everyone's entourages. My mother and my others were safely on Deck Seven, the level with ten of the fifty VIP guest suites, including mine. My stateroom attendant had arrived. My butler and personal chef weren't in the suite just yet, but they'd be along shortly. All was well. Thanks to her.

She led me through a wide arched doorway into a solid gold atrium, six stories high with a sweeping gold staircase in the middle, where four porters flanked the entrance, three men in navy blue suits stood at the foot of the staircase behind gold desks, two clusters of rich people sipped champagne, and one lady played a golden harp under a blinding crystal halo chandelier. Everyone stopped what they were doing to look at Jessica and she was very happy.

She made me feel so pregnant.

* * *

The ship ran on a central processor somewhere I'd never see, and the passengers were connected to the processor, thus the ship, by personal electronics. I wasn't issued a room key; I was given a Saygus V2 five-ounce handheld computer. One of its many features was that it operated as a telephone too, which was way down the app list from V2's primary purpose—that of being the major component of *Probability*'s security system. It made perfect sense that you couldn't put this much wealth in one place without a security system to rival that of the Heaven Embassy in Hell. The passengers were connected to all this safety by individual 60GHz mobile transceivers in the shape of a phone. A phone with GPS, gyroscope, accelerometer, compass, proximity and vital statistics sensors. A phone, without which we couldn't move around the ship, eat, sleep, or gamble. Take every electronic spec you've ever heard of or imagined, add ten years of technology, then stuff it into a device barely bigger than a credit card. And that's how you stay safe, enjoy, and navigate *Probability*.

My mother, who had to relearn the television remote every single day of her life, would surely love it.

A man behind a gold desk named Corwin, who was a dead ringer for Hugh Grant—the hair, the teeth, the accent—did a quick facial recognition and fingerprint scan on me, then waved a V2 in front of my nose. "You understand this replaces your personal electronic devices."

"Yes." I knew that. Guests were warned well in advance that

the ship's system wouldn't recognize any signal not connected to *Probability*'s central processor.

"You can't lose it." He passed it to me.

"I won't." It weighed two cotton balls.

"If you lose it," he said, "you'll have to swim home. And in your condition, I wouldn't recommend it."

Jessica hid a yawn.

Hugh Grant passed me a leather-bound encyclopedia. Gold stamped on the cover: *The Compass*. The pages were gold-leaf edged. "It's a passenger directory," Hugh said. "Inside you'll find information about the ship and short dossiers on your fellow shipmates."

Short? The book weighed ten pounds.

Jessica made a big show of looking at her watch.

"Does it tell me how to get to my room?"

"Press the map on V2, Madame."

I pressed; the phone pointed.

"Your concierge will arrive momentarily to escort you," Corwin said.

"I've got this, Corwin," Jess said.

"No, I've got this." I'd had about enough of her. Just then, the computer in my hand buzzed. The screen said I was getting a call from the Bianca Casimiro Sanders Suite.

"So, your thumb," Jessica said. "You answer the call with your thumb."

I pressed my thumb against the sensor.

"It's me." My partner, Fantasy. "Do you know what I've been doing for two solid hours? Getting your mother and Anderson Cooper in this room. You'd better get your pregnant self up here before I jump off this boat."

"It's a ship," I said. "You call it a ship."

"You're going to need what I call a lifejacket if you don't get here and take care of your mother and Anderson Cooper."

"I'm on my way."

* * *

Probability's transportation system, Zoom, consisted of individual spaceship capsules that seated six and ran on a suspended oval track around the perimeter of Deck Three. Just above the water line. Think Disney monorail, but private, with plush carpet, chocolate brown leather seats, and Ultra HD 4K televisions displaying *Probability* amenities. Of which there were many, including Zoom, which felt like flying. If my mother didn't pass out on this, I'd be surprised. Of more concern to me, at the moment, was how Anderson Cooper fared, because that was a stowaway smuggling situation.

Zoom stopped and I stepped off. A red dot popped up on V2, with a corresponding red dot blinking above one of five glass-door elevators in front of me. I scanned V2 against the elevator control panel, the doors opened, and I stepped into the casino. Not the actual casino—the back wall of the elevator was an LED screen panning the casino on Deck Eight that would open at seven tonight. This was my first peek and *Probability's* casino was spectacular.

The promenade featured larger-than-life ice sculptures; I saw Neptune, Captain Jack Sparrow, and either one of the Weeki Wachee Springs mermaids or Morticia Addams. I couldn't tell. Along the west wall were table games: poker, blackjack, roulette, craps, and baccarat. The east wall held a massive glass bar and plenty of luxurious lounging, the color scheme throughout was navy and silver, waterfall prism lights floated and twinkled above everything. The best part was in front of the bar. Back to back in two rows of twenty-five were the stars of the show—*Probability's* slot machines—Knot On Your Life—one with (Bianca's) my name on it.

I studied V2, wondering how to ask for a casino pit stop; might as well (avoid my mother) check it out on my way to the suite. I love casinos. But before I could talk myself into it or out of it, the elevator doors opened and spilled me out on Deck Seven. So I took the path I was destined for: Suite 704.

The casino wasn't going anywhere.

I had a whole week.

With my mother.

Standing at the door, I had no idea how to get in. I shook V2 trying to figure it out, but before I did I heard gear clicks and bolt slides. It opened.

"Get in here. Do something with your mother. Look at you! You're so cute!"

"Thank you!" (Finally.) My partner, Fantasy Erb, whom I'd seen about twice in the past six months, held out her arms and I began filling them: V2, my sunglasses, the encyclopedia, my purse, little sweater, then grabbing her arm for balance, my shoes.

"Are you going to take off your clothes too?"

"Maybe."

The vestibule was like a museum, and just to prove it, directly in front of me was a statue of some sort. "What is that?"

"A Chinese antique," she said. "You break it, you buy it."

"I don't want it."

Our heads whipped the other way when the front doors began beeping and flashing red warning lights from the thick steel frame. "Oh, good grief." Fantasy's V2 was in the pocket of her jacket. She juggled my things until she could get to it, pulled it out, then pointed V2 at the doors. They hushed, then closed decisively, with the whir of motors and a notable catch.

We stared at the doors.

"This way," Fantasy said. "Are you ready?"

"No."

From the narrow vestibule we stepped into the salon, a magnificent room with an exterior wall that was a seamless wraparound window separating this room from the terrace. Like being inside and outside at the same time. The salon was sparsely decorated, showcasing spaces rather than things. What struck me first was the simplicity of the interior design and the clean lines, the overall unassuming feel of a space so magnificent. Everything I could see was either white or very close to it. In the middle of the room on a silver rug, four long white linen sofas formed a square around a large slab of glass sitting on an ancient fishing boat propeller. The only thing on the table was a tall clear vase holding a dozen perfect white tulips. I got a little misty; I knew exactly who they were from.

My mother sat at one end of a sofa staring at Anderson Cooper, who sat at the other end, staring at her. Mother looked as angry as I've ever seen her. Not that Anderson Cooper looked happy. Without taking her eyes off Anderson my mother said, "It's about time."

My mother thinks that next week, after the cruise, she's being admitted to St. Vincent's in Birmingham, Alabama for a complete mastectomy and simultaneous breast reconstruction surgery. Caught by diagnostic mammogram at Stage 1A, Mother's tumor was the size of a pea, completely contained, and zapped out of existence. She was on the freedom side of chemo and radiation, all follow-up tests were back and clear, and according to my father, the surgery was my mother's idea. He said she sat down at the breakfast table one morning and announced, "Samuel, I believe I'd like new bosoms. I'm tired of looking at these old ones." He told me she approached the subject no differently than if she'd said, "Samuel, I believe I'd like new shoes. The heels are worn down on these old ones."

Two weeks later, the scheduling nurse called Daddy. Mother denied having been recently treated for cancer ("Poppycock," she told the nurse), insisting her medical records were confused, and refused to discuss it any further. It caught the attention of the augmentation consultants. They ordered a pre-op psych evaluation, fearing Mother wasn't "providing informed consent" and when they tried to discuss it with her, she excused herself, saying she'd be back in a jiffy.

She got in her car and drove home to Pine Apple. The scheduling nurse told Daddy that unless Mother could be honest with herself about why she was having the surgery, she'd need to have it somewhere else or reschedule with them after counseling.

Daddy sent her on a Caribbean cruise with me in lieu of counseling.

"Daddy, just find another surgeon."

"One with less scruples?" he asked. "One who doesn't care about your mother's wellbeing?"

"That's not what I mean."

"Davis, I want you to take her with you. Get her out of the kitchen. Take her on a beautiful vacation and help her deal with this."

I don't have enough influence over my mother to help her deal with a paper cut. Much less what she'd been through or the surgery she'd signed up for. At the time, just weeks before the cruise, I wasn't even sure I could get her on the passenger list, and there was no getting her out of the kitchen.

I didn't agree to it fast enough.

"Don't worry about it, honey." Daddy looked so tired. "I'll find another way. I understand if you don't want to spend a week with your mother."

Well, when you put it that way.

I didn't think there was even a remote chance Mother would agree to spending a week with *me*, and I was stunned when she went along with it. A week? Me and Mother? Together? She started packing and I wasn't about to protest. Her diagnosis had scared us all to death. And here we were. Scared to death.

The problem was my mother doesn't particularly enjoy my company.

And she sure didn't like Anderson Cooper's.

Anderson saw me and jumped into my arms. We found a seat on the linen sofa opposite Mother.

"Davis." Mother clasped her hands in a prayer and leaned my way. "I can't believe you snuck a cat on this boat."

"It's not a boat, Mother. It's a ship." Anderson tried to get comfortable in my shrinking lap, gave up, and settled in beside me.

"You have a contraband cat on this *ship*, Davis."

"Mother, everyone on this ship thinks I'm Bianca Sanders."

"What does that have to do with your cat?"

"The Bellissimo owns this ship," I said. "Bianca can sneak her cat onboard if she wants to. She sneaked *you* onboard."

"I'm not a house cat, Davis, and you're going to get us all arrested."

"Who's going to arrest us, Mother?"

"The Coast Guard. Or the casino. Surely someone will." She eyeballed me from just over the edge of her peeper glasses. "And I'll tell you something else. I don't know what in the world you were thinking when you named that cat. If I'm going to spend the next week with it, you better believe I won't be calling it Anderson Cooper. I am worried sick about what you'll do when the day comes that you're responsible for naming a human."

I stole a sideways look at Fantasy. See?

She barely batted an eye in acknowledgment. She saw.

Not only had my mother refused to face her own truth, she had yet to acknowledge mine. Which I believed to be the real reason Daddy pitted us together in the middle of the Caribbean. So my own mother might notice I'm pregnant.

"I named her Blizzard, Mother, but it didn't stick. Because she looks just like Anderson Cooper."

"Well, Davis, that's ridiculous."

If I had a nickel.

"And before this boat drives off—" Mother was on a roll, "—you call Bradley and have him come get your cat or I will. Either me or that cat is getting off this boat before it leaves."

"Mother, it's a ship, Bradley's on his way to China, and Anderson is deaf."

"So you say."

"She's stone cold deaf. She can't hear a thing."

"I understand what deaf is, Davis."

"I couldn't leave her. I can't leave her. I wasn't about to leave her. I'm the only one she talks to."

Fantasy, a mile away on the other end of the long white sofa, whistled a little tune and studied the beadboard ceiling.

"I have news for you, Davis," my mother said. "That cat doesn't talk to you."

I suspected Anderson couldn't hear when she was six weeks old. Her veterinarian confirmed it. It's called Waardenburg Syndrome, and it's something about the gene for deafness being located between the genes for white fur and blue eyes on the DNA ropes. The hearing gene gets skipped. And she really does look just like Anderson Cooper.

"Where does Bradley think your cat is?" Mother asked.

I didn't answer.

"He doesn't know, does he?"

Mother slept for four months. We had to wake her up to get her in the car, then wake her again to get her in the outpatient doors of the Cancer Center in Greenville, Alabama, twenty miles from my parents' home in Pine Apple. She slept the whole time. For four months she didn't wake up until noon, then she was back in bed an hour later. "It's just a stage," my father said, over and over. "She sleeps all the time because she's feeling a little blue." (I guess so.) (We all were.) (We were purple-black-blue.) Mother finally woke up when her treatments were complete, and boy, did she get up on the wrong side of the bed. She woke up mad. Mad at the world. Mad at my father. Mad at Donald Trump. Mad at telemarketers. Mad at the weather. Mad at her bosoms. Mad at me, which really wasn't anything new, but she was also mad at my sister Meredith who she never got mad at. "It's a stage," my father explained. "Her bad temper is a defense mechanism. She's trying to distance herself."

Mother and her defense mechanism stared at us. We squirmed under the scrutiny. My Caribbean cruise was off to a choppy start. First Jessica, now Mother, what next?

THREE

Probability Stateroom 704, all three thousand and eight hundred square feet of it, had one owner's and two grand suites. In addition, there were crew quarters somewhere: one for the butler, one for the stateroom attendant, and one for the chef. The owner's suite was (Bianca's) mine. Fantasy and Mother were in the grand suites on the opposite end, a good jog away. Between all the suiteness were luxuriously appointed living spaces, including a totally private veranda that ran the length of 704 on the starboard side of the ship. The balconies were staggered from deck to deck, so we were the only ones with access to ours and no other passengers could see us. In the middle of the veranda, a pool. Behind the pool, a private sundeck. Each of the fifty suites on *Probability* were just as secluded as ours and had private pools. In spite of things not going quite swimmingly just yet, we had everything we could ever need or want for a fabulous vacation.

Let the fabulous part begin.

"How long have you been here?" I asked Mother and Fantasy.

"Not long," Mother said.

"A while," Fantasy said.

"Have you looked around?" I asked.

"I unpacked," Mother said. "Then I pressed my blouses with my travel iron. They were creased from my Samsonite."

"I snooped," Fantasy said.

"What'd you find?" I asked.

"I just poked my nose in the doors," she said. "I didn't dig through anyone's luggage."

"Well, I should hope not," Mother said. "That's rude."

"Which way is my room?" I asked.

Fantasy pointed. "It's gorgeous. And I would've snooped through your luggage but you have too much."

"Davis." Mother said. "It took those men an hour to bring in your luggage. Ten minutes for everyone else's and an hour for yours."

"It's for the photography, Mother."

"Well, it's ridiculous."

"Fantasy, when you were snooping, did you find anything to drink?" I asked.

"Fantastic idea." Fantasy stood and crossed the room to a fully stocked sidebar. "What's your poison, ladies?"

"Surprise us," I said.

"This will surprise you." Fantasy pushed a button somewhere near the sidebar and with a swoosh, the wraparound glass wall slid into the ceiling. Now we really were inside and outside.

Probability Suite 704 was magnificent.

We stepped all the way out with our drinks and settled around an iron bistro table in a chocolate finish, sinking into thick cushioned chairs under a canvas umbrella. In the distance, I could see the Bellissimo—my husband, my home, my work—and it looked so far away.

"This is delicious." Mother knocked back half of hers in one long pull. "What is it?"

"It's a cranberry sparkler," Fantasy said. "Cranberry juice and champagne. Davis, yours is sparkling with ginger ale."

"Cranberry juice and champagne," Mother said. "This would be nice at Christmastime."

I picked up the pitcher and topped off Mother's sparkler.

"Nice weather."

"Very nice."

"Perfect."

"Not too hot."

"No."

"Just right."

"Not too cool."

"No."

"A beautiful afternoon."

Fantasy crossed and uncrossed her long legs three times, Mother nervously twisted the gold anchor buttons on her jacket, and I petted Anderson in long smooth strokes, waiting for the ice to crack. Before it could, the table vibrated. Even Anderson felt it; her ears stood up. It was V2, letting us know the front door had opened. V2 said Jessica DeLuna and Andrew Burnsworth had entered Suite 704.

I wasn't in the mood for any more Jess.

"Who is Andrew Burnsworth?" Fantasy stared at her V2.

"He's our butler," I said.

"Which means?"

"I'm not sure. What do butlers do other than open doors?" I asked.

"Why do we need someone to open the door?" Mother asked. "Are we expecting visitors?"

"Surely he does more than open doors," Fantasy said.

"Does this mean we're going to have a *man* here?"

"We have a butler, a stateroom attendant, and a chef, Mother. I think the butler is a man."

"What in the world is a stateroom attendant?" Mother asked.

"She cleans," I said.

"We have a *maid*?" Mother asked.

"I feel like I've won the lottery," Fantasy said. "An entire week of not worrying about anything or anyone, no kids, no dishes, no laundry. Just fun and sun."

"How are we supposed to fun and sun with a *man* here?" Mother asked.

"It's not like he'll be with us the entire time," Fantasy told her. "The staff gets several hours off in the afternoon."

"And we won't be in the room the whole time, Mother."

"So we're leaving a *man* in here while we're gone? All day?"

"And all night," I said. "He's part of this suite's staff. The staff stays in the suite."

"A *man*? Where's he supposed to sleep?"

"That way." Fantasy pointed. "Three small bedrooms that way."

"Three small staterooms that way," I said.

"They have beds, dressers, and closets," Fantasy said. "I call that a bedroom."

"A *man*?"

I poured Mother another sparkler.

"And what do we need with a chef?" Mother reached for her glass. "I thought there were restaurants."

"There are, Mother. We have a chef because we have a kitchen, so we have the option of eating in."

"A butler, a cook, and a maid?" Mother rolled her eyes. "Which one of you intends to make a big mess? I don't know about you, Fantasy, but Davis was raised to pick up after herself. And surely, Davis, you can still make yourself a salad or a sandwich. Surely to goodness you're not so spoiled by all this," she gestured wildly, "that you've forgotten how to heat a bowl of soup or make yourself cheese toast. And I'll tell you another thing." Her crooked index finger took off, aimed at no one in particular. "I don't want anyone making my bed. I make my bed as soon as my feet hit the floor in the morning. I strip back the comforter and top sheet and pop up that bottom sheet. I give it a good shake and tuck it back in all four corners." She pantomimed her precision tucking. "Every day. And I strip the bed to the mattress on Thursdays mornings." Mother paused to check her mental calendar. Scheduling her maritime bed stripping. "You can't tell me there's a maid in the world who will take the time to pop up my bottom sheet. You've heard of bed bugs? That maid isn't touching my bed."

"She's on edge," my father reminded me again on the phone this morning, something I already knew and had been smack dab in the middle of (my whole life) for months. "She's wound tight as a tick, Davis. Be patient with her and don't say or do *anything* to upset her. No stress, no surprises. Give her a day or two and she'll settle down and relax."

"I'll tell you something right now," Tight as a Tick said. "I'm not exactly fond of the idea of sleeping under the same roof with three strangers. Especially a strange man." She appeared, however, very fond of the cranberry sparklers. I poured her another. Maybe if I liquored her up she'd settle down and relax sooner than the day or two Daddy said it would be, because it had only been an hour or two and I wasn't sure I'd make it a day or two.

The V2s buzzed again, telling us the door to 704 had closed.

"What's up with the front door?" I asked Fantasy.

"It's the only way in and out of here," she said. "Which, if you ask me, is a bad idea. Not to mention a fire hazard."

"Oh, forevermore." Mother added five-alarm fire to her worry list and polished off her third sparkler. My mother had never touched a drop of alcohol or allowed it in the house until the day she was on the receiving end of a positive biopsy result. In the months since, she'd discovered that "a little something for her nerves" went a long way. And everyone agreed.

"Well, there are security doors and then there are security doors," I said. "The doors here are a little much. Like Alcatraz doors."

"What a great idea," Fantasy said. "Repurpose this boat as a prison, just don't give the prisoners a V2."

"It's a ship, Fantasy. And you could fit five thousand inmates on it. This would make a hell of a prison."

"You should know."

"Thank you, Mother."

"And watch your language."

This was going to be a long long week. My mother could bring up every mistake I've made in my life at a single red light. Yes, I've been incarcerated.

Several times. All work-related misunderstandings.

And somehow, she managed to remind me of it ten minutes into our week together. Lest I forget. It's a good thing 704's pool deck was so big; Mother would need every inch of it to air my dirty laundry.

"So!" Jessica DeLuna stepped out of the salon. "Burnsworth is here!"

The man beside her, Burnsworth, was built just like me, short and pregnant with twins. He wore a starched white tuxedo shirt with a little black bow tie and black pants. Shiny black shoes. He was olive skinned, with a two-inch track of clipped black hair that wrapped behind his head from ear to ear, a little black moustache, and widely spaced dark eyes.

Jessica was busy taking a head count. "Where's Poppy?"

"Who?" Mother asked.

"Poppy Campbell. Your stateroom attendant." Jess's fingers flew across the screen of her V2. "There was a last-minute stateroom attendant shuffle and you got Poppy. Three hours ago."

"I've been here two," Fantasy said. "I haven't seen a Poppy."

From absolutely nowhere, a Poppy appeared. "Right here." She waved.

I don't know if the girl dropped out of the sky, materialized out of thin air, or if she'd been somewhere on the veranda the entire time. I do know Poppy Campbell couldn't possibly have been old enough to drive. Her blond hair was pulled back into a high ponytail, her bright face free of makeup, and she had a definite athletic air about her. Nothing about her said maid. Everything about her said high school cheerleader, surfer girl, teenage teleporter.

"Poppy?" Jessica said. "Where'd you come from?"

A very good question. Along with where had she been?

Poppy opened her mouth, possibly to explain, but didn't get a word out before the table buzzed again. Jess's V2 vibrated in her hand. She stared at it curiously. "It's dead. My V2 went dead."

I leaned over. The screen on my V2 was black.

Fantasy gave hers a bang against the table.

Jess shook hers. "So, no! No!"

"Hold on." I picked mine up and examined it all the way

around. I found what might be a pin dot power button. I used the stud of my David Yurman Chatelaine earring to depress what might be the power button on V2. Let's reboot this fun-sized computer.

Nothing. The V2s had no power.

"The system must have overloaded," I said. "I'm sure they're working on it and it will be back up in a minute."

"I don't even know what that means," my mother said.

"It means," Fantasy said, "we're locked in this room until the phones come back on."

"Well, that's ridiculous."

FOUR

Bianca Sanders had been in comfortable maternity loungewear for six straight months. She wore Swiss voile cotton, cashmere, and silk ensembles from Séraphine in London. She looked pretty, she moved around the bed easily as she had no zippers or turbo elastic to deal with, and in true Bianca fashion, she never wore anything twice. Maybe because she dribbled pizza sauce on everything, but more likely because she was bored out of her skull and didn't want to look at the same $2,000 jammies again.

With her, comfort and expense were king. The more it cost, the better it felt. On the flip side, when it came to what I wore to represent her in public, photographs, and on social media, it was all about cutting-edge style. I tried to steer her in a more Kate Middleton Duchess of Cambridge direction when it came to my wardrobe, but she wouldn't have it. "Please, David." She dismissed the glossy magazine coverage of expectant Kate. "She looks like she splits atoms all day. And those absurd hats."

"Bianca, she's a maternity fashion icon. She looks elegant. And regal."

"Says you, David."

Bianca had yet to choose actual maternity clothes for me to wear. The Vera Wang jumpsuit she had me in for the Welcome Aboard party was a two-tone scuba knit and silk, cream on the top, black everywhere else. V-neck, sleeveless, banded waist above the babies, and overall a beautiful piece. If, that is, you don't buy it in size linebacker, then have an alteration team slash it to size five-foot-tall pregnant. It lost a little in translation. My mother nailed it.

"Davis. You look ridiculous."

"Thank you, Mother."

"I think you look great and I like your positive attitude." Fantasy checked her watch. "The party starts in thirty minutes."

We gathered in the salon. It had been an hour since our V2s went black and in that hour, the sun had set, I'd put Anderson Cooper to bed, located Vera Wang, changed into her, and in all that time the phones didn't budge. No one knocked on the door. There'd been no ship-wide communiqué to tell us all was well. Nothing. I'd checked my V2 every two minutes and it hadn't made a peep. Given that this was the inaugural voyage of *Probability*, hiccups were to be expected. But who would ever dream they'd include communication and captivity?

Fantasy and I returned to the sofa we'd claimed earlier. Mother sat across from us, trying to kill a piece of chewing gum, her jaw clenching, unclenching, clenching. Jessica DeLuna was totally occupied with her V2, stomping the length of the room. She went one way, tried her V2, made a two-point turn, then tried the V2. Then again.

"How long has she been doing that?"

"The whole time," Fantasy said.

"That man and that girl have disappeared, Davis," Mother said.

"They went that way." Fantasy tipped her head in the direction of the crew's quarters.

"They're probably in their rooms getting settled in, Mother."

From behind us, Burnsworth cleared his throat. He hadn't been in his room. He'd been lurking in the shadows of the dark veranda. Fantasy and I exchanged a quick look.

"Burnsworth?" I asked.

"Adjusting the outdoor lighting, ma'am."

Dots of soft flickering light illuminated 704's outdoor living space.

"Would you mind finding Poppy?" I asked Burnsworth.

When I turned around she was standing in front of me.

"Poppy?"

"Yes?"

Again, out of thin air. My nerves were shot. "Everyone have a seat. Let's talk."

Burnsworth took two giant steps forward; Poppy took one. Jessica claimed an empty sofa and threw down her V2 on the table in front of her.

I addressed my fellow 704 hostages. "Chances are, like us, most of the passengers were in their suites settling in when the system went down. I'm sure someone is working hard to get the V2s back up and everyone out. In the meantime, we need to make the best of our situation and be patient. It's not like we're stranded in a dinghy in the middle of the ocean with no food or water."

"So, what about *me*?"

I'd seen this side of Jessica the day I met her. It wasn't attractive from a distance and decidedly less attractive up close. "What about you, Jess?"

"I so don't want to be here!"

"Oh, brother."

"Mother." I turned to her. "Please. Jessica's upset. She'll be fine. Won't you, Jessica?"

"I am so not fine."

"Yes, you are," I said. "We're all fine."

A fine silence settled over the salon of 704.

Mother, who just couldn't stop herself, broke it. "Are there not regular wall telephones here?" she asked. "Why isn't there a phone on the kitchen wall? Has anyone checked the kitchen for a regular phone? Like a house phone?" Her head whipped around. "Where *is* the kitchen, anyway? Why can't we pick up a good old-fashioned telephone and call the front desk? You young people and your portable phones." She slapped at thin air. "It's ridiculous. Look at every one of you, lost without your playthings. Davis, get your regular portable phone and call someone. Tell them we're locked in here."

"Mother." This would be the fourth time I explained the same thing to her. "The minute we stepped on the ship, our personal devices stopped working. It's part of the security system. The broadband on the ship doesn't recognize any digital signal that isn't directly connected to *Probability*'s system."

"Which is SO DOWN!"

I took a deep breath of fortitude. "We know that, Jess." Like talking to a six-year-old. "And you need to settle down."

"Well, my portable phone works just fine."

All heads whipped Mother's way.

"*What?*" Fantasy asked.

"Mother! Where's your phone?"

She'd had the same phone for twenty years, an old-school flip phone, nothing smart about it. It was the dinosaur of mobile communication, with no Wi-Fi, camera, or texting capabilities, which hardly mattered because Mother would text a message exactly never. The *Probability* system hadn't recognized her old analog phone, so there'd been nothing to disable.

"It's in my room," Mother said. "I called your father and told him you brought a cat on this boat."

Six months ago I would have been up and had the phone in my hand in under a minute. Today, I needed a crane. Before I could even think about getting myself and the babies off the sofa, Fantasy flew past me in a blur. "I've got it!"

"It's on the nightstand," Mother called after her. "And I'd appreciate it if you'd leave my bed alone."

Short of breath, Fantasy returned. She dropped Mother's Casio flip phone into my waiting open hands. I stared at the relic, as dense as a rock, and was overwhelmed with unexpected emotion at the thought of just how much communication had passed between Mother and me on this one prehistoric device. My eyes found hers.

"What, Davis? What are you waiting for? World peace?"

Moment over. I flipped open the phone and for the life of me had no idea what to do. Whatever directions had been on the raised black buttons were long gone, and I'd had a phone similar to the Casio four hundred phones ago.

"Well, Davis," Mother said, "turn it *on*."

I depressed the black circle in the middle, which was clearly the wrong choice, because it triggered a long and loud horn blast that reverberated through the open terrace and scared the living daylights out of everyone. I yelped, tossing the phone through the air, and like a bolt from the blue, Jess dove for it, screaming, "No! So, no!" She landed on the glass table; tulips, V2s, and water went everywhere. Mother, Fantasy, and I were plastered against our cushion backs, staring at Jessica, who was facedown and spread eagle across the glass table, her shoulders heaving, her head hanging off one end, long dark hair pooled on the silver rug. Her hand rose as she displayed the phone she caught midair and my mother broke the shocked silence when she said, "There was no need for that. You can't hurt that phone, young lady. I've run over it with my Chevrolet twice."

Fantasy and I exchanged wide-eyed looks of wonderment. Before we had a chance to (get Jess off the table) recover, three staccato horn blasts shook the walls *again*. So loud Anderson Cooper had to have heard it. The horror-movie scream was courtesy of Jessica, who wound up on the floor at my feet, the F-bombs were courtesy of Fantasy, and my mother shrieked, "Oh, my stars! Oh, my stars! Oh, my stars!"

Fantasy straddled Jess, pried the flip phone from her claws, and handed it to me. "You don't have much time." She peeled Jess off the floor and lobbed her back onto the sofa she'd flown off of a few minutes earlier. Then she dusted her hands and took a deep breath. "The ship must have pulled up anchor," she announced. "We're leaving. The horn blasts mean were leaving. Everyone calm down. It's all fine."

"It is NOT FINE!" Jess lunged at her. "You need to SHUT UP! You are SO not in charge!"

Fantasy pushed up her sleeves, balled her fists, and was on her way to get a piece of Jessica, me yelling "Stop! Stop! Stop!" the whole time. My mother, trying to disappear into the corner of her sofa, said, "You'd better believe I'm telling your father about this."

I propelled myself to my feet by sheer will and caught Fantasy by the back of her shirt. "Everyone please settle down! Just settle down!" I pushed Fantasy back down into her seat and started with Jessica. "Really, Jess, dial it back. You're making it ten times worse." Next, my wild-eyed partner. "Fantasy, I understand you're not in a good place and you'd love nothing better than to kick someone's ass—"

"You watch your mouth, young lady."

(Really?)

"—but not hers," I stabbed a finger at Jess, "and not now. Right now this phone," I shook Mother's Casio, "might be close enough to a cell tower on land to pick up a signal, and if the ship has pulled up anchor, it means I have very little time to make a call. So everyone calm down and let me do this. Mother?"

"What?"

"How do I use this phone?"

* * *

I didn't know anyone's number. I could dial 911 (not a bad idea), but I didn't know individual phone numbers. I programmed numbers into my phone, seeing them once and immediately forgetting them. I knew Bradley's number by heart because (I'm married to him) his is the number our Mr. Lau's Dim Sum delivery account is set up under and I have to repeat Bradley's number to the Dim Sum operator who's standing there looking right at the caller ID with my number displayed. As if I would lie about what phone I'm using to call in our hot chicken peanut and beef and broccoli with extra fried rice and eggroll order. But Bradley was somewhere over Ohio or North Carolina right now, and even though he probably had cell service, I didn't want to panic him. There wasn't a thing he could do but have the pilots turn the plane around, and by the time he got to us, which would take landing in Biloxi again, then getting on a boat, or at that point, a helicopter, to reach us, chances are we'd be well out of our luxury prison by then and I'd have worried him and disrupted his schedule for nothing. The person I needed to talk to was my immediate supervisor, No Hair. Whom others call Jeremy Covey. (Long story, but easy to figure out: Jeremy Covey has No Hair.) I couldn't call No Hair. Even if I knew his number, he was somewhere on this ship and his personal phone was disabled. I could only communicate with No Hair by V2.

Which wasn't an option.

We had no options without V2s. So, I did what I've done all my life when I ran out of options. I called my father.

"Daddy! Daddy! It's me!"

The phone dropped the call. I pulled it away from my head and looked at it.

"What?" The collective question from my very attentive audience.

Mother's phone was so old it didn't display signal strength, but I didn't need to be told I didn't have much reception. "I'm going outside."

Fantasy helped me up and we marched out to the deck single file. I immediately dialed Daddy's number again, too soon for Mother's old phone, and got clipped beeps. Poking buttons until I ended the call, I tried again and got through.

"Sweet Pea? Is that you?"

"Daddy! It's me! We need help!"

"What, honey? What? You're breaking up."

"Daddy! We're locked in our suite on the ship. We can't communicate with anyone. Call No Hair, Daddy. Find a way to call this ship and have No Hair get us out of here!"

"Yes, your mother said the ship is beautiful."

His words were drowning in static.

"Daddy, we're STUCK in our suite! We're *STUCK!*"

"You're what, honey? I can't hardly hear you."

"STUCK, Daddy! *STUCK!*"

"Davis, I hope you're not using that kind of language in front of your mother."

And the phone gave up.

First it was a single pop, like a toy gun. It came from the dark sky. The initial pop was followed by ten more. We rushed toward the deck rail to see a starburst of multicolored explosions lighting up the night, the ship, and the water. Then another, then more, then hundreds. A dazzling fireworks display celebrating our departure burst a thousand feet above our heads and spilled down for the next fifteen minutes. When silence and night fell around us again, Mother asked, "Why would they be shooting off fireworks when they're supposed to be opening the doors?"

Why, indeed.

"And if everyone's locked in their room," Mother said, "who's up there at the fireworks party?"

Who, indeed.

FIVE

There are three Bellissimo Super Spies: me, Fantasy, and Baylor. We report to No Hair, who's the head of Bellissimo security at all times and the head of *Probability* security this week.

When I'm not pregnant with twins, I'm a little more than five feet off the ground, and when I am pregnant with twins, like now, I'm also a little more than five feet around the middle. I felt that way, anyway. My hair is red—cinnamon, not tangerine—and my eyes are the same cinnamon color. Put me next to Fantasy, who is six feet tall, and whose skin is both light and dark—think Halle Berry—with slate blue eyes and new blondish highlights in her short layered hair, and we are a visual interpretation of opposites attract. We don't look like we belong, but we do.

Baylor, just Baylor, and I'm beginning to suspect Baylor might be his last name instead of his first (I've been meaning to nose into that), is the third member of our team and our resident manchild. Fantasy and I are close to the same age, thirtysomething, and Baylor is, on paper, twenty-six. In real life he's twelve. He's fearless, strong, and based on popular speculation, very much in the wrong job. No one looks at Baylor and thinks law and order. They look at Baylor and say, "He's a country music singer, professional football player, or male stripper." He has thick dark brown hair and rascally brown eyes, a lazy way about him, and he's a ninja sharpshooter. He sleeps with everything that owns a pushup bra, it's humiliating, he has a sixth sense when it comes to danger, and he's always hungry. He's more like a two-hundred-pound puppy than anything else. Fantasy and I have spent years getting him good and housebroken, and we were almost there when my husband took him. More and more, including this week, Baylor stayed by Bradley's side in a security capacity. It couldn't be me, because I love Bradley too much and I'd shoot anyone who looked at him sideways. It couldn't be Fantasy, because her personal life had taken a front seat to her work life for months now with no end in sight. And it couldn't be No Hair, because he was in charge of everything else security at our seventeen-hundred-room hotel casino, and this week, he was everything security on *Probability*. All that to say this: Our happy spy family was in major transition and why hadn't our happy spy father rescued us?

No Hair was the glue holding things together for six months of me being pregnant, back and forth to Pine Apple helping with Mother, and publicly representing Bianca Sanders's pregnancy. The whole time, Fantasy had been trying to patch up her marriage and Baylor has been with my husband. We'd been a scattered crew of spies for a long half-year, relying completely on No Hair. Who was somewhere on this ship, and he had to be looking for me. He just had to be. There are three men in my life I know I can count on: my husband, my father, and No Hair. My husband was forty thousand feet in the air and over Missouri or Minnesota by now. My father was in the middle of Alabama without a clue. No Hair was somewhere on this ship, and why he hadn't busted through the door of Suite 704 and rescued us was curious at best and disconcerting at worst.

At eleven o'clock, with *Probability* well underway and still no communication in or out, Mother, Fantasy and I sat quietly on our appointed sofas in the salon. Burnsworth had "retired" to his quarters, Poppy excused herself five minutes after he did, while Jess had done nothing but drink vodka, whine, and beat on the front door, demanding someone let her out, which was a total waste of time. The companionways were private from the elevators to the individual suites; there was no foot traffic to hear her. The only reason someone would be outside our door would be to open it, so screaming unnecessary. After two solid hours of it, she gave up and stretched across her sofa. The steady lull of the ship moving through the dark Gulf waters, sheer exhaustion, and the ongoing hysteria (Jess) had numbed everyone.

I looked up from the babies and caught my mother's eye.

"I'm dead on my feet."

I hated that phrase. "You should go to bed, Mother."

"I believe I will."

She stood, and without another word, made her way down the hall.

"Mother?"

She hesitated.

"Lock your door."

She waved acknowledgement.

"That's it?" Fantasy stared after Mother. "No sleep tight, don't let the bedbugs bite?"

"She's not exactly the touchy-feely type, Fantasy."

"I heard that, Davis."

"Goodnight, Mother."

I love you.

* * *

"So, I don't have my stuff."

We were hungry and the kitchen was white. White subway tile walls and white glazed porcelain floors, with round rugs and rectangular runners in thick white shag scattered here, there, and yon. White stone waterfall-edge countertops, solid white high gloss cabinets, a round white dining table with six white molded chairs. White pendant light fixtures dangled at the ends of white leads from the white ceiling. The only hints of color in the room were from the stainless steel appliances, all Miele, all obscured by the blinding white, and if I were to put Anderson Cooper down in this room and she closed her eyes, I might never find her.

"Your stuff?" Fantasy was deep into a bag of Cheetos. "What's your stuff, Jess?"

"My *meds*. My *clothes*. My *lipstick*. And so, where am I supposed to sleep?"

"There's an empty staff room," I said.

"I don't think so." Jess pulled a chair from the table and plopped down, while Fantasy and I foraged for her dinner.

"It's the staff room or a sun chair on the deck," Fantasy said.

Our first meal aboard *Probability* was sliced from a whole honey ham and a wheel of Colby cheese. We had sandwiches on thick white crusty bread with a peppery spring pasta salad. There was enough food in the white kitchen to feed an army, including odd things, like a full array of spices, a seven-pound sirloin tip roast, fresh fruits and vegetables, several whole chickens, and a summer-camp-size box of Captain Crunch. That was just the first layer. Of many. There were thirty-one flavors of ice cream in the freezer and a wine closet behind a white glass door that was half cellar, half cooler, and the whole wine list at a five-star restaurant.

Jess picked at her food, moving it around on her plate, while Fantasy and I wolfed ours down like it was The Last Supper. For one, we were hungry. For another, we were trying to hurry Jess along so we could do something. I wasn't sure what, but something needed to be done.

"Jessica?"

She dropped a crust of bread and looked up. "What?"

"You're not supposed to be here," I said.

Her head swiveled as she studied the four white walls. "So, where do you want me to go?"

"That's not what I meant. What I meant was you're the only person here who should be somewhere else. Where are you supposed to be? Surely someone is wondering where you are."

She twirled a length of long dark hair. "I doubt it."

"Are you not *Probability*'s Miss Congeniality?" I asked. "There have to be passengers who noticed you weren't at the Welcome Aboard party."

"So, you think it's just us?"

"Is what just us?" I asked.

"Do you think we're the only ones whose V2s don't work?"

I didn't say that, and I certainly didn't intend for her to jump to that conclusion. "I think, Jess, as big as the ship is, there's no way every single passenger was in their suite when the V2s went down. And if anyone's looking for anyone, it would be you."

"Who's looking for me?"

Fantasy drummed impatient fingers on the white table.

"There has to be someone who's noticed you're missing."

"Probably not," she said.

"But the cruise is your job, Jess."

"My job was to get people *on* the cruise. So, they're on it."

She had a point. "What about your husband?"

"He's a bloodsucking bastard."

That shut things all the way down.

I cleared my throat. "In spite of that, Jess, don't you think he's noticed you're missing?"

Unprovoked ugliness had flown out of Jess's mouth for hours on end without her so much as taking a breath between them, while it took her forever for her to say the one word, "No."

Fantasy, who'd recently learned far more than she wanted to know about marital discord, spoke up. "Jessica, even if your husband hates your guts, he's still going to notice you're not where you're supposed to be."

Her face clouded in confusion, as if she couldn't possibly imagine who hated her guts or where in the world she was supposed to be, then without any warning she slammed face first into the table. Our chairs scraped, we shot up, and our mouths dropped open. Fantasy and I looked at each other. *Is she dead?*

I inched over, pushing miles of dark hair away from her neck, and cautiously dove in with two fingers. "She's alive." To prove it, Jess made a strange sound. A rumble. Then again. It was a snore. She was snoring. The woman had passed out. "Jessica." I shook her. "Wake up."

"How much has she had to drink?" Fantasy whispered.

"Not enough for *this*." I shook her again. "Jess. Wake up."

She slowly peeled herself off the table and scanned our astonished faces as if she had no idea who we were or why we were staring. "So? What?"

"What just happened?" I asked.

She checked her immediate vicinity, unsure if the question was hers. She spread a hand across her ample chest. "So, me?"

"Yes, Jess," I said. "You."

"Did I crash?"

"You did," I said. "Are you okay?"

"I'm a narc." She yawned, deeply.

"What?" I asked. "What does that mean?"

"I have narcolepsy. I need my meds."

Fantasy and I took a step back.

"So? I microsleep."

We took another step back.

"I fall asleep!"

"Jess." I didn't know what to say. "Should we—?" I couldn't find a way to finish the question. Should we...what?

"What exactly is narcolepsy?" Fantasy asked.

"If I sit still, I fall asleep." She yawned again. Deeply. So deeply, Fantasy and I couldn't help but join her. "Music puts me to sleep. The Hallmark Channel. Red lights. Lots of things. I fall asleep. There's nothing you can do but get me out of here so I can get my meds. Or deal with it."

I was entirely too exhausted to deal with one more thing. I was too tired to think another thought and she needed to lie down somewhere so she didn't break her neck the next time she decided to slam asleep. "It's been a long day and it's late," I said. "We need to get you in a bed."

The word "bed" must do the trick too. Luckily, we caught her.

"Now what?" I was having trouble holding up my half of Jess.

"Come on." Fantasy was carrying more than her half of Jess.

Past the salon, we took a left and thumped Sleeping Beauty down three short steps. It wasn't hard to figure out which was the empty crew cabin, because between the three, there was one open door. A thin light shone from under the door of the room at the end of the narrow hall and the door directly in front of us was dark and closed.

We tucked Jessica in the bed and got out of there as fast as we could. We fell on our sofa in the moonlit salon.

"What is going on?" Fantasy whispered.

"I don't have a clue." I whispered back.

*   *   *

At midnight, the clock clicking from Saturday to Sunday, I locked the door to my stateroom behind me. I gathered my cat, pajamas, prenatal vitamins, and toothbrush, and was in a hurry for the bed when I stepped into the gold bathroom and saw an envelope taped to the mirror above the vanity. It was addressed to me. I recognized my name right away; I've had it all my life. The problem was—I took slow and steady steps toward the envelope—no one outside 704 knew my name. Correspondence to me aboard *Probability* should have been addressed to Bianca Sanders. Not Davis Way Cole. I reached for it, curious and apprehensive at the same time. I opened it to find a photograph of my boss, No Hair. My knees gave way and the vanity caught me. Hands bound behind his back, legs secured at the ankles, clothes disheveled, his tie gone, and his lower lip split wide open, he was in a straight chair against a wall between two dark porthole windows. No Hair was someone's prisoner. He looked straight at me when the picture was taken, his eyes apologetic, but everything else about his expression and posture was livid.

My head swam and I saw stars. I backed up to the square porcelain bathtub in the middle of the gold floor and sat down on the wide edge. I read the letter.

Mrs. Cole,

To ensure your safety and that of your guests and loved ones, sit back and settle in, because you're not leaving your suite. Rest assured no harm will come to anyone as long as you follow these simple instructions: Do not attempt to escape or make contact with anyone. Jeremy Covey will be detained for the duration of the cruise, as will you and your party. You will walk off this ship unharmed if you cooperate.

Unfortunately, the medical staff accompanying you tried to board with controlled substances and was refused passage. They're not looking for you. Your photography crew has been reassigned. They're not looking for you. No one is looking for you. There's no way out. Not only is escape impossible, you will most assuredly jeopardize everyone's welfare if you attempt any overt attention-seeking endeavors. In other words, Mrs. Cole, don't start a fire. You'll burn.

Arrangements have been made to communicate with your husband for you. Should you try to contact him directly and by some miracle succeed, you run the risk of never seeing him again.

Relax, follow these simple instructions, and all will be well. Attempts to escape, alert your husband, the authorities, or other passengers will be met with deadly consequences. It's up to you.

And that was it.

We were hostages on a luxury cruise liner.

SIX

I clapped my hand over Fantasy's mouth and pinned her to the bed so she wouldn't kill me. Instead, she bit the fire out of me. Anderson Cooper jumped to my defense and onto Fantasy's face. There was wrestling and meowing. Anderson didn't vocalize often and when she did, because she couldn't hear herself, it was loud, raw, and cannon-shot unexpected. I grabbed for (my cat) a pillow and slammed it over Fantasy's head to muffle the language. "It's me, Fantasy! It's me!"

We both panted for a full minute.

She clicked on a bedside lamp and sat up. "Davis! What the *hell*? What happened?"

"Shhhh!" I scream-whispered. "Be quiet!"

"Me be quiet? How about that crazy cat of yours?" She gave Anderson a very dirty look. "Besides," she whispered, "who's going to hear us?"

My mother.

"Come with me."

"Davis, what's wrong?"

"Do you have your gun?"

"No." She swung her legs over the side of the bed. "I smuggled your cat on, which was hard enough, thank you. No Hair has my gun."

I doubted that.

"What's happened? Who do we need to shoot?"

"Just get up," I said. "I need you to see something in my room."

She read my face. "Uh-oh."

"Don't make a peep." I stepped toward the door. "We do *not* want to wake up my mother."

Fantasy, wearing almost nothing but a tank top, tied her robe around her waist, but her robe was so short it didn't do any good. She stepped into her fuzzy slippers. "What the hell is going on?"

*　*　*

We tiptoed from one end of 704 to the other by the light of the moon. When we reached my stateroom, I closed and locked the door. I held a finger to my lips and led her through the sitting room to the bedroom.

"You're freaking me out, Davis."

I passed the envelope. She passed out. (No, she didn't.)

She went back and forth between the picture of No Hair and the letter. "Oh my God. We're prisoners."

Yes.

"Who is this? Who's doing this?" She shook the letter. "And where is he?"

She shook the picture.

I had no answers.

We sank to sit on the edge of the bed.

"Do you think they mean it?" she whispered.

"Which part?" I whispered back. "Yes, I think they mean it. We're trapped and they have No Hair."

"Who are *they*?"

"I have no idea," I said. "Whoever it is, they want us out of the way."

"Of what?" she asked. "A heist? A con?"

"Or a target," I whispered. "One of the bazillionaires. Extortion. Blackmail. Kidnapping."

"It could be escaped prisoners hitching a ride," Fantasy said. "Or there's a Bernie Madoff on this boat. A homicidal first wife. It could be anyone with any number of agendas."

"A homicidal first wife wouldn't lock us in here. Or No Hair there."

We stared at the photograph of our boss.

We stared at the photograph of our friend.

"Where's there?" Fantasy asked. "And where did you find this?"

"It was taped to the bathroom mirror."

"Who taped it to the mirror?" She grabbed my arm. "Davis! Either Jessica, Poppy, the butler, or all three of them are in on this! One of them did it!"

"No." I shook my head. "Not necessarily."

"I didn't put it on the mirror. Your mother didn't put it on the mirror."

"It could have been on the mirror when we left Biloxi, Fantasy. *Anyone* could have put it on the mirror."

"But you just found it."

"That doesn't mean it wasn't there earlier."

"Well, think, Davis. Was it or wasn't it?"

"I don't know! I can't remember. I didn't see it before we left, but I didn't *not* see it before we left."

"Which is it, Davis? You did or you didn't?"

"I don't know." I fell back on the bed. "I know I went in there, but I wasn't looking for a note on the mirror. I found it ten minutes ago and I have no idea how long it's been there."

"Oh, holy crap." She fell beside me. "This can't be happening."

"It's happening." We stared at the ceiling until it got a whole lot worse. "My mother."

"What?"

"We can't breathe a word of this, Fantasy. Not one word. My mother *cannot* know."

"Considering your mother doesn't know you're pregnant, I don't think it will be too hard to hide this from her."

We lay there, staring at the ceiling, until Fantasy raised herself on an elbow. "What are we going to do, Davis?"

"Get out of here. And rescue No Hair."

*   *   *

We armed ourselves on the fly, me with a lamp base and Fantasy with a satin nickel towel bar she ripped right off the wall.

"Let's start at the front door."

"You're not going first." She pushed in front of me. "You're too pregnant."

We crept through the salon barefoot, catching a moonbeam, which sent our distorted shadows across the floor and up the walls, making the entire endeavor as spooky as possible. We finally reached the foyer. Pitch black. I patted the wall until I found a round dimmer switch. I rolled it to the right, illuminating the silver statue display enough for us to see the cabin door.

"There's a panel here," I whispered.

Fantasy was facing away from me, standing guard with her towel bar. She looked over her shoulder. "What is it?"

"It's a number pad. I bet it's—" I popped off the panel, "—an override. Like an emergency way to open the door." I turned to her. "What's the code? We don't know the code. We could stand here the whole week and not guess it." I poked the keypad anyway: seven, zero, and four. "It doesn't matter. It's dead."

"What?" Fantasy asked.

"The numbers aren't lighting up."

"What?"

"Find me a screwdriver," I said.

"Where am I supposed to find a screwdriver?"

"Hold this." I turned the lamp around, she held the base, and I unscrewed a crystal ball finial from the top.

"Good thinking."

If it had worked.

She smashed the crystal ball with the towel bar; I used a shard of glass to pry the number pad off the panel. "It's cut."

"You cut yourself?" She turned to look.

"The electrical." The red and blue twist of lines behind the number pad had been snipped clean.

Back to our sofa.

Anderson Cooper, who'd wandered out my stateroom door, pounced on us, back and forth.

"We need to sleep in shifts," Fantasy said. "You go first, because your cat is driving me out of my mind."

Sleep wouldn't be easy, in spite of the fact I couldn't remember being this tired in my life. Neither of us had a gun. I'd stopped carrying one the minute I passed the pregnancy test, because babies and guns don't mix. Fantasy didn't bring a gun onboard, because as Bianca Sanders's guest, it would have been too hard to explain to the embarkation people why she was packing. We were both lost without our heat.

"We need to check on my mother."

"Check for what?" Fantasy looked down the hall. All was quiet.

"I don't want her all the way down there by herself."

"Well, let's go get her."

"Under what pretext? A slumber party? Fantasy, we can't tell her."

"At this point, how do we *not* tell her, Davis? You need to tell her."

"I say we don't say a word to anyone until we know what we're dealing with."

"We're hostages," she said. "That's what we're dealing with."

"I mean the enemy within."

"As in here?"

"Right," I said. "Chances are someone in this suite is in on it. Where was Poppy for three hours? She could easily be in on it."

"And that creepy Burnsworth," Fantasy said. "He could too."

"Plus the fact that Jessica didn't leave our side all day. Until she passed out."

"Meaning?"

"There are two ways to look at it," I said. "One, she probably didn't put the letter on the mirror because she was with us the entire time. Or two, she's behind everything which is why she was with us the entire time."

"I don't see that airhead behind anything," Fantasy said. "Much less this."

One of my babies bumped into another one of my babies. "Look." I pointed.

She placed a warm hand on the babies and was rewarded with a kick.

"Davis. We have to get you out of here."

We listened to each other breathe for the longest.

"We need to set a timer," she said. "A limit on how long we're going to wait before we make a move. There's got to be something we can do."

"Like what?"

"We can throw all the furniture off the deck. Someone has to notice a trail of white sofas in the water."

"Sofas don't float, Fantasy. And even if they did, it's the dead of night. If we throw all the furniture in the ocean, we'll be locked in here with no furniture," I said. "We could throw ourselves overboard right now and no one would notice."

"Okay," she said, "we Rapunzel. We tie bed sheets together. Make a rope. Climb down."

"The ship isn't built that way. Didn't you get a good look at the exterior? The decks are designed to *prevent* anyone climbing around. And the terraces are built for privacy, tiered and staggered, so it's not like we could drop off our deck onto someone else's. We'd have to go up or down *two* decks to get to anything or anyone. Let's say we did. Let's say there are that many bed sheets in here. Then we'd have to dangle over the ocean and somehow gain enough momentum to swing in fifty feet to land on a deck that's fifty feet down, and we're moving at almost forty knots an hour. There's no way. Whoever we send down will be lost at sea. And that's if they don't land on a Zoom car and splatter at sea."

She looked at me in the quiet dark. "I didn't say it wouldn't be dangerous. Obviously you can't do it. You can barely walk." (Thank you.) "We'll elect someone by secret ballot. I'm ready to vote right now."

"Face facts, Fantasy. We're stuck here. With Jess. That said, do you think you could hate her a little less?"

"I don't *hate* her," she said. "Much."

Anderson Cooper had fallen asleep.

"We could build a bomb," she said. "Blast our way out."

I studied her face by the light of the moon to see if she was serious. "Do you think for one second this suite is stocked with bomb-building supplies? Even if it was and we built one, this unit is probably as strong as a vault. We already know the door is. If we build a bomb and set it off we'll still be locked in, but at the bottom of a pile of rubble after we blow ourselves up. Which will set off the sprinklers. So if we don't kill ourselves in the blast we'll drown."

"There you go." She snapped her fingers. "We figure out a way to flood the casino. You know if a blackjack table took a drop of water they'd find the leak, which means they'd find us, and we'd be out of here in ten minutes."

"Fantasy," I said, "the casino is on the deck above us. We can't defy gravity."

We were running out of late-night escape options.

"For now, we need to sit tight." I tried to get comfortable. "Think about how we solve problems at the Bellissimo. It's not by setting off bombs."

She raised a questioning eyebrow, mentally tracking our three years of Super Spying, thinking surely we've blown something up at one point or another. And she was probably right.

"We've been in some scrapes, Fantasy. Tight spots."

"Very tight."

"And every single time No Hair believed in us. He let us see things through. Think of how many times he could have pulled the plug when it didn't look like we'd find our way. Think of how things would have turned out differently if he'd set off a bomb on us. We have to return the favor. As bad as this looks, taking a desperate or drastic measure right now might do more harm than good, especially since we've been warned not to. Did you read the part in the note about being *dead*?"

"This is horrible," she said. "We're helpless."

"We're not. We need to hit it from another angle," I said. "We play along, pretend we didn't even find the note, don't let on we realize we're prisoners, and approach it from behind."

"Sneak up on it," she said.

"Right."

"How is that going to help?"

"We can flush out the bad guy," I said. "And find out why we're locked in here. There's a *reason* No Hair's being held and there's a *reason* we're hostages, and we need to find the reason. And until we find the reason, we hang onto this: Who do we know that's tougher than No Hair? Have you ever known anyone tougher than him?"

"No."

"You have to believe he can tough this out until we can get to him. Because if you don't believe, I won't be able to believe."

"I believe, Davis. I believe."

We hooked pinkie fingers.

We believed for five quiet minutes until I said, "Here's the plan."

"I'm listening."

"We figure out who locked us up and why."

"Okay," she said.

"We turn this place upside down and find a way out."

"Got it."

"Then we rescue No Hair."

"First thing in the morning, Davis. We'll knock off your list. One, two, three. After that, let's go try on jewelry we can't afford at Tiffany's."

"I thought you said you believed."

She sighed.

"Okay, then this," I said. "No matter what, we'll be out of here sometime tomorrow. We'll get out, then rescue No Hair."

"How?"

"I don't know exactly how, when, or what we're going to have to deal with before. But we'll be out tomorrow."

"How can you be so sure?"

"When Bradley's plane lands in China the first thing he'll do is call me. When he doesn't reach me he'll call No Hair. When he doesn't reach either of us he'll send Navy SEALS."

"Since when does Bradley have the authority to engage SEALS?"

"You know what I mean."

"I appreciate your confidence," she said. "But whoever's behind this has done an impressive job setting it up. They've managed to take down No Hair and lock us up. When they say they have communication with Bradley covered, they might have it covered."

"I know my husband."

"The husband you know so well is halfway across the globe."

"Okay," I said, "last resort. We have Mother's phone. Whoever disabled our V2s doesn't know we have a phone. Tomorrow, we'll cruise close enough to Cuba to see land. We'll be close enough to pick up a cell signal. And if that doesn't work, we'll absolutely be able to call for help Monday."

"Why Monday?" Her words were hidden behind a yawn. "What happens Monday?"

"On Monday we'll be in the Caymans. We can definitely get a call out when we get to the Caymans."

SEVEN

Probability's itinerary included one port of call—the offshore financial haven of the Cayman Islands. We were going straight there, stopping for two days, then heading right back to Biloxi. The Caymans were one of the monetary capitals of the world with forty of the fifty largest international banks in operation, and our destination was George Town, the capital city, on the southwest coast of Grand Cayman. Collectively, the passengers on *Probability* had more than a small stake in the Cayman's $1.5 trillion in financial transaction liabilities, and a very vested interest in visiting one, or several, of the six hundred George Town banks. The Caymans had more registered corporations than people, and the banking accompanying all that incorporation ran the gamut, including day-to-day trading, general commercial transactions, investment activities, hedge fund formation, structured securitization and financing, captive insurance, plus any and all other broad-spectrum corporate financial activities. Not all Cayman banking was aboveboard and sanctioned by the United States Federal Government. But all Cayman banking was tax free on profits and capital gains with no withholding taxes for foreign investors, in addition to being free of estate and death duties. It was the ideal location for the mega wealthy to set up trust, annuity, and savings accounts, and the fifty invited guests on Probability had one thing in common: They banked in the Caymans.

There were three reasons *Probability* was only making the one stop.

First, anchorage—where to park the big thing. The draft of a ship refers to the distance between the waterline and the keel, the rock bottom. The draft on *Probability* kept it well away from the shoreline. In other words, what you couldn't see went too deep to dock the ship anywhere near land without running aground. It had to stay in the ocean; there weren't enough tug boats in the whole Caribbean to pull *Probability* off a sandbar. The bazillionaires would be ferried to George Town on luxury commuter speedboats with three-piece Jing Ping bands housed in *Probability* garages. (The boats were housed in *Probability* garages.) (Not the Jing Ping bands.) (Surely they had staterooms.)

The second reason we were only making one stop was interest level. The passengers on this cruise had upcountry estates on Maui, chateaus in the south of France, penthouse condos on Bora Bora, and beach-front mansions in Monaco. They cared very little about the tourist traps of Jamaica, Cozumel, and Montego Bay, because the activities and amenities aboard *Probability* were greater than the activities and amenities in all of the Antilles, Greater and Lesser.

And the third reason *Probability* had one destination: security.

"Only one passenger on the entire guest list won't be bringing private security."

"Which one?" I asked. "Me?"

No Hair and I were in his office and the countdown was on. T-minus six weeks before *Probability* would set sail. I'd parked my car ten minutes earlier, having just driven back from Pine Apple. I'd gone upstairs to Bradley's and my twenty-ninth floor home to put Anderson Cooper to bed, then straight to No Hair's office. He gave me a bear hug with one massive arm around my shoulders and patted my babies bump. He asked about Mother, he asked about Daddy, then we took seats at his corner conference table covered with hundreds of *Probability* dossiers.

"Not you," he said. "The passenger who isn't bringing security is actually in the security business. He's his own security. You have security. You're taken care of."

"Fantasy?" I asked.

"Fantasy is definitely security," he said, "and she's definitely booked in your suite."

"What have we heard from her?"

"We've heard exactly nothing."

Fantasy had been working the bare bones minimum, showing up only when it was absolutely necessary. Between my pregnancy, managing Bianca Sanders's pregnancy, and running back and forth to Pine Apple, I'd spent a whopping hour with her over the last six months. I had no idea what was going on in her marriage, I missed her, and I was looking forward to spending time with her on *Probability*. "So it's been you and Baylor all week?"

He nodded.

"Are we sure Fantasy's going to make the cruise?"

"Davis, they filed."

My heart hit a wall. We'd been holding our collective breath waiting for Fantasy and her husband Reggie to work it out, and filing for a divorce wasn't a step in that direction.

"Who they?" I asked. "He filed? He's divorcing her? On what grounds?" The last time we'd talked, a good six weeks earlier, Fantasy's greatest fear wasn't that Reggie would divorce her—she felt certain he would. Her main concern was that of every mother: the fate of her children. To be determined in a courtroom based largely on *how* he divorced her: fault or no-fault. I'm a little of a divorce expert, having been through a few. Okay, three. Three divorces (humiliating), two previous marriages (even more humiliating), and in all that only one ex-husband. (Humiliating all the way around.) (But I'm not one to dwell on the past.) (What's done is done.) (Move on.) Fantasy wasn't a divorce expert. She'd been married to the same man, the father of her three sons, for fifteen years. She had an accidental affair with a psychotic surgeon and it cracked her marriage wide open. With this news, it looked like there'd be no repairing it.

"I don't know the details." No Hair rubbed his bald head. "She's not talking. Not that I've heard from her for her to talk."

"She hasn't called at all?" I asked.

"Not only that, she's not taking my calls."

"Mine either." She returned text messages in the middle of the night. She returned emails days later. Obviously, she didn't want to talk about it. "I'll go knock on her door," I said. "I'll just show up and make her talk. And I'll do it as soon as I see my husband for five minutes, check in with Bianca, and bottom line, I need more hours in the day."

"Me and you both," he said. "When we ever get this *Probability* business out of the way and before you have the babies, I'll need your help restructuring this team. I can't do this alone. I haven't been home in time for dinner in two months. I haven't had a day off in three. Grace is about to have a fit."

I felt my eyes sting. "I'm so sorry, No Hair."

He placed a big meaty paw over my hand. "This isn't on you. But I do need this boat business out of the way so I can have my life back."

"Don't you call it a ship?" Sniff.

"Does it make any difference?"

"The difference is a ship can carry a boat but a boat can't carry a ship."

"Why does it matter?"

"It's just, you know," I said, "the right word versus the wrong word."

"How long do you want to talk about this, Davis?"

I picked at my Pea in a Pod sweater. "I'm done."

"When we get off the *ship*, you'll be on maternity leave, Baylor's pretty much set with Bradley, and Fantasy's going to have to decide if she's coming back to work or not. Thank goodness I still have you for a few weeks." He tapped a stack of *Probability* files. "I need you to dig up dirt on these people."

"Again?" This was back when the babies had plenty of room to lunge and lurch. One or both did one or both. It was hard to tell. "Whoops!" I sat back and watched.

"I can't imagine," No Hair said.

"Swallow two squirrels," I said. "It's just like that."

"No thank you." He leaned in. "Hello little Jeremys! It's Uncle Jeremy."

My hands hopped all over the babies trying to cover their ears. "No Hair, stop scaring them."

Since the day we told No Hair about the babies, he's worn me out asking me to name them Jeremy. Both of them. Jeremy.

"What if we have girls, No Hair?"

"It's the twenty-first century, Davis. Why don't you know what you're having?"

"We don't want to know."

"Well, Jeremy works both ways. If you have a girl, or two girls, just spell it with an I."

"Really, No Hair? Twin girls both named Jeremy with an I? No."

"Why not?"

We'd had this conversation countless times and we had it again today until I picked up a *Probability* passenger dossier and smacked him with it. Which led us back to work.

"We've got the usual," he said. "Hedge fund, dot-com, real estate, big money."

"I know already. I could recite the list in my sleep. Why do you need me to look at them again?" I'd run them through the wringer ten times already.

"I don't," he said. "I want you to run backgrounds on their guests and their personal security. Let's see what pops. The fifty suites have two guestrooms and they're booked out." He pushed a stack of a hundred blue folders at me. "We need to know as much, if not more, about the entourages as we do the One Percent." He piled a smaller stack of red folders on the blue ones. "These too."

"Who are they?"

"Ship security," No Hair said. "I've pulled twenty-five from our casino floor, the vault, and hotel security for my team. Our guys. We know them. But *Probability* has its own security, also twenty-five. They'll report to me and I want to know who they are."

"How will a security staff of fifty cover so much space?"

"They don't have to," he said. "The surveillance on the ship is so severe, Davis, we could probably get by with half the security we're taking."

"Severe?"

"Let me put it this way," he said. "Don't try to hide anything. It can see through your clothes and down your throat. It's military-grade imaging. Eight thousand cameras with proprietary microelectronic surveillance watching every breath every passenger takes."

"Surely not in the suites."

"No." He shook his big bald head. "The public access areas only. The suites are so secure they don't need it. They're fortresses," he said. "They can't be breached."

Is that so.

"What about the casino?" I asked. "A security staff of fifty can't patrol the traffic, the gaming, and the cage."

"There is no cage."

"How can there not be a cage?" Casinos are about money. The money is kept in the cage. No cage means no money. No money means no casino. "I don't understand."

"The boat is electronic, Davis, including the casino. Not a penny of cash will change hands. Everyone will be issued a phone, or a reasonable facsimile thereof, and one of its many functions is banking. It also operates as a direct and unlimited line of credit for the players."

"The V thing?"

"Right."

"With no cash and unlimited credit, the gambling will be outrageous, No Hair. They'll have a few drinks, they won't keep track, the players will swipe themselves stupid."

"They can afford it. And someone has to pay for the boat."

"Ship." He shot me a look. "Do I get one of the V phones?"

"Of course," he said. "Everyone does. Everyone has to have one. It's the only way to get on and off the elevators and it's the only way to gamble. All transactions are electronically deducted from personal *Probability* accounts. And all wins are paid back into the accounts electronically. It's the wave of the future."

"Where does all this waving happen?"

"What?"

No Hair had so much trouble keeping up with conversations.

"Where does all this electronic exchange of money happen? At kiosks? In the submarine?"

"Right in the gaming chair. Every seat at the gaming tables has a reader. The player swipes to buy chips and then swipes to cash the chips out."

"There you go," I said. "There *is* money. Chips are money."

"Not *Probability* chips. They don't have a long enough shelf life to be considered money," he said. "They're only currency when they're in play. The second they're won or lost, they're done. They're electronically encoded. They have an imbedded funding chip that can only be activated for gaming once."

"The chips have a chip?" Encoded casino chips and tokens aren't new. RFID tags—radio frequency identification—have been used in casinos worldwide for years, but for the purposes of security and inventory. Not to deposit and deduct wins and losses from individual accounts. I was impressed. "They cash them out then throw them away?"

"No," he said. "They give them away. The chips actually have one and a half lives. After the player cashes out the chip to his or her account, they can assign it a one-time value, then use it for a tip."

"Who is it they're tipping?"

"Casino servers, porters, concierge, the maître d', anyone. It could be five dollars, it could be five thousand dollars, or fifty thousand dollars. And that's how the staff is tipped. The chips are swiped to the receiver's V2, and *then* it's a dead chip."

"Holy moly." I drew big circles around the babies. "Who dreamed this up?"

"It's proprietary software written by the processing bank."

"Which bank?"

He patted folders on his desk. "It's in here somewhere. It's a Hawaiian bank with a branch in the Caymans."

"Why?"

"Why the Caymans?"

"No," I said. "Why go to so much trouble?"

"So there'll be no currency. I doubt there'll be a ten-dollar bill on all of *Probability*. No cash means no converting, exchange rates, or counterfeiting issues. But the main reason, Davis, is security. There'll be no cash to guard, there'll be no cash to steal, but the best news is how easy the banking will be. We won't have to conduct transactions with fifty different banks. Just the one."

All the eggs in one basket.

"Let me see if I've got this straight," I said. "*Probability* is the middle man for all the money between the players and the bank."

"Yes."

"And that's money in *and* out?"

"Correct," he said.

"How in the world were fifty billionaires talked into letting *Probability* do their banking for them?"

"They love it, Davis. They're gambling in international waters and their U.S. banks won't know a thing about it."

And there was the brilliance of the plan. Uncle Sam and all.

"If all the money is on the phone, what happens if a V-thing is stolen?" I asked.

No Hair shook his head. "The money isn't on the phone, Davis. Just the balances. The money is in the bank." He glanced at his watch.

"What happens if the system goes down and bank transactions aren't recorded?"

"That," No Hair said, "would be a problem, but it won't happen either."

"How do you know?"

"From what I understand, the computer system is state-of-the-art processing, designed by the greatest nerds around, run by a

geek squad in California, and it has four different backup systems."
He checked the time again.

"Do you have somewhere better to be, No Hair?"

"Not better," he said, "but I do need to run. Get back with me as soon as you can on these." He gave a nod to the stack of folders in front of me I could barely see over. "And you can skip two of them."

"Which two?" I began making arrangements to hoist myself and the babies out of the chair.

"Your guests. We're sneaking your mother in too late to load her into the system and I'm pretty sure Fantasy is clean."

"You never know."

"Hey." Again with the watch. "You might want to come with me. The Knot on Your Life slot machines were delivered this morning. I'm on my way to sign off on them."

You never have to ask me to look at a slot machine twice. "Why are they here?"

"To be programmed with player account numbers."

"Who's programming them? That sounds like a job for me."

"It is a job for you." He pointed at my Pea in the Pod sweater.
Right.

"And you've been in Pine Apple," he said.
Right.

"And doing your Bianca business."
Right.

"So?" I asked. "Who's programming the slot machines?"

"The Cayman bankers."

Something stopped me dead in my tracks. "Here?"

We were at the door of No Hair's office. "Yes," he said. "Here. Why?"

"I don't know." And by I don't know, I meant I had a funny feeling. "It seems crazy to me that they'd do it here. Wouldn't it be easier for them to program the slot machines at their own facilities? Or on the ship? Why here? How is it a good idea to let Cayman bankers in our house, No Hair?"

"Davis." He patted my back. "You worry too much."

As it turned out, I didn't worry nearly enough. Not anywhere near enough.

For the next week I put portfolios together on *Probability*'s guest's guests and the extended security detail. Nothing popped. I peeked in every medicine cabinet, under every bed, and high and low in every closet. Before *Probability* pulled up anchor and left the Mississippi Sound, I could tell you where everyone on this ship placed in their fifth-grade spelling bee and their mother's mother's maiden name. But somewhere along the line, I'd missed something. I knew I had (because No Hair was being held prisoner) and I knew where I missed it. It was when No Hair and I left his office and took a service elevator to the slot machine staging area below the casino. I got a little caught up in how much fun the Knot on Your Life slot machines were—I lined up the anchors three times!—when I should have been paying attention to the Cayman bankers. They were the only people on *Probability* I didn't know. But they knew me. And they knew No Hair. Because we'd let them in our house.

EIGHT

Anderson Cooper was a thief.

I woke up Sunday morning on (*Probability*) the high end of the abject terror scale. I'd spent a restless night in a strange bed with petrifying images of No Hair having dominated the snips of dreams I sneaked in between tossing, turning, and trading places with Fantasy. Between the two of us, we might have pieced together three hours of sleep. Before I could shake the cobwebs, I was hit with bacon and a $5,000 *Probability* casino chip. A gift from Anderson Cooper. I was familiar with (bacon) casino chips, so it took me a minute to understand how strange, and miraculous, it was to see one in my alternate universe. I was locked in 704 looking at something that belonged outside of 704. My head fell back on the pillows when I remembered the velvet gift bag on a mirrored table in the sitting room. Rumored to have more than $25,000 worth of goodies in it, including a Roberto Coin pave diamond bangle bracelet. A welcome gift. Which probably included the casino coin. "Have you been snooping, Anderson? Did you open my prize?"

She balanced on the babies and pawed the chip, flipping it on my chest, wanting praise. I tapped her nose twice in thanks. I picked it up. "What did you do with the Roberto Coin bangle, young lady?"

She'd shown her burglar proclivities way back. It started with a necklace. My older sister and only sibling, Meredith, and my niece Riley, who lived in Pine Apple a block from my parents, came to visit one weekend when Anderson was just a few months old.

Meredith busted into our bedroom the first morning at the absolute crack of dawn. "My diamond necklace is gone."

"What?" The two-babies news was very new, the reason Meredith had come—we needed something to celebrate—and it all came flying at me too fast that morning. "Is Mother okay?"

"Dammit, Davis!" She was staring and pointing at my still relatively flat stomach.

Was this about the twins?

She snatched her necklace from the bedspread I was under. "Do you not have enough jewelry of your own?"

Anderson stole all kinds of goodies and brought them to me. If she thought it was important to me and if she could carry it, she snatched it. She was forever taking things from Bradley—his socks, his keys, food off his plate when his head was turned, then landing them in my lap. "Be glad," Bradley said, "she's a thief and not a hunter. If she were a hunter she'd bring you birds, gophers, and snakes."

I'll take pizza crusts, diamonds, and casino chips over gophers every day of the week.

I said good morning to the babies, promised them I'd do whatever it took to keep them safe until we were back on dry land, palmed the casino chip, and tried to prioritize what all I wanted to accomplish in the first five minutes of my second day of captivity on a luxury cruise liner. (Get out, bust No Hair out, and go home. All in five minutes.) Swinging my legs off the bed, I made a more reasonable game plan: calm myself down, somehow wrangle into my maternity yoga pants, then find the bacon. I'd figure out how to get out of 704 and rescue No Hair after breakfast. It was, after all, the most important meal of the day. This would be a big day. It would take a big breakfast.

With a heavy heart, I brushed my teeth, my eyes not leaving the reflection of my cat's eyes in the mirror. The same mirror that had broken the news of our imprisonment. The questions that had haunted my sleep hit me harder and faster in the light of day: What all could I accomplish without engaging the deadly punishment clause of the letter? What was this about, who was behind it, where was No Hair, and was someone in 704 aiding and abetting? Then there was the biggest question of them all: Could I accomplish *anything* without my mother catching on? Anderson watched my dark introspection. "Who came in here?" I asked through toothpaste. "Who left us a letter?"

She yawned.

* * *

Good Lord, my mother owned a swimsuit. And she was wearing it.

"Mother?"

She looked up from the frying pan full of bacon and said, "Fantasy slept on the couch with a bathroom towel bar, of all things, and there's not one knife in this kitchen."

"What, Mother? What? Start with the knives."

"There's not a knife in this whole kitchen. Butter knives. That's it. Not a knife one. I'd like to know how I'm supposed to cut up the chickens without a knife or kitchen scissors."

"Why would you *want* to cut up chickens, Mother?" I pulled open the drawer that had been full of knives last night. I'd used one to slice ham. "And what are kitchen scissors?"

"You know good and well what kitchen scissors are, Davis Way, and how is it you cut up your chicken when you make chicken?"

"Mother, I don't *make* chicken. I *order* chicken. And I cut it with a knife when it's on my *plate*."

"Well, you're plum out of luck because we don't have any knives."

There were knives in this kitchen last night. Carving knifes. Steak knives. Butcher knives. Big knives, little knives, and now no knives. The drawer was empty.

"Have you looked in there?" Mother interrupted my panic attack, waving a plastic spatula at the refrigerator. "That's the biggest Frigidaire I've ever seen in my life. Two people could fit in there. Can you imagine the electric bill for this boat? And there's enough food in this kitchen to feed an army. I took one look in there and I knew good and well why the cook didn't show up. That's a lot of cooking. It's a good thing I'm here, Davis. A good thing."

"Yes, it is, Mother."

"I woke up famished. How'd you sleep? I slept better than I have in six months. Must be the boat rocking or this ocean air. Are you hungry, Davis? And did you even think about combing your hair or putting on a housecoat before you came out here? Are those your pajamas? Did you not bring pajamas to wear?" She shook her greasy spatula at me. "I don't know what happened to you. When you girls were little you wore nothing but freshly pressed cotton pajamas."

I never understood ironing something you wore to bed, I don't miss cotton pajama sets, who took the knives, and I had to hold it together. "Let's start over."

"Come again?"

I sat down in a white chair at the table. "Good morning, Mother."

She hesitated. Then she poured a steaming cup of coffee and placed it in front of me. "Good morning, Davis."

I pushed the coffee away with a whimper and said, "No thank you."

"You young people and your picky eating habits."

"Not drinking coffee doesn't make me a picky eater, Mother." Of my list of pregnancy sacrifices, coffee was very high up the list. When the babies are five minutes old, I'm going to have someone hook me up to a dark roast pipeline.

"Suit yourself," she said. "It's the Starbucks and you're missing it."

I was missing the Starbucks and she was missing the reason. Mother refusing to acknowledge my pregnancy was one of the two objectives my father had when he planned this Mother-Daughter Getaway—he had no idea what he'd gotten Mother into—so we could "work it out."

How? How was I supposed to force my fifty-nine-year-old mother, who'd just fought the hardest battle of her life, to admit that life goes on? Number one, hers. Number two, these *new* lives. Her grandchildren. She woke up from her treatment and there I was, bigger than life, out to there, and she didn't say a word. She still hadn't said a word. We'd all tried to broach the subject and she'd changed it immediately. "Give her time," my father said. "She's not out of the woods yet. Even if she were it's going to be a good long while before she feels out. She's not ready to talk about it and you have to give her time." How much? The babies would be here in less than three months.

Have you *ever*?

"While we're alone," I looked over my shoulder, "let me talk to you for a minute, Mother." Every bit of her froze. "About our cruise." She melted.

"What about it?"

How to put this. "There's a chance we'll be locked in here again today." And tomorrow. And the next day.

"This is very unusual, Davis. I don't quite know what to think. I doubt this would have happened if your father was here."

"I don't know how Daddy could have prevented a computer system from going down or what he could do to get it back up."

"Don't you speak ill of your father to me, Davis Way." I wasn't and the bacon was killing me. If I reached for a slice from the piled-high platter, she wouldn't hesitate to slap my hand with her hot spatula. I got to eat when Mother told me I could. Since the day I was born. "I'll tell you something about your father. When the going gets tough, he gets going."

This was an indirect reference to Mother's four months of chemo and radiation. Daddy had refused help outside our immediate family. He opened the back door for casseroles and pound cakes from Mother's Sunday School class, but he refused to hire a nurse or household help. Related to Mother's illness and the running of their home, if he didn't do it, Meredith or I did. Although, truth be told, early in my pregnancy I slept as much as

Mother did, so I wasn't much help. And Mother telling me Daddy was a good man was a total waste of her breath. For one, I've worshiped him since the day I was born. I was a police officer in Pine Apple for seven years, working side by side with my police chief father, so for two, she didn't need to tell me Daddy had my back. I knew it better than anyone. Regardless, Mother suggesting our current situation wouldn't be happening if our hero were here wasn't exactly true. Daddy would have been just as helpless to see this coming, stop it, or correct it any more than I was. (And I'll tell you something else. Mother has ridden Daddy like a broom since the day I was born—his disinterest in her garden/hairdo/bunions, his interest in football/muscle cars/Fox News. All my life, I've listened to my mother complain to my father about the way he blinks: "Maybe if you didn't blink so *slowly*, Samuel, you wouldn't blink so *often*." This "Your Father is the Greatest Man in the World" business was fresh and new.) (Welcome, and brand new.)

She held the last of the bacon over the frying pan until the final drips fell, then flipped it onto the platter. "Well, personally, Davis? I don't care a thing about going anywhere. My bedroom is beautiful and so is my powder room. I even have my own coffee pot and a nice rocking chair with a big wide footstool on my balcony. Very comfortable. I woke up at six, like I always do, and made myself a hot cup of coffee and took it outside for my Daily Devotionals. It was peaceful and beautiful, and now I know why so many people go on the Carnival cruises. The ocean is very soothing. I don't give a care about that casino or the public pools or the restaurants. Public pools are filthy and I don't appreciate how modern restaurants go so far out of their way to serve the oddest food they can, things I can't even pronounce, and everything cooked in olive oil, like there's something wrong with Crisco, and rosemary and pesto, whatever that is, and saffron all over everything. A good cook needs two spices. Are you listening to me, Davis?"

"Two spices. Salt and pepper."

"That's right. And all this raw fish is ridiculous. One long weekend in the hospital with a good bout of food poisoning from raw shellfish and you young people will get over your love of raw fish."

"I don't love raw fish, Mother."

"Country-style steak and gravy, mashed potatoes, a pan of dinner rolls, and a fresh salad tossed with Miracle Whip and a squeeze of lemon is a fine dinner. Maybe a nice cobbler for dessert. I can't imagine anyone who wouldn't enjoy a dinner like that. What's wrong with that, Davis? You tell me what's wrong with that."

"Nothing, Mother."

In fact, nothing at all. I was fifteen, back in Mother's kitchen, and officially starving to death.

"We have everything we need right here, plenty of space, plenty of food, and plenty to do. You might have noticed I'm dressed for reading my magazines by the pool today."

"You look very nice, Mother."

"Thank you."

The skirt on the swimsuit went almost to her knees. The matching floral cover up with silver tassel ties covered everything else. On her feet, orthopedic flip-flops.

"Now, there is a problem." Mother poured the bacon grease into a ceramic bowl and there wasn't a doubt in my mind she'd find a use for every glob of it and figure out a way to pack any leftovers and take them home. A lump of cloudy congealed bacon grease was the first ingredient in most of Mother's recipes. She poured several dozen scrambled eggs into the hot bacon dregs and began whipping them into shape. I'd never been hungrier in my life than I was at this exact moment in time. "And I'm talking about a problem other than your cat." She gave me The Eye, dropping her chin and cocking one eyebrow. "It's that loudmouth whiner. I'm not listening to that bull hockey all day long."

"What do you want me to do with her, Mother? Throw her overboard?"

"That girl needs to stuff a sock in it." She turned the eggs with her spatula until they were perfect, then tipped them onto a platter and sprinkled a pound of grated cheese on top. She stood over the eggs and said, "That one's lost her marbles."

Jessica DeLuna, the loudmouth whiner who'd lost her marbles, filled the kitchen door wearing a plush white *Probability* bathrobe, wide open, belt trailing behind her, so we could see her pajamas: a blood red demi bra and matching panties. "Has anyone seen my clothes?" She tipped her head back and sniffed the air. "I smell crab cakes."

Mother and I watched, both a little dumbfounded, as Jess rambled around at the butler's bar and mixed herself a stout Bloody Mary. She plopped down beside me. "So, do you smoke? Do you have any cigarettes?"

Fantasy showed up before I could think of how, or even if, I should answer Jess.

Mother pulled a pan of biscuits from the oven. "Davis, go get that man and that girl. I didn't cook all this for my health."

I kicked off our first official 704 meal by stating the obvious: The door was still locked; the V2s were still dead. I asked if anyone had any bright ideas. They didn't. I asked who took the knives. (No, I didn't.) The next twenty minutes were marked by the clinks of forks, dull butter knives, and whimpering. (Jessica.) The food disappeared and we sat around a white table full of dirty dishes.

Mother stood and pushed her chair in. "We're going to make the best of this situation and have a lovely day by the pool." Then she passed out marching orders. She started on her left. Jessica. "Young lady, get some clothes on." Next was Poppy. "I guess you do whatever it is you're supposed to do, then you're welcome to join us." She got to Burnsworth. "I don't believe in mixed bathing. No offense." He surrendered—none taken. Then me and Fantasy. "You two do the dishes."

"Why do we have to do the dishes?"

"We're splitting the kitchen chores, Fantasy. I cooked; you and Davis can clean."

Fantasy opened her mouth to protest and I cut her off. "It's fine, Mother. We'll do the dishes."

"Lunch is at twelve sharp by the pool. I've made us a nice chef salad," Mother said. "I'll see you all at the pool. Except you," she said to Burnsworth. "But you're welcome to join us for lunch."

Fantasy waited to kill me until everyone else left the kitchen.

I looked around to make certain we were alone. "Someone took the knives! Every knife in the kitchen!"

"I know! It was *me*, Davis! I took the knives!"

NINE

We couldn't find the dishwasher.

"If I'd known it was you who took the knives I would've fought the dish fight harder." I was under the kitchen island.

"You didn't fight it at all. And how was I supposed to tell you in a room full of people?" She was under the sink. "Was I supposed to butter a biscuit and say, 'Oh, by the way, Davis. I hid the knives so these people won't stab us'?"

"Did you hide the dishwasher too?"

We looked in the least likely places, having struck out in the most likely. I looked inside the cabinets while she pulled open the warming drawers between the wall ovens. I looked in the skinny cabinet to the right of the refrigerator while she disappeared into the walk-in pantry. "I found an herb garden," she called out. "How can I find an herb garden and not find a dishwasher?"

It had been twenty minutes on the dishwasher search already—wasted precious time, considering we'd been ordered to the pool and I knew better than to keep Mother waiting. It wasn't that I was in such a hurry to get there and act like (I wasn't pregnant) nothing was wrong, it was that I had way bigger and better things to worry about than the dishes. Not to mention I had to find something to wear to the pool. I didn't own any poolside fashion for the truly expectant.

"We need a bucket," Fantasy said.

"A what?"

"A big basket. A big container. Something we can fit these dishes in."

"And then what?"

"We hide them until we find the dishwasher."

"Let's just wash the dishes in the sink, Fantasy, with Dawn, like people do."

"Yeah? Where's the Dawn?"

Another thing we couldn't find—a drop of dish soap.

We stared at the tall stacks of dirty white plates, serving bowls, coffee cups, silverware, and greasy skillets.

"Would a tote bag work?" I asked. "I might have a tote bag."

She snapped her fingers and shot out the kitchen door. She was back in a flash. She popped open a Louis Vuitton bandoulière, held it against the edge of the kitchen counter with one arm, then wrapped a crooked arm around the plates and slid them into the bag. They did not go quietly. "What the hell are you doing, Fantasy?"

She stopped. Dead cold. "The dishes."

We peeked out the kitchen door, right and left, the $3,000 Louis between us. We didn't see a soul, so we made a mad dash to my room. We closed the door behind us and fell against it.

"Good news." She nodded to the pile of clothes and loose scattered jewelry, probably a million dollars' worth, she'd dumped out of the Louis Vuitton and onto the floor of the sitting room. "I found you a swimsuit."

"Yay." I rolled my eyes.

We lugged the bag full of busted dishes between us to the balcony doors, slid them open, poked our heads out, cleared the area for witnesses, scooted across the deck, then lobbed Bianca's Louis bandoulière into the Caribbean Sea. The wind caught it like a vacuum and it was gone. Forever. Fantasy dusted her hands. "Well."

"I can't believe we just did that."

"Davis?" I was facing the Caribbean, from which Bianca Sanders's Louis Vuitton bandoulière would never return. Fantasy was facing my bedroom. "Look there." She pointed. "Look at your cat."

Anderson Cooper stood at the open balcony doors. With a $25,000 *Probability* poker chip between her front paws.

* * *

"I don't like that man."

"Mother, there aren't many men you do like."

She'd saved me a perfect sun chair. One that gave me a panoramic view of the glorious Caribbean on one side and a full view of the salon on the other. I'd be able to see the Navy SEALS my husband was surely sending if they dropped from the sky, climbed over the deck railing, or busted through the front door.

"Davis, that's mean spirited and not true." Mother slapped her *Woman's Day* closed, tipped the brim of her sunhat, so big it looked like an open umbrella on her head, and got a good look at me. "Heavens to Murgatroyd. What are you wearing?"

I was wearing the only swimsuit option I had. I was supposed to be in a photoshoot in front of a Picasso in the ship's art gallery on Deck Eight all morning wearing a Saint Laurent lace mini dress, and in another photoshoot at a waterfall in the middle of the ship's botanical garden on Deck Ten all afternoon in a Givenchy hot pink satin cape blouse over hot pink satin pencil capris. My cruise itinerary looked exactly the same every day: photography sessions in different inappropriate outfits all over *Probability*. The only clothes I'd packed for myself were of the comfort variety to wear between the shoots, in the suite, or to sleep in. No lounge-by-the-pool time had been built into my schedule, so I had to wing it. I was at the pool winging it in the only thing Bianca packed that would even halfway work, a string bikini (I know...) (you should see my bellybutton) she actually sent with the intent that I have my picture snapped in it (not a chance in all holy hell), and the only thing I could find to wear over it, a sheer gauze Madonna robe fringed in thousand-foot-long white silk ribbons. The train on the robe trailed a half mile behind me and was earmarked for yet another page in the Pregnancy Album, this one shot in the *Probability* portrait studio and against a solid white backdrop and a pose Bianca called "Baby Belly." My instructions were to wear the robe, barely wear the robe and only the robe, wide open, the shot a profile of my naked body with the mile of robe sprawled out behind me. Bianca had an instructional note card with the robe, handwritten on her gold-foil Dempsey & Carroll stationery: *"In Baby Belly, you are to gaze lovingly at Ondine as you caress her, David, and it aggravates me to no end to have to REMIND you to have a daily manicure. Essential for this particular photograph and for God's sake, have a salt scrub at least 12 hours beforehand. GLOWING, David. I want to GLOW in this photograph."*

(No.)

(No. No. No.)

"Could you not have gone to the shopping mall, Davis? Could you not have gone to the T.J. Maxx or the Marshalls and bought yourself a decent swimming suit?"

"I really didn't think about it, Mother."

"Well, you look ridiculous."

(I knew.)

The air was pure, the view spectacular, the soundtrack of slicing through the sea in a luxury liner glorious. Because of the cool breeze blowing the fringe of silk ribbons all over my face, and for a split second blowing away my terror, I couldn't really gauge the temperature. Definitely warmer the farther south we traveled, but not blazing hot, and without a single puff of a cloud in the sky. I could see where, under any other circumstances, this would be the vacation of a lifetime. And because she was who she was, more comfortable at home than anywhere else and uncomfortable in any social setting outside of Wilcox County Alabama, my mother was enjoying herself tremendously. Making herself right at home in 704. Her face was smooth and unlined, her posture relaxed, her temper tucked away. She was still my sharp-tongued mother, but she didn't appear to be the least bit upset at being confined. With one caveat, the loudmouth whiner, and now, she informed me, two.

"Why don't you like him?" I asked.

"Who?"

"You said you didn't like the man. Burnsworth."

"Well, I got sidetracked by you being out here in your birthday suit."

We'd covered that. "Burnsworth?"

"He has buggy eyes. I don't trust men with buggy eyes."

"How are buggy eyes an indication of trustworthiness, Mother?"

I slipped off the Madonna robe, because I was tired of batting down the billowing silk ribbons, and if ever there was a time for her to say something about the two humans inside my body and right in her face, it was now.

She didn't.

I carefully positioned myself for the drop to the sun chair and, not without sound effects, lowered myself and stretched out. All belly.

"How long has she been doing that?"

Jessica DeLuna, having shed her *Probability* robe and now parading around shamelessly in her blood red skivvies (I'm one to talk), was on the other side of the pool, her body bent double, the top half of her hanging over the deck railing. With great flourish, she righted herself, gulped in as much sea air as her lungs could hold, and flung herself over the rail again, mouth moving furiously. Screaming for help. I was twenty feet away and couldn't hear her. There wasn't a doubt in my mind no one else could. Next, she flipped over and screamed up, her back bent over the rail, trying to get someone's attention above us, again, to no avail.

"For half an hour, at least," Mother said. "That girl doesn't have the sense God gave a goose. And how do you lose your clothes? Where's Fantasy?"

Following Anderson Cooper around in my stateroom to find the stash of *Probability* casino chips. The velvet gift bag in the sitting room was intact—Roberto Coin bangle bracelet and all. The casino chips were coming from somewhere in my stateroom and Fantasy stayed behind to find out where. "She's changing. Why?"

"I hope she had the good sense to pack a decent swimsuit."

The exterior styling of *Probability* 704's deck space was minimalist, with a strong artisan touch. Running the length of the suite, there was, now that I gave it a good look, almost as much outdoor gathering space as there was interior, with three separate social areas made up of loungers, chairs, and fire pits, a private sun terrace, and an outdoor dining room that seated eight, all on wide-plank spice-colored teak decking. The fabric covering the furniture, the many outdoor rugs, and the dozen sun umbrellas was all the same parchment color, and everything pointed to the sparkling pool. Past the pool, as far as we could see, the Caribbean.

"I think he's been in my room." Mother talked to me from behind her *Woman's Day*.

My heart stopped beating.

"Who?" I knew who.

"Buggy eyes."

"Did you see him in your room?"

"No."

"Is something missing? Is anything disturbed?"

"Not that I could tell." She rolled her magazine into a weapon. She shook it at me. "But that doesn't mean he's not a rapist. And I don't know why he'd bother me with that around." She aimed her magazine at Jess. "She's his best bet."

It was official. I would need to keep Mother close. Very close.

Jessica took a break from calling for help and flung herself facedown on a double chaise lounge, her dark hair spilling down to the teak, her limbs slack and dangling, the physical definition of utter defeat.

"If I could get up I'd go get her."

"Don't you dare go get her."

"She's pitiful."

"Leave pitiful alone."

"Are you talking about me again?"

Fantasy could wear a one-piece on a New York runway. This one was an off-the-shoulder maillot in mocha, almost the exact color of her skin. Long and lean without an ounce of fat, everything fit Fantasy, which I'd never paid much attention to until recently, because nothing fit me. And she had *three* children. Three boys, whose father was leaving their mother. Something she had yet to say a single word to me about. She took in the scene. "Is this beautiful or what?" She pulled her sunglasses down and peered over them. "Is Jessica passed out again?" Then she looked at me, barely shaking her head no. She hadn't found Anderson's casino chip stash.

"Fantasy, you sit over here." Mother pointed to the chair on her right. "I don't want you two ganging up on me, whispering and giggling. This isn't high school. I want to talk to you anyway."

"And I want to talk to you, Mrs. Way."

Uh-oh.

"Start at the beginning," Mother said. "Tell me everything. I want to know why you're getting a divorce. Everything. Spill the beans."

"Mother, Fantasy doesn't want to talk about it."

"Davis," Mother said, "this is a conversation between me and Fantasy. Stay out of it."

I stayed out of it and cracked open *The Compass*, the big blue book I was given when I stepped aboard *Probability*. I was looking for a chapter on "Secret Stairways in Your Suite" or "Hostage Holding Station."

"Are your parents divorced?" Mother asked Fantasy.

"What does that have to do with anything?" Fantasy asked.

"I'm wondering if you had a good example set for you growing up," Mother said.

"It doesn't seem to have worked for Davis. You and Mr. Way aren't divorced and look at her."

I propped *The Compass* against the babies and did my best to lunge in Fantasy's direction. "Leave me out of this."

"Well, Davis is a different story altogether. You can't use her for an example of how to tie your shoe."

"I'm right here, Mother."

Then Burnsworth was right there.

"Burnsworth!" Fantasy snapped. "Don't sneak up on us!"

He cleared his throat. "I thought you might like something to drink."

"No," I answered too fast. "We're fine."

"Speak for yourself, Miss Manners," Mother said. "Yes. We'd like drinks. Fruity drinks. With umbrellas."

If Burnsworth was in on it, we'd be dead after one sip.

He took our order, then crossed the deck to Jessica, who'd already had three breakfast Bloody Marys. "I hope she's ordering water," I said.

"That's a strange bird," Mother said.

"Jess?" Fantasy asked. "She's out of her mind. I wonder what her story is."

"Don't you have a big enough story of your own, Fantasy?" Mother asked. "Don't go courting a bigger one and don't meddle in other people's business."

"Don't meddle? What is it you're doing, Mother?"

She turned her hat my way so deliberately it's a wonder I didn't hear every bone in her neck snap. "Is anybody talking to you?" I stuck my nose back in *The Compass*.

"I was talking about that man," Mother said. "He's weird."

"Fantasy, Mother thinks Burnsworth has been in her room."

"Did you catch him?" she asked.

"No." Mother shook her magazine. "But that doesn't mean he's not a serial killer."

Fantasy and I made a silent agreement over our sunglasses: Keep two eyes on Burnsworth. One on Jessica, one on Poppy, two on him.

"Has anyone seen Poppy since breakfast?" I asked.

"That one's not any bigger than a minute," Mother said.

"Well, have you seen her, Mother?"

She looked at me from under the brim of her hat. "Somebody's gotten so big for her britches, you know it? Don't start smart mouthing me, Davis."

"I saw her with a feather duster sticking out of her back pocket," Fantasy said. "She said she was on her way to make my bed."

"She's not making mine. I made my bed this morning at six."

Which launched Mother into a speech about bed sheets. No-iron, percale, and thread count. Then she gave us her opinion of Egyptian cotton sheets. "That's just a big rip-off. Do either of you honestly believe the sheet people go to Egypt and buy cotton? Let's say they do. Is cotton from Egypt any better than good old American cotton?" She smacked Fantasy's leg with a *Family Circle*. "I'm talking to you, Fantasy."

"What about Egypt?" Fantasy asked.

"You know, Fantasy, this might be a big part of the reason your husband is divorcing you. You don't pay attention."

"Mother!"

"Davis, mind your own business. Read your book." Back to Fantasy. "Now, where's your mother in all this, Fantasy? What does she have to say about this divorce business?"

"My parents retired to Florida ten years ago."

"Is that your answer? They're retired?"

"I haven't told them yet."

"Oh, boy." Mother didn't like this news a bit. "Well, it's a good thing I'm here. Now, start at the beginning."

My mother was having a ball.

I went back to peeking over my big blue book into the salon. Burnsworth was at the bar mixing the world's slowest drinks. Poppy had crossed through twice, back and forth. No SEALS.

Fantasy launched into her life story: six pounds, ten ounces, twenty-two inches long. So she was tall and skinny from the get-go. She went to a private Catholic preschool and I turned the page and went to Dining Services. The kitchen on *Probability* was almost as large as the casino and on the same deck, eight, just above us. The one kitchen serviced all seventeen restaurants and covered room service. I read through the restaurant descriptions and decided everyone on this ship would gain ten pounds, which for me, if I weren't a prisoner, would be forty. I flipped pages back and forth, trying to determine if we were under the casino or the kitchen. Flip flip. The casino. We were somewhere below and behind the ice sculptures in the casino. Maybe closer to the main bar.

"Cotillion Ball." My mother blew a raspberry. "So your problem is you're spoiled."

"I'm spoiled?" Fantasy shot up and her long legs straddled the sun chair. "Have you taken a peek in Davis's closet lately? Davis?"

"Yo." *The Compass* had an entire chapter on the building of the ship. Blueprints, diagrams, and the timeline, illustrated. First, a hangar was built in a port city in Germany on the Baltic Sea, and it took more than a year to build the hangar. Then the bones of *Probability* were laid out in the hangar, it went on and on, fascinating, and two years later here we were. On this half-billion-dollar prison.

"If you had to say how much money you have tied up in handbags, just handbags, what's your guess?"

I looked up from *The Compass*. "What does the cost of my purses have to do with anything?"

"Your mother is accusing *me* of being spoiled."

"You're missing my point, Fantasy," Mother said. "What I'm trying to say is this seemingly perfect childhood of yours didn't prepare you for adulthood. You're spoiled. You think your life should be like a Cotillion Ball. It doesn't sound to me like you ever had to tough it out. Davis didn't get a brand-new car when she turned sixteen, and she didn't go to a fancy college like you did, and Samuel and I certainly didn't buy Davis her first home or any other home."

I tried to sit up. "Why are you telling her all this, Fantasy? She's just going to use it against you for the rest of your life."

"You zip it, young lady."

I opened my mouth.

"Zip it."

Probability had a diving center full of water sports equipment. Somewhere near the submarine, far from the helicopter pad, and for whatever reason, on a ship built out for VIPs, there was a separate and invitation-only VIP deck. How very important were the people invited there? The ship was powered by twin 4000hp Yanmar diesel engines and held four hundred and fifty thousand gallons of diesel fuel. So not only was No Hair hidden somewhere on this huge ship, so were four hundred and fifty thousand gallons of potential inferno. Terrifying.

Mother had a finger going very close to Fantasy's nose. "Stepping out in a marriage happens, Fantasy. I'm not saying I go along with it. I am saying couples survive it every day. Now it's usually the man stepping out, and you have to learn to look the other way—"

"What, Mother? *What?*"

She ignored me completely.

"—but with *you* being the cheater and all, what you've done is taken away his manhood. You need to apologize to him and really mean it, and I'm not saying you're not going to spend the rest of your life giving him his manhood back, but if you'll take my advice and just tell the man you're truly sorry, maybe he will forgive you."

Dead air.

"And you may have to make it up to him in ways you've never dreamed of. Acts against God and nature."

"Mother! *Stop!*"

She turned to me. "I'm talking about the oral sex, Davis, and I don't mean discussing it. Your generation didn't invent it and I wasn't born yesterday."

I might drop dead today.

She turned back to Fantasy, whose head was hanging off the other side of her sun chair; her shoulders were shaking and she was slapping her own leg. "What are you snorting about? You think this is funny? You slipped up, young lady. That's all there is to it. You need to get over yourself and make it up to him for the sake of your children."

Burnsworth scared us to death again when he appeared with his silver tray of refreshments we'd totally forgotten, and for the first time since the day I passed the pregnancy test, I wanted a drink. Mother took a sip and wanted several.

"What is this?"

"It's a Vodka Fizz, Madame."

"Well, keep 'em coming, Mister."

I took a sip of mine and it was more straight pineapple juice than it was antifreeze. Or rat poison. Or arsenic.

I made it to the chapter describing the fifty staterooms on *Probability* and found the two pages dedicated to 704 just as Mother geared up to talk to Fantasy about the birds and the bees, a talk she'd never bothered having with me when it could have done some good.

"Mother, Fantasy has three children. I think she knows all about the stork."

After slamming her magazine down she turned to me and said, "When you start a story, Davis, you start at the beginning. I'm trying to make a point here, if you don't mind." Back to Fantasy. "Do you know what my mother said to me ten minutes before I married Samuel? She said, 'Men are nasty, but it's your duty. The way you get through it is by thinking about your garden.' Which is where I believe the cabbage patch business started. All those women lying there stiff as boards thinking about canning the cabbage, cabbage soup, cabbage slaw, cabbage casserole, and stuffed cabbage rolls. Now I found out quick my mother was wrong. It wasn't that way in my marriage bed."

I slapped my hands over my ears.

Fantasy caught Burnsworth's eye as he crossed the deck and toggled a finger between herself and Mother for another round. I watched over the top of my sunglasses as Jess dove into the bottle of Petron tequila she'd ordered for her mid-morning poolside refreshment. Mother finished explaining how fulfilling marital relations could be, not a bit worried about me slowly dying beside her, and moved on to her second Fizz and more timely matters. "You tell me what happened, Fantasy. How you met him and what was so special about this total stranger. And particularly I want to know if you had him take the AIDS test beforehand or if you used protective prophylactics. Because I can see your husband calling it quits if something was rotten in Demark."

I might be hallucinating. I was certainly hearing things, because surely to goodness my mother didn't just say what I think she did.

"Even then, Fantasy," Mother said, "you could still clean up that mess. So to speak. I believe if you try hard enough you can talk your husband out of this divorce business. All he has to do is call his lawyer and take it back."

I turned the page and almost fell out of my sun chair. Page sixteen. *Onboard Communications*. There were two subtopics, the first V2. (Pfffffft.) The second entry was email. Channel seven on the interactive television located in the library. I'd been in every room looking for an emergency exit, including the library, and I hadn't seen an interactive television in the library or anywhere else. But according to *The Compass*, I could send and receive email from the library. Relief flooded me. Email. If I could get just one email out of 704 this would all be over. I was on my way there, but before I could get halfway up, Fantasy beat me to it. She swung her brown legs over the side of her sun chair to face me and Mother. Her bare feet slapped down and her long shadow fell over me. She pulled off her sunglasses. "He didn't call a lawyer, Mrs. Way. I'm the one who filed for the divorce."

I dropped *The Compass* and it landed on the deck with a thud.

"Wait," my mother said. "I thought—"

"I filed. I'm divorcing Reggie."

"*What?*" I scrambled up in as much of a hurry as I could. I sat on the side of my sun chair facing Fantasy, Mother's big sun hat swinging back and forth between us. "Why, Fantasy? *Why?*"

"I'm giving him his freedom, Davis. I want him to move on with his life."

"But you *love* Reggie."

"I do. With all my heart, 'til death do us part. Which is why I'm letting him go."

Mother's hat sliced back and forth.

"Try it, Davis. Break Bradley's heart, then try to pick up the pieces. Sit across from him at breakfast every morning and get a good look at what you've done. Wait for him to walk through the door all day hoping it will be the day you've been pardoned. Climb into the bed every night with a man you've wrecked."

"Fantasy." My breath was coming in short bursts. "These things take time. Wait it out. Don't be a martyr. Don't nail yourself to some righteousness cross."

"It's done, Davis. I can't spend the rest of my life waiting for him to forgive me. I want Reggie to move on with his life. He won't until I'm gone."

My hands were all over my children, protecting them from this. "What about the boys? What about your innocent little *boys*?"

"Do you think I want them to grow up thinking this is how it works? Davis, if I don't get out of their faces they'll *never* trust a woman. Ever. I'm not going to turn my back on my boys. I will always love them and take care of them, but not under the same roof with Reggie. Because someone has to pay for what I did. And that someone is *me*."

"Fantasy, *no!*"

"This isn't your call, Davis. This is *my* life. *My* marriage."

"And you're throwing it away!"

Mother's arms spread slowly and she landed a bony hand on one of my knees and the other bony hand on one of Fantasy's. "Both of you pipe down and listen up." She pulled off her ginormous sunhat and a shock of bright Caribbean sun hit my mother's head and I could see her bleached scalp through her whisper-thin hair. I grabbed for my heart, lodged somewhere near my throat, because I thought it might burst.

"Marriage is a two-way street." Mother's voice was even and steady. "And it takes two to tango. If you'll take a harder look at what happened, Fantasy, you might discover it wasn't all your fault and there's no need to walk out on your husband for something that might have been just as much his fault as it was yours. These things don't happen by accident. You didn't just fall into that other man's bed. Dig a little deeper and you might find out you had a little push. There isn't a divorce out there that's all one person's fault, and you taking all the blame on yourself might be the worst example you could ever set for your boys. The problem isn't that your husband hasn't forgiven you. The problem is you haven't forgiven yourself. And all your cockamamie 'the greater good' isn't serving anyone but you. He can forgive you all day long, Fantasy, but until you forgive yourself you're going to be no good to anyone."

TEN

Fantasy took a little personal time behind the closed door of her stateroom. She needed it, and I let her have it while I sent an S.O.S. email from the library. Or I would have sent an S.O.S. email from the library if there'd been an interactive television. I looked high and low—no interactive television—until Mother rang the lunch bell, and I decided I'd have an easier time finding it when I wasn't starved out of my mind. I might have been more upset about the missing interactive television if it weren't for the fact that Bradley's plane should have landed at Macau International Airport on Taipa Island two hours ago. Which meant this was almost over with or without an interactive television.

"Guess what?" I asked my lunch buddies.

"What?" Fantasy asked.

"It's rude to read at the dinner table and I raised you better, Davis."

"There's a wedding tonight." I turned *The Compass* around for everyone to see. "The theme is Tie the Knot. It's in the wedding chapel on the ninth deck from eight until midnight. Everyone will be there. It's the New York hedge-fund man," I tapped his face, "who left his wife for the nanny." Tap.

"I read about that," Fantasy said. "They're on this boat? Big scuttlebutt."

"Ship," I said. "It's a ship."

"Well, that's ridiculous. You young people know nothing about commitment."

"Mother, I think we've covered that subject thoroughly and no one here is responsible for the hedge-fund man's actions."

"Whose actions are you responsible for, Davis? Because you certainly don't take responsibility for your own."

"So, can anyone do anything about her?" Jessica pointed straight at my mother.

"How about I jerk a knot in your tail, young lady? How about I do something about you?"

Like a squall, it came out of nowhere: the gloves were off. Mother and Jess were sitting there one second and ready to fly across the table at each other the next.

"Do something," Fantasy whispered.

"I'm not getting in the middle of this," I whispered back.

Jess blinked first. She didn't blink so much as she closed her eyes and the next thing we knew, she was on the way to her plate. Poppy, who moves at the speed of light, bolted across the table and caught her, easing her back against the chair. We stared as Jessica's head lolled, the bluster blowing her long dark hair, until Fantasy said, "Here she comes."

Jessica sat up, shook it off, raised her empty shot glass and stared into it, wondering where the tequila had gone. "*So?*" She looked around the table. "Stop looking at me."

The drama died down and lunch picked back up under miles of wisteria weaving through an overhead iron pergola providing a leafy canopy for the outdoor dining area. We lingered under the wisteria and around the table long enough for me to eat all of my chef salad and most of Fantasy's. For dessert, we had chocolate mousse with raspberries in chilled martini glasses. I was polishing off my third, Poppy and Jess having donated theirs. "This is delicious, Mother."

"You're eating like a truck driver, Davis," she said. "If you don't watch out you're going to be big as a barn."

"She already is big as a barn," Fantasy said.

Mother refolded her napkin.

"Listen to this," I said, flipping a page of *The Compass*. "The reason the deck railing is bowed and curved isn't to keep us from jumping or climbing to another deck, or even for privacy." All of which it did, in fact, accomplish. "It's aerodynamically designed to keep the wind down. *Probability* was built for interoceanic crossings, which, as it turns out, is a windy proposition."

My audience wasn't nearly as impressed as I was.

"So, does it say how to get out of here? So? So? Does it?"

We stared at the inoperable V2s stacked in the middle of the table.

"They could come back on any minute," I lied. "Let's try to be patient and make the best of it until then."

"Where is that man?" Mother's sunhat whirled. "He needs to clear this table. Why is he forever sneaking off? Davis, you and Fantasy do the dishes." She looked at her watch. "I'm going to my room to rest my eyes. We'll have a swim in the pool in one hour. Two o'clock. Don't be late."

* * *

We used the first half of our hour doing the dishes. Most of it on another dishwasher search.

"Was there anything in the book about the dishwasher?"

"I didn't see anything," I said.

"Can we wash dishes with shampoo?"

Five minutes later we were lugging a Louis Vuitton Keepall between us. Price tag $4,200.

The $4,200 Keepall was full of silverware, salad bowls, and martini glasses. After we tossed it, I gave her a look. A big look. A hard look.

"I don't want to talk about it."

"You're in luck," I said. "We don't have time to talk about it."

The dressing room in the master stateroom of *Probability* 704 was as large as the bedroom. It had two interior arched doorways, one leading to the Hers closet and one to His. The walls were painted gauntlet gray. The back wall was made up of four full-length mirrored panels, the middle two stationary, the ones on the right and left on hidden tracks allowing them to pull away from the wall for 360-degree viewing.

Anderson Cooper had been in the dressing room with the door closed all morning. Between Save This Marriage and Chef Salad, I'd come back to the dressing room to find something, anything, else to wear, because the Madonna robe was driving me out of my mind, but instead I found my kitty girl sleeping with a $10,000 *Probability* casino chip. We were up to $40,000 in chips Anderson had swiped. Clearly, the casino chip stash was somewhere in the dressing room or my cat was sneaking in and out. And I was still wearing the Madonna robe over my string bikini.

We checked the closets, top to bottom. We tapped the walls, shook the shelves, and checked for loose carpet corners, finding neither a stash of casino chips nor an entry or exit. In His, Fantasy pointed to the smaller of Bianca's two Louis Vuitton trunks. "If we have a big enough dinner tonight, this can be our dishwasher."

"No, it can't. Bianca is going to kill me."

"We have to get off this boat for her to kill you, Davis."

"Ship."

"I've about had it with that."

"Then call it a ship." And don't divorce your husband.

We checked the gauntlet gray walls, top to bottom. They were solid.

We studied the ceiling. Nope.

The floor. Nothing.

"It's the mirrors." Fantasy flopped across the white linen ottoman.

"Has to be." I started on the right, dragging the mirrored panel across the carpet as far as I could, exposing a length of gauntlet gray. "How in the world is my cat getting in and out of here?"

"There." Fantasy lobbed an arm. "Look by your foot."

"I can't even see my feet, Fantasy. Could you possibly get up and help?"

She rolled off the ottoman, her body slack, her energy zapped by our predicament, the sun, my mother, the Vodka Fizzes, or her pending divorce. She crossed the six feet of carpet between us in two long lazy steps, then dropped to the floor. She splayed out flat on her stomach beside me to examine the dark open space at the baseboard between the mirror and wall. "Your feet are so fat."

I nudged her with one of my fat feet. "They're swollen, thank you. Not fat. And if you think my feet are fat you should see Bianca's. They're pillows."

Fantasy dove behind the mirror. "Her pillow feet are going to come unglued when she finds out what you did with her luggage."

"What I did?"

Fantasy, afraid of nothing, at the moment sharks, minnows, or any other sea creature that might be lurking between the ship's walls, had an arm all the way in the dark unknown behind the mirror, slapping away. "That luggage business is between you and her." Slap slap. "God be with you." She pulled her arm out of the black hole. "There's nothing back there. Let's check the other one."

I helped her up and we crossed to the opposite side where she gave the left mirror several pulls. It didn't budge. "How'd you do this?"

"I just slid it away," I said. "Is it caught on something?" I leaned in to help the very second her tugging efforts were rewarded. And I got hit in the head with a nine-foot-tall, three-foot-wide flyaway mirror. I landed on my butt, splat, on the dressing room floor.

"Dammit!"

"I didn't do it on purpose!" Fantasy flew to my side. "You walked right into it!"

"Wait." I placed a hand over Baby B and sat very still.

"What! What? Are you okay? Should I get your mother?"

"Are you kidding me, Fantasy? Why would you do that? Are you mad at me?" I poked. "This baby has the hiccups." My hand jumped to the other side. "And now this baby does too."

Fantasy sat on the floor with me, relief flooding over her. "You scared me to death."

"Sorry." Both babies had the hiccups, and not at the same time, off by half a beat of each other. "It's like popcorn popping in here."

She patted her chest.

"You are the scariest pregnant woman in the history of childbirth."

"No, I'm not." I propped myself up on my elbows. "I've had, as twin pregnancies go, a very easy time. I don't need to fall again, though. Or you'll be delivering babies at sea."

"That's not funny, Davis. And that's what's so scary, how casual you are about your pregnancy."

Hiccup hiccup.

"I am not."

"You are," she said. "I was a textbook first-baby nervous wreck every single minute with my first. You aren't at all. And you should be twice as nervous as I was."

"Fantasy, I fell on my butt. I'm fine. The babies are fine."

She stood and I held up both arms.

"There you go again." She pulled me up with a grunt. "I never raised my arms above my head when I was pregnant the first time. I made Reggie reach for everything."

"Why?"

"Because my grandmother told me the baby would be born with the umbilical cord around his neck if I raised my arms above my head."

"Well, my grandmother told me not to look a monkey in the eye or the babies will look like monkeys."

"That's a horrible thing to say."

"Are we going to be like that when we're old, Fantasy?"

"We have to get off this boat to get old, Davis."

And with that, a hush settled over us. We were halfway through this day—no SEALS, no No Hair, no V2s. We didn't take the time to discuss it, per se, but it was there.

"You're sure you're okay?"

"I'm way more okay than you are, Fantasy."

"Look." She leaned against the runaway mirror. "I would have told you, but I didn't want to talk about it."

"Because you didn't want to tell me your secret."

"I have no secrets, Davis. What I did made the news."

True. She had to testify to all the intimate details of her extramarital fling in open court. Her husband Reggie in the front row for every minute of her testimony. Staring at his shoes.

"You kept your decision a secret, Fantasy. You didn't decide to divorce Reggie just now by the pool."

"Are you suggesting, Davis, that you don't keep secrets from me?"

"That's exactly what I'm suggesting. There's not a thing about me you don't know. Name one secret I've kept from you."

She rolled her eyes.

Right.

She snapped her fingers. "No Hair told me you were pregnant. Not you."

She had me there.

"And Bradley told me your mother had breast cancer. Not you."

"Those weren't secrets. If you hadn't been avoiding me you'd have heard both from me."

We heard a tinkle, which effectively ended the contest about which one of us kept the most secrets, and we both looked up to the crystal chandelier. But the jingle was coming from below. It was Anderson Cooper's collar bell. She came out of Hers kicking and flipping a $10,000 Probability casino chip all the way to my (fat) feet.

I scooped her up. "Good girl," I signed. "This makes an even fifty thousand. Where in the world are you getting these, Anderson?"

"From back here." Fantasy had ducked behind the mirror.

I put Anderson Cooper down and followed Fantasy. "Can you see anything?"

"I need to get on the floor."

I dropped to all fours behind her. "Can you see anything now?"

"Nothing," she said.

"You have to see something."

Her head barely fit into a ten-inch-wide gap. She carefully pulled it out. "Back up. I don't have enough room to turn my head. I need to lie down and look up."

I tried to put it in reverse, but I was stuck between Fantasy and a gauntlet gray wall. "I can't move if you don't get up."

"Well, stay there." She flipped, pulled her knees up to her chin, then shot her legs between mine and there we were, Davis and Fantasy, playing Twister in the dressing room. The babies were brushing her thighs. "I swear I can feel their hiccups and it's freaking me out." She gently lowered her head back through the opening to the carpeted floor. "Good grief."

"What?"

"Gimme a minute."

"Can you see anything?"

She lifted her head an inch to find herself nose to nose with me as I'd managed to creep up an inch or two. "Will you back up?"

"I have nowhere to go."

She grunted and her head went back into the dark space. "What's above us?" She sounded like she was in a cave.

"I think it's the service area behind the bar."

"Why do you think that?" she asked.

"*The Compass*," I said.

"You and that book." I could barely hear her.

"What does it look like?"

"It's a long dark way up." Her voice echoed around. "And it's tight. The only one of us who'll fit up there is Poppy. Go get her."

"Seriously? Surely it's not that small."

"Yes, it is," she said. "She's the only one of us who'll be able to move in here. The whole way up it's made of material that looks like concrete but it's not. It's moldy."

"How could it be moldy? This ship isn't old enough to be moldy."

"Mold*ed*," she said. "Shaped funny. It's not the regular wood or metal framing you'd expect to see behind a wall."

"That's because it's a bulkhead, not a wall."

"Your cat must be climbing it."

"How?" I asked.

"It loops around," she said. "It's not straight up and straight down."

"Maybe she's jumping."

"Whatever." Then she yelled, "HEY! HEY!"

"Who is it! Who is it? Do you see someone?"

"Davis, shut up. HEY! HEY! CAN YOU HEAR ME? CAN ANYONE HEAR ME?"

"Can they? Can anyone hear you?"

Her face appeared in the opening. "If they heard me and tried to answer, how would I hear them with you jabbering? And would you please get off me?"

I heard footsteps and got off her in a hurry.

"Davis?" My mother filled the doorway. "Where is that thieving cat of yours?"

Fantasy froze behind the mirror.

"What are you doing on the floor?" Mother asked.

"I'm resting."

"On the floor?"

I heard Fantasy snicker.

"Where's that cat of yours?"

"She's in the closet." I pointed. "Why?"

"Because my portable phone plugger is gone."

"What, Mother? *What*? Someone took your phone plugger?"

"I didn't say someone. I said your thieving cat."

"Where was it, Mother? Did you have the phone plugged in?"

"In what?"

"An outlet? In the wall? Where was your phone plugger?"

"Don't you take a tone with me, Davis."

Sigh. "I'm sorry, Mother. Your phone plugger is missing. When did you see it last?"

"In my powder room."

"And it's not there now?"

"Davis, did you get too much sun? I just told you my phone plugger is gone. And your cat took it."

My cat did not take it. My cat hadn't been out of this room.

"But your phone still has power, right?"

"Just a little bit," she said. "Which is why I wanted to plug it up. So I could call your father later."

She made it sound so simple.

"Where is it now, Mother?"

"My phone?"

"Yes." Sigh. "Your phone. Where is it?"

"I hid it and I hid it good."

Great.

"And you can dial down the sass, young lady. There's soap on this boat, you know. If you think you're too big for me to wash your mouth out with it, just keep trying me. Get up," she said. "It's two o'clock. You can't swim in here."

I sat there panting, my head between my knees, until Fantasy asked if the coast was clear. She crawled out.

"She's wrong about the soap," she said. "Dish soap, anyway, and what the hell is a phone plugger?"

"She means her charger."

"Davis." We sat side by side on the floor of the dressing room. "I hate to state the obvious. But the envelope didn't tape itself to the mirror and now your mother's phone plugger is missing. One of these people, either Jess, Poppy, or Burnsworth, or all three, are in on it."

Before we left the dressing room we stuffed the hole in the wall behind the mirror with Bianca's Monique Lhuillier strapless gown. It occurred to me later that we should have blocked Anderson's path with a *Probability* bath towel.

ELEVEN

"I won't fit," Fantasy said. "I'm too tall. Even if we knocked out enough wall for me to climb through, I'd get stuck. I wouldn't be able to get a leg up. Or even move."

Fantasy and I were whispering over Mother's sun chair while she swam laps, the translation of which is as follows: Mother, wearing a bright yellow rubber swim cap and mirrored swim goggles, was hopping across the shallow end of the pool on the pads of her feet while furiously dog paddling, water shooting up and out in a three-foot fountain around her. Fantasy and I were using the time wisely.

"We need a kid," Fantasy said. "Someone half my size."

"Which any other day would be me."

"Davis." She looked over her sunglasses. "We can't knock out enough wall for you either, and even if we could, I wouldn't let you."

"I wouldn't let myself."

We watched Mother.

"And to think we were talking about sending Poppy up the wall."

"Yeah." Fantasy let out a long breath. "That's not happening. We've got a phone-plugger-stealing rat in this suite and it may very well be her."

"Jessica is too tall," I said.

"Jessica might be the rat, Davis."

"Seriously, Fantasy? I don't see it. We're getting way ahead of ourselves anyway. Let's not worry about who to send up the wall just yet. If we can get close enough to land to get a call out, we won't need to climb the wall. That's going to take getting the phone away from Mother, which won't be easy, because she won't let us out of her sight." Just to prove my point, Mother took a timeout and waved from the pool. We waved back.

"Your mother is having the time of her life."

"I know."

"We have to make a call before her phone runs out of juice, Davis. If we can't get a call out, sending someone up the wall will be our only option. And we have to get away from your mother long enough *to* knock out the wall. Before that, we've got to find something to knock out the wall *with*."

We sat quietly, thinking about jackhammers.

"Tell her, Davis."

"I can't."

"Then let me."

"No. You just said it; she's having the time of her life. We're not telling her."

Fantasy dribbled a line of Hawaiian Tropic Sheer Hydration SPF 10 down one leg, up the other, then rubbed. "If we're going to rule out Jess," she whispered, "who do we think it is? Poppy or Burnsworth? Or do we think they're working together?"

"It looks to me like they're avoiding each other," I whispered back. "I haven't seen them exchange one word." The only thing either of them had done all day was stay busy looking busy. Either could have taken Mother's phone plug, because unlike Jess, they didn't constantly make their presence known. I'd get a bead on one, then the other, only to look back to see the first one gone. "If either of them are in on it and their job is to kill us, they've failed miserably. They could have tossed us overboard last night, yet here we are."

"And Burnsworth could have spiked our drinks."

"Obviously, that's not the plan," I said. "The plan, so far, isn't to hurt us. They need something from us."

"How can you be so sure?" she asked.

"Because we're alive."

Mother was trying to float on her back and the strange noises coming from her were her laughing at her own failed attempts.

Fantasy sunscreened her arms. "Poppy's jumpy," she said.

"She doesn't seem too upset."

"Davis, if upset is the criteria, Jessica wins."

"What about Burnsworth?"

Fantasy no more had the words out of her mouth before he sneaked up behind us. I almost had a heart attack. "Burnsworth!" I slapped my chest, trying to stop my heart from jumping out of it. "Please stop doing that!"

His face reddened. "I apologize."

"What do you need?"

"Just checking on you."

"Well, I'm fine."

He stood there.

"Is there something else?"

He looked at his watch. "It's almost three o'clock."

"And?"

"He's off," Fantasy said. "He's off duty from three until five."

I'd forgotten.

"If you don't need me, I'll report back to work at five."

"Take your time," I said. "There's not much to do."

He evaporated. Like smoke.

"He's way too calm," Fantasy said. "And slippery. He wants us to think he's taking all this in stride. And have you noticed he's always watching us?"

Of course I'd noticed. It was impossible to miss.

"Your mother might be right about him."

My mother was right about several things.

"You know what we need to do?" I asked. "Figure out a way to toss their rooms."

"There's nothing in Jessica's room to toss."

"True," I said. "Maybe we could find her clothes. And then she'd put them on."

"If they get the next two hours off, with absolutely nowhere to go, there's no tossing their rooms," I said. "They'll be in them."

Jessica DeLuna stepped out from the salon in her blood red undies and *Probability* bathrobe. Her hands full of V2s. And she was anything and everything but taking it in stride.

"That nutjob isn't going to give it up, is she?" Fantasy asked.

"Nope."

"Maybe we should tell her."

"Tell her what? About the wall?"

"That she's a nutjob," Fantasy said.

"Go ahead."

Jessica looked at the sun chair she'd enjoyed her tequila from early, decided it was too close to Mother, and turned her dark head in our direction.

"Come on, Jessica," I said. "Come sit with us."

Fantasy growled.

"We'll send her to Mother's room to get the phone," I whispered. "Mother will notice if one of us goes inside. She won't notice or care if Jessica isn't here. And we can see which team Jessica is playing for."

"Good thinking," Fantasy said. "If she shows up with the phone she's not the rat," Fantasy said. "If she palms the phone and tells us she couldn't find it, we put her out of her misery."

I peeked over my sunglasses. "Fantasy? You have anger issues."

Jessica remained in the doorway weighing her many undesirable options and decided, of all the bad choices, we were the least offensive. She made her pitiful way to us, dragging her bare feet across the deck. She pulled up a chair and collapsed into it. "So," she said. "My life isn't worth living."

I reached for *The Compass*. "Jessica." I went to the directory at the front of the book, ran my finger down the list, found what I was looking for. "How good are you at math?"

"Very." She squinted in the sun. "I can calculate conventional loans in my sleep. Why?"

The oddest words I'd heard the woman say yet. Were they a reference to the narcolepsy or was she shopping conventional loans?

"Why?" she asked again.

"I'm trying to distract you with something other than how unhappy you are." Flip flip. "Cheer up. Stop acting like it's the end of the world."

"You don't understand."

"What don't I understand? I'm locked in here too."

She banged her two stacks of dead V2s against each other.

"Listen, Jess." I found what I was looking for. "A nautical mile is a little over a regular mile."

"So?"

Fantasy chimed in. "So?"

"We've been on the move since seven o'clock last night."

"So?" (Both of them.)

"And this says our cruising speed is thirty knots per hour."

"How many miles do we go per knot?" Fantasy asked.

"A little more than one," I said. "I'm trying to figure out how far we've traveled. We're going thirty knots per hour with Cuba five hundred and fifty miles from Biloxi," I pushed my sunglasses up on my head so I could think better, "and we've been traveling for roughly nineteen hours."

"We've traveled six hundred and fifty miles," Jess said.

Fantasy and I stared at her.

"Give or take," she said.

Fantasy and I stared at each other.

Jessica tipped to the edge of her seat, V2s hitting the deck, and peered over the railing. "So, where's Cuba?"

Fantasy was counting on her fingers and toes, trying to keep up with the math. "She's right. We should be there."

"Yeah, but we're not crows flying to Cuba. We're swinging way east. We're taking the long way."

"So?" Jess twirled a thick strand of dark hair. "We're not even going to Cuba."

I was back in *The Compass*. "No, but we're going to get close enough to the city of Arroyos de Mantua to see it." Total lie. The guests on the port side of the ship would see Arroyos de Mantua. We were starboard. We'd never see it. But we needed Mother's phone, and if it took lying about which way the ship was pointed to recruit her to get it for us, I wasn't above it. "I think we'll get close enough to Cuba to pick up a signal." Which wasn't so much of a lie; regardless of what side of the ship we were on, we might still be able to make a call. "The thing is," I said, "someone has to sneak into my mother's room and get the phone."

"Me." Jess bounced up and down in her seat. "I'll do it."

"Perfect."

"So, where is it?" Jessica got so excited her arms and legs shot out, then with no warning whatsoever, she totally deflated. She flopped everywhere. It's a wonder she didn't slide right out of her chair.

"Holy shit," Fantasy said. "How does she do that?"

"The better question is how did she do the math?" It didn't fit. I sat straight up. "The bank."

"The bank?"

"Jessica and her husband came from a bank." I checked our immediate area: Jess was out like a light, Mother was doing the backstroke, Burnsworth and Poppy were off duty. "Their background is in banking."

"And?"

"What if this is about the bank?" I asked. "Specifically, the bank upstairs?"

"Upstairs?"

"The casino bank, Fantasy."

She clapped her hand over her mouth and talked through it. "Oh, dear Lord. This is about the casino. And *she's* the problem?"

"I doubt she's the problem, Fantasy, but she may very well be the solution."

"Wake her up!"

"No," I said. "Let her sleep. When she wakes up, she won't

remember what we were talking about. It's like she loses her short-term memory. I'm going to try something."

"Go for it."

Several minutes passed before one of Jessica's legs flew up in the air and slapped right back down. Her head snapped up. She blinked fifty times. "So? What?"

"You were telling us about your husband," I said.

"That greedy bastard." She waved him off. "What a dick."

I hoped my babies couldn't hear through *The Compass*. "You were saying he knows who I am. He knows I'm not Bianca Sanders."

"So he tricked that out of me, Davis. He total snow-jobbed me, because he's a total prick. I hate him so hard."

I was beginning to hate him pretty hard myself.

"The phone, Jessica."

"The phone?"

"You were going to go to my mother's room and find her phone."

"I was?"

"Get the phone and we'll call Cuba."

"Right. Where do I look?"

"She hides everything in her underwear drawer. Find her underwear and you'll find the phone."

"So. Ewwwww."

"We need it, Jess."

"Right."

We watched her hurry away.

"We may have stumbled onto the very reason No Hair is being detained and we're trapped in this suite," I said. "This may be nothing more than a simple casino heist."

"There's nothing simple about fifty billionaires in a casino, Davis."

Which would make it a very complicated casino heist.

"I hope she doesn't fall asleep in your mother's room."

"Let's hope she doesn't make a mess in my mother's room."

"That too," Fantasy said. "We'll have a dead body on our hands."

"Let's hope it doesn't get to dead bodies."

* * *

Ten minutes passed and Jessica hadn't returned. I spent five of the minutes trying to remember everything No Hair had told me about *Probability* banking and the other five trying to remember everything I could about Jessica's husband. Mother was stretched out along the slick edge of the pool after her vigorous workout, soaking up the sun and patting her feet against the top of the water.

"Davis?"

"Yes, Mother?"

"Look how the sky and the water are the same color."

"It's beautiful."

"I wish your father could see this."

She looked like my much younger mother, content, happy, and carefree, to the extent she ever allowed herself to be free of care. Maybe I was time traveling and my much younger father, the strong and handsome father of my childhood, who was genuinely content and happy as a rule where Mother was only situationally satisfied, and not all that often, would walk up behind her and kiss the top of her head. Or push her in the water and jump in after her. Daddy was the only person who could make Mother let go, and I never realized how genuinely affectionate my parents were with each other until I was happily married myself and understood how much the smallest of touches or locked eyes across a crowded room meant. I always thought of marriage as something that started out with a giddy bang, then diminished, every minute, a little more every day, until I married Bradley. It was only then I realized nothing about my parents' relationship had paled through the years. Several weeks ago, on my last trip to Pine Apple, when Mother had been given the green light by her doctors after her tests came back clean, my sister Meredith and I watched our parents from the porch swing as they returned from a tour of Main Street. (They were gone all of two minutes.)

"You know, Davis?" Meredith said. "Mother and Daddy are the grow-old-with-me couple. You know, from the song?"

"The best is yet to be," I said.

"That's them."

I'd seen my father worry plenty—it went with his job—but I'd never seen him panic like he had at the idea of losing Mother. And the count was at two on the road to my parents' next station in life: Daddy had a massive heart attack and bypass surgery three years ago and now Mother's health had been compromised by cancer. I thought of the past and I thought of the future, drawing lazy circles on my babies, who were barely stirring, lulled by my warmth, soothed by the imperceptible rocking.

I thought of my husband.

I thought of Cuba.

I asked Fantasy how long she thought it took to go through someone's underwear drawer.

"It depends on how much underwear your mother packed. If Jess isn't back in two minutes, I'll go look for her," Fantasy said. "Your mother is ten feet from the balcony door to her room. She's going to get up any second, walk through that door, and catch Jess."

"Mother isn't going anywhere," I said. "She'd never go inside in a wet swimsuit. It's not allowed."

She must have felt us talking about her, because she stood, peeled off her yellow swim cap and traded it for her afternoon sun hat—how many did she bring?—slipped into her floral cover up, and padded our way. "I'm going to sun myself for a few minutes, let my bathing suit dry, then go to the kitchen to see what we might want for our supper."

Behind her, against the glass separating the salon from the veranda, Jessica DeLuna jumped up and down in her red undies. Waving victory through the air.

Fantasy scrambled off her chair to get her out of sight before

Mother turned around and caught Jess with her portable phone. It was close.

I wasn't sure how much more I could take.

Mother settled into her sun chair.

"How was your swim, Mother?"

"So refreshing." She cracked open her *Good Housekeeping*. "So refreshing."

Time ticked sluggishly away until Mother's swimsuit was Maytag dry. She slapped her magazine closed and said, "Well, dinner's not going to cook itself."

I waited until I heard pots and pans, then scared Fantasy and Jess out of hiding. We hugged the wall and sneaked past the kitchen to my stateroom where we turned on Mother's phone. It was dead. There could be a cell phone tower on top of *Probability* and we wouldn't be able to call anyone. The SEALS weren't here and it was time to face the fact that they weren't coming. Bradley landed hours ago; that clock had run out. Our captors had apparently done such a good job of communicating for me, my own husband had no idea we were in this predicament. No one was coming to save us. We had to save ourselves.

It was time to bust through the wall.

TWELVE

"Leeward," I said. "We were leeward and now we're not."

"So? What does that even *mean*?"

"The wind has been hitting the other side of the boat all day," I said. "But we changed course. We're pointed at the Caymans, so now the wind is hitting this side of the ship. Or maybe the wind changed directions."

"We've all had enough sun and outdoors anyway." Then Mother had a few words for Jessica. "You need to cool your jets and pipe down. I'd think you'd be exhausted by now from all your bellyaching. Why don't you rest? Do you know how to rest?"

"So, hello? I have a sleep disorder? I rest all the time?"

"I believe you play possum all the time, Missy. I don't believe a word of your mystery 'disorder.' You young people and your food disorders, your sleep disorders, your short attention disorders. It's all in your head."

"SO?"

"Mother?" She turned my way. "Would you like to go to your room and read or rest your eyes?" So I don't have to listen to this? And I can pump Jessica for information about her husband?

"I've already rested my eyes, Davis," Mother said. "Do you want to rest yours?"

I wanted one thing: out. More to the point, I wanted to be with Fantasy, who was working toward that end. Between us, one needed to keep Mother and Jessica at bay while the other executed the demolition work order in my dressing room. I'd had just about all the excitement I could take for one afternoon so I got the babysitting job, the less physical of the two chores. Mother and Jess might wear my mental health down to the wire, but at least my unborn children and I wouldn't be knocking down a wall.

"Davis?" Mother asked. "Where is Fantasy?"

"She's resting her eyes, Mother." She was busting through a wall was what she was doing.

"This is a beautiful room," Mother said. "She's missing it."

We were in 704's library just off the salon, the one without the interactive television, but with a bird's-eye view of the door that led to the crew's quarters and far far away from the activity in my dressing room. Mother, Jessica, and I had been driven indoors because with *Probability's* shift in course, the pool deck was breezier by one puff. When we stepped out, Mother's sun hat ruffled with a wisp of wind and you'd have thought we were in the middle of a typhoon. ("Get back! Get back! We'll catch our death of cold.") I talked them through the salon to the library. For a change of scenery. The interior room was so dark we had to turn on the floor lamps to see each other, making it feel later than it really was, but it was quiet and peaceful, Jess and Mother at each other's throats notwithstanding.

We were deep in three of four dark leather armchairs surrounded by four dark walls of bookshelves with hundreds of beautiful hardcover books whose spines had never been cracked. I was out of the string bikini and in a soft gray 3.1 Phillip Lim jersey knit sleeveless drape dress, and over it, I wore a million-dollar creamy cashmere cropped cardigan by Brunello Cucinelli. My afternoon *Probability* prison ensemble was outrageously expensive, roomy, comfortable, and covered me. All of me.

"So, Davis." I looked up from the jersey knit. "I never understood why you and Mr. Cole were married but I get it now. You and Mr. Cole are alike. The way you're both so solid. That's what I like about him so much," she said. "He's so solid. He makes me feel more solid. And so now I see it. You're solid too."

It hit me like a freight train, Jessica saying his name. I was running on fumes and desperation and panic, and it was for him, for our children, for No Hair, for my father, for my mother, for Fantasy's family, for Jess even, and everyone else remotely connected to 704 that I kept propelling myself forward. But the flood of emotion that poured over me at the unexpected mention of my husband threatened to undo me. I'd made it through six months of pregnancy and Mother's breast cancer without shedding a tear, and it was right here and right now, and at the hand of Jessica DeLuna, that I almost lost it. And I would've. If she hadn't passed out.

Which effectively hit my reset button.

"Does she have a mother?"

"I'm sure she does," I said. "How can you not have a mother?"

"Well, there are mothers and then there are mothers," my mother said. "Everyone needs a mother."

Yes.

I had to get us out of here.

"When she wakes up, I guess you should say thank you," Mother said. "That was very kind."

I didn't trust myself to speak, so I nodded.

"Maybe she's not as harebrained as she thinks she is."

I smoothed the jersey knit, nodding again.

"Davis, it's four o'clock."

Mother had a single cup of afternoon coffee every day of her life at four o'clock and with that, we'd been 704 prisoners for exactly twenty-four hours.

"Stay there, Mother. Let me make you a cup of coffee." And check on Fantasy.

*   *   *

The dressing room door was wide open. "Fantasy! You're going to let Anderson Cooper out!"

She came out from behind the mirror covered in gauntlet gray dust. "All we have to worry about and you're worried about your cat." She shook the only thing we could get our hands on in all of

704 to knock out a wall—the statue from the foyer. "Worry about this." She shook it again. "We're probably going to get sued."

According to *The Compass*, my constant companion, she was shaking a $52,000 piece of antiquity dating back to the Ming Dynasty. It looked like hammered silver grasshopper antennas mounted on a silver dinner plate, and it was doing the job of destroying the wall. She slammed it in, then raked it through the gauntlet gray. And the wall came tumbling down. She sat back on her heels, pushed her hair out of her face, and rubbed her eyes with the pink sleeve of her summer sweater.

"Is it me, Fantasy, or are you growing more hair?"

She looked at herself in the mirror. "It's the humidity." She patted it down. "Give me a few more days. I'll have another foot."

"No."

"No, what?" she asked.

"You can't have a few more days."

"Right," she said. "We've had enough vacation."

I took a step to the left, inspecting the destruction. "How's it going?"

"As well as can be expected. How'd you get away from your mother?"

"I'm making her a cup of coffee."

"Any sign of Burnsworth or Poppy?"

"Not a peep."

"Jessica?" she asked.

"Cat nap."

Fantasy stretched her neck and rolled her shoulders. "What are we going to do when I get through destroying this boat?"

(Oh, come on. How hard is it? Ship. It's a ship.)

"Next up, we need in Burnsworth's room. I found a lifeboat." On my way to the Ming Dynasty statue in *The Compass*, I stumbled on a closet behind a closet in the butler's room of every suite that held ten life jackets, a comprehensive first-aid kit, and the lifeboat.

Fantasy flecked gauntlet gray off her sleeve. "What are we going to do with a lifeboat? If our plan is to escape by lifeboat, why am I knocking down a wall? Davis, surely you understand that we can't climb into a lifeboat and drop a hundred feet to the water. You get that, right? We'll get sucked out to sea like Bianca's luggage."

"Fantasy, the lifeboat has LED lights and a flare gun."

"How are LED lights going to help us?"

"They're not. But the flare gun will."

She pinched the bridge of her nose and shook her head. "And you want to do what with it?"

"Neither of us can get up the wall. But maybe we can get *in* the wall far enough to shoot a flare."

"That'll get someone's attention."

"Exactly."

"How are we going to get in Burnsworth's room?" she asked.

"One of us keeps him busy, the other one goes to his room."

Five minutes later I was back in the library with Mother and Jess, who'd nodded off again.

"Davis?" She placed the last *Probability* 704 coffee cup in the last *Probability* 704 saucer.

"Yes, Mother?"

"That coffee was good to the last drop."

"I'm glad you enjoyed it."

"Thank you very kindly."

"You're welcome, Mother."

"I need to put my chickens on."

"Do you need me to help?"

"I'll do it." She pushed up from the chair. "I need to preheat the oven and set the table. If you come with me to the kitchen, you'll probably find something to eat and ruin your dinner."

I picked up *The Compass* in the dim quiet of her wake to keep from joining Jess and falling asleep. I'd made it almost all the way through the big blue book without finding a magic way out. I was at the end, the indexes at the back, and they started with the employee directory. It led off with the Captain. It went on to list the ship's officers, then department heads, so on and so forth, Sommelier This and Curator That. Then it listed employees by stateroom.

Decks Five, Six, then Seven. I found ours, Burnsworth first. His name was Andrew Burnsworth and he was from Jackson, Mississippi. Just like No Hair. And they were about the same age. I was about to turn the page to meet our missing chef or learn a little more about Poppy when I heard quick footsteps coming down the hall. I looked up to see Fantasy and her $52,000 statue breeze by. I heard her stop and back up, then she poked her head in the door. "What are you doing?"

"Waiting. Waiting for her to wake up." I nodded at Jess. "Waiting to get out of here. Waiting on you. Just waiting." I caught her eye. "All we can do is wait." She waited. "What are you doing?"

She checked the hallway, right and left, then whispered, "I've got the hole ready. It's big enough to climb through."

"If only we had someone small enough to climb through it."

Right, her face said. "We'll go with the flare gun and we need a vacuum cleaner. I'm hiding this in my room." She shook the statue, curves long gone, now a mangled Ming Dynasty silver fork with sharp straight tines. "We might need to throw it overboard. Where's your mother?"

"In the kitchen."

She aimed her statue at Jess. "How long has she been out?"

"This time? Five minutes." I tilted *The Compass* to show her Burnsworth's picture. "Come look at this."

She rolled her eyes and sat the statue down at the door. "You and that book."

"Look at Burnsworth's picture. Have we ever seen him before?"

She was over my shoulder. "No."

"Are you sure?"

"No."

I turned the page and found the missing chef. Her name was Dawn Frazier. She learned to cook in Vermont at the New England Culinary Institute, and while I didn't know if she was any better a cook than Mother, I did know she was a luckier cook than Mother. Because she wasn't locked in 704. I turned the page to meet our stateroom attendant, Colby Mitchell. Not Poppy Campbell at *all*. Not even a little bit. I gasped and Fantasy smacked my shoulder. Before we could even speculate as to why we had Poppy Campbell instead of Colby Mitchell, my mother let out a roar that rang through all of 704 and a gunshot blasted through on the exact same beat.

"DAVIS WAY! WHERE IN THE *WORLD* ARE THE DISHES?"

Fantasy and I froze—what was that?

"So? So? SO?" Jessica's legs flew out of the *Probability* robe and into the air.

"Stay right where you are, Jessica." I pushed up from the leather. "I mean it. Don't move a muscle."

"Go back to sleep," Fantasy said. "Right now." She grabbed her statue and ran into the hallway; I was on her heels. She pointed at the door that led to the crew's quarters where the shot had come from. "I'm going in alone, Davis."

"No, you're not."

"Yes, I am." Her hand was on the doorknob.

"Fantasy." I tried to hold her back. "There's a gun down there."

She shook her Ming Dynasty giant-sized fork. "And it's about to be mine."

Who takes a Ming Dynasty fork to a gun fight?

Fantasy.

We piled onto the steps and looked down the short hall. Light spilled from the door at the end of the hall. "Burnsworth! Poppy!"

"In here." It was Poppy, the fake stateroom attendant, her voice giving nothing away.

Fantasy's arm shot out, holding me back and trapping me on the third step. "Stay here."

I did. I owed it to Bradley, to my babies, and to my mother to stay out of harm's way, which meant sending Fantasy in alone. My mouth went dry and my heart was in my throat as she took tentative steps in the direction of the light, statue first. I barely heard my mother bellow my name again and at the same time I heard a struggle, a thud, then my partner.

"Davis, come on. I've got her."

I hugged the wall, creeping toward the bedroom, then peeked. Fantasy had her down; Poppy wasn't giving her a fight. "You've got this all wrong," she said. "He pulled a gun on me. He was going to kill me."

I ran for Burnsworth and dropped to my knees at his side. "I don't think so."

Fantasy had a forearm on Poppy's neck, ready to snap it. "I don't either."

I got out of my sweater as fast as I could and pressed it against the fountain of blood flowing from Burnsworth. The air was thick with the acrid smell of impending death. I put all my weight into stopping the flow, but blood poured through the cashmere and my fingers. His eyes found mine and we both knew he wasn't going to make it. In fact, he only lived long enough for me to watch him die, and his last gurgled words were so faint I was the only one who heard them. "It's up to you."

THIRTEEN

Face of an angel—this was not her first kill. She couldn't care less about the dead body at her feet and she was even less concerned that we had her.

The bullet ripped through Burnsworth's carotid artery; he bled out in minutes on the white carpet at the foot of the bed. The room was small and there were too many of us in it. We strapped Poppy to a desk chair with the belt we took off Burnsworth's dead body.

"Don't you even breathe hard, Poppy, or I'll take your ass down." Fantasy yanked one more notch in the belt and had the gun, a Hi-Point C-9 semi-automatic 9mm with seven of eight rounds in it, tucked in the waistband of her jeans.

"It was a good shoot." Poppy tested her constraints. "He was going to kill me."

"Good shoot," Fantasy scoffed. "Who are you?"

She wasn't emotional, that much was for sure. I couldn't believe my unborn children were witnessing this. I was shaky, dizzy, and covered in blood. "Where's the gun he pulled on you, Poppy? He doesn't have a gun."

"I took his gun." She had no remorse. Zero. "Then I shot him with it before he could shoot me."

"You're a liar." Fantasy took a step to the left, her eyes darting around as she mapped the door and the body. "You walked in here and took him out in cold blood."

"You made a big mess too." If my mother saw this she'd flip. And I was making it worse—digging, tossing every drawer, every inch of the small space. I found it in his nightstand.

I used the wall to hold me up as I studied Burnsworth's Mississippi Bureau of Investigation identification, his last words ringing through my ears with so much truth I was almost blind with it.

"Fantasy." I held out the ID.

Fantasy took it, then showed it to Poppy. "You're never going to see the light of day. You just took the life of a federal agent."

"He's state, not federal," she informed us, "and we're in international waters. Good luck." Then she laughed.

I looked into Poppy's eyes, cold metal blue, and knew she'd kill every one of us and never look back. Who was this girl?

Fantasy made sure this girl wasn't going anywhere, then sat down in front of her to find out. Nose to nose. She waited a long beat, long enough for Poppy to get antsy, which she didn't. Nerves of steel, this one. "Right here and right now, Poppy," Fantasy said. "What's this about?"

Poppy declined to answer.

"Whatever it is," I, good cop (never works except for in the movies) said, "maybe we can help."

"You can't even help yourself, Davis. And who says I need your help?"

Fantasy leaned in closer. She whipped out the gun and let the barrel rest on Poppy's smooth forehead. "If that's how it's going to be, fine by me. You can hold that chair down for as long as you want, but shut the hell up. Not one more word. And call her Mrs. Sanders."

Mrs. Sanders needed to sit down.

"So?"

Jessica—she might have been sleepwalking—found us. Her eyes rolled around the room and landed on the pillows, the huge red oval of blood on the white carpet under them and Burnsworth's splayed legs sticking out from them. She opened her mouth so wide we could see her tonsils, then she let out a hair-raising scream, the stuff of Hitchcock, she broke the sound barrier, I'm surprised Anderson Cooper didn't hear her. She collapsed into a puddle on the floor, fainting dead away, or sudden-onset sleeping, and in her place stood my mother.

I tried so hard to say something, anything, to Mother about the scene she'd stumbled upon, but there were no words. I think I said, "Bububububu."

"Davis?" Mother demanded. "Where are the dishes? There are only four dinner plates in the whole kitchen. And I guess I know one of us who doesn't need one. Is he dead?"

It took everything I had to nod.

"All the way?"

I nodded again.

Mother pointed to Poppy in the chair. "She did it?"

I nodded.

"Jiminy Cricket." Hands on hips, Mother said, "Davis, pull that bedspread off the bed and roll him up in it. I'll get some white vinegar." She shook a finger at Poppy. "You're not coming to dinner either and you can scrub this carpet." To the rest of her stunned audience she said, "What? You think I don't know what's going on right under my nose?"

*   *   *

The pièce de résistance of Bianca Sanders's brand-spankin' newly commissioned Louis Vuitton luggage was the large trunk. It was silk lined, thirty-six by twenty-five by nineteen, and fabulous. It took a half hour to secure Poppy, who promised us we'd never walk out of 704 alive, and afterward, as if we hadn't been through enough, we had to dispose of a dead man. My own mother helped Fantasy drag Burnsworth's linen-wrapped body up three steps, down the hall, through the salon, down another hall to my sitting room, through my bedroom, and into my dressing room. After much further ado they got him in Bianca's trunk. There was no dignity in the process—("If you hold up his arm, I can get his leg in," and "How's it going to hurt to break his foot if he's already dead?")—and we would surely all face abuse of a corpse charges before this was over, but it's not like we could lay out his dead body on one of the white sofas and throw a blanket over him. My only contribution was being helpful from the safety of the ottoman. ("Try rolling him in a tight ball and put the trunk on top of him.") ("Yeah? Then what?") ("Slide something under him and flip him over.") ("Davis, just sit there and be quiet.")

Not a bad idea, but then I noticed it was too quiet. "Do you hear that?"

"What?" Mother stared at a smear of dark dry blood on her forearm.

"Nothing," I said. "That's just it. I don't hear Jessica."

The whole time we'd been figuring out what to do with Poppy and transporting poor Burnsworth, Jessica had run a loop through the salon, *Probability* robe flying, screaming her lungs out. And she'd kept it up. When her trail brought her around to this end of 704, we could hear her shrieks as they swelled then faded. Now we didn't hear a thing.

"Maybe she fell asleep." Fantasy said every word on a grunt as she got the last of poor Burnsworth inside the trunk.

"That one's cheese has slid right off her cracker," Mother said.

"I'll do the honors." Fantasy stared down at the trunk. "I'll check on Poppy while I'm at it. Maybe you two can figure out what to do with this." She gave the trunk a pat.

"Why do we need to do anything with it?" Mother asked.

"Mother, I'm not sleeping twenty feet from a dead man."

"Well, he can't hurt you, Davis."

"I'll let you girls work it out." Fantasy stretched her achy arms. "Be right back."

"Would you mind checking on my chickens?"

The request stumped Fantasy, who hadn't given dinner the first thought, and certainly wasn't thinking of it then. "What exactly is it you want me to check for?"

"Golden brown skin and clear juices running in the bottom of the roaster."

Fantasy shook the chicken juice details into her head.

"The roaster?"

"Did you make potatoes, Mother?"

Fantasy's head swiveled between us. "We're covered in blood." (We were.) "We have a killer in the laundry room." (We did.) "And you two are talking about chickens and potatoes like we didn't we just pack a dead man into a trunk." (Yes.)

"And I'm not sleeping with that trunk," I said.

"There's the walk-in refrigerator." Mother scratched just above her left eyebrow. Her thinking move. "But then I might trip over him going in and out."

"Let's take the trunk outside for now," I said. "It's closer than dragging it to the kitchen."

"And we have dinner in the kitchen at six. I'll check on the chickens myself." Mother was on her way out of the dressing room when she noticed the gauntlet gray rubble on the floor beside the mirror. She gave us the suspicious eyeball. We shrugged innocence. She didn't believe a bit of it and stepped around the mirror to see for herself.

"Oh, boy." She turned to me. "Did your cat do this?"

I rubbed my babies bump.

"Answer me, Davis."

"No," I said.

She turned to Fantasy. "Did you do this?"

She whistled Dixie.

"You two," she rocked a finger back and forth between me and Fantasy, "don't necessarily bring out the best in each other."

"Mother, we have a situation."

"Davis, we have several situations."

Fantasy was tugging on her earlobe. "How about I run check those chickens."

I patted the ottoman. Mother sat down. I started at the beginning, and for the first time since the day I was born, I told my mother everything.

* * *

We changed clothes. We stuffed the bloody clothes and bedding into Bianca's Sirus 45, one of my favorites in her new Louis collection, price tag $3,800, a zipper bag with rounded leather handles that Delta approved as a carryon. We approved it as an overboard.

"Watch this, Mrs. Way." Fantasy tossed the Louis. The wind caught it and swept it out to sea.

Mother said, "That's a crying shame."

"I know," I said. "Bianca's going to kill me."

"I meant the clothes, Davis. It's a crying shame to throw away good clothes. There are naked children in Africa."

"There will always be naked children in Africa," Fantasy said. "It's the hottest continent in the world."

"It's hot in Pine Apple too, Fantasy, and the children don't run around naked."

It had taken Fantasy just one day to figure Mother out: Let it go.

The three of us stared out to sea. "I'm down to four or five pieces of that luggage," I said. "I hope I can stuff everything in the small trunk."

"Let's worry about Poppy right now." Fantasy checked her watch. "She's had plenty of time to think about it. We'll worry about luggage later."

"Be careful," Mother said. "That girl is the devil in disguise."

We didn't leave Poppy in poor Burnsworth's room scrubbing the carpet with white vinegar. We dragged her and her desk chair to the laundry room. Between Burnsworth's and Jessica's rooms was a utility closet. Easy to miss with its flush pocket door. It was small and square, with a low ceiling and white oak hardwood floors. One wall held a stacked washer and dryer and a long folding table. Bolted to the opposite wall was a wire shelf unit. The long silver shelves were full of 704 sundries: glass cleaner, linens, paper products galore, and wouldn't you know it—dish soap. We strapped

Poppy's chair to the wire shelves. She was secure in the chair and the chair was secured to the shelves and the shelves were bolted to the wall. It was all very Boy Scout—Burnsworth's leather belt and six *Probability* Egyptian cotton bathrobe belts tied in figure-eight knots. She wasn't going anywhere.

Mother took a left for the chickens and Fantasy and I took a right past Jessica, passed out on one of the white sofas.

"Anderson Cooper is in the dressing room with a dead man."

"Who's locked in a trunk, Davis. It's fine."

"Promise me you'll help me get that trunk out of my room, Fantasy."

"I promise."

"Or let me sleep with you tonight."

"I am not sleeping with Anderson Cooper. No way."

We stopped at the door leading to the crew's quarters. I had *The Compass* and Fantasy had the Hi-Point 9mm in the waistband of her jeans and a bottle of water poking out of her pocket.

"Okay." Her hand was on the doorknob. "We give her a two-minute break, then we interrogate her."

"We're not going to get anything out of her."

"Why do you say that?"

We stumbled down the steps.

"Fantasy, she's like Special Forces cold. And she's strong as an ox."

Fantasy's hand was on the laundry room door. "We've gone up against worse."

True.

"You ready?"

I nodded.

I felt my babies nod.

Fantasy slid open the door and said, "Oh, holy shit."

Special Forces Cold and Strong as an Ox had managed to rip the metal shelves away from the wall. There were gaping holes in the plaster and the whole unit was down. Poppy was somewhere underneath.

"*Poppy?*" It came out several octaves higher than I intended it to.

Fantasy kicked through Clorox and Bounty Select-A-Size. "Stay out of the way, Davis."

Poppy hadn't made a peep.

"You can't lift the whole thing by yourself, Fantasy."

"The shelves are empty." She had a grip on the wire rack and she assumed heavy-lifting posture. She heaved it with a loud grunt and got the wire shelves several feet off the floor. "I can hold it for three seconds. Can you get her out?" Fantasy's voice was strained beyond recognition.

"Oh, dear Lord, Fantasy. Her head is—"

"What, Davis? I can't hold this thing up forever! Hurry!"

Poppy was still strapped to the chair and the chair was still secured to the wire shelves. The problem was Poppy's head. Or, more specifically, her neck.

"DAVIS!"

"Something's wrong with her neck, Fantasy. It's hanging there like a little bird neck. It's," terror collected in my throat, "flopping. Her neck is floppy. Her neck is *broken.*"

"Is she—POPPY?"

"Fantasy, she's gone!"

My words rang out through the lavender-scented air.

"Get that, Davis." Sweat rolled down Fantasy's face.

I tore my eyes away from dead Poppy. "What?"

"That." Her eyes were on a large canvas-covered laundry bin she spotted under the folding counter. I rolled it out and positioned it under the racks of shelving and Fantasy let the shelves fall. The laundry bin caught them with a thud.

I backed up and let the wall hold me, fanning my face with *Probability* hand towel, while Fantasy bent to see for herself. "Good God, she's dead."

And there went the smaller of the two Louis Vuitton trunks.

We had to get out of 704 before it killed us all.

FOURTEEN

We each took a sofa in the salon. We came clean with Jessica. She took it pretty well, considering she was sure she was next on our hit list. "So, is this what you do at the Bellissimo? You kill people? Are you going to kill me? Are you going to wait until I microsleep and smother me with a pillow? SO?"

"Jess, we didn't kill Burnsworth or Poppy," Fantasy said. "Poppy killed Burnsworth, her death was an accident, and we don't like it any more than you do."

"How are we ever going to explain this?" I asked.

"That's mighty hopeful of you, Davis," Mother said.

"What?" I asked.

"That we'll actually speak to another human to explain it to."

"This is so cray." Jess had twirled a length of her hair so tight it looked like twine twisted around her finger. "So cray."

"What?" Mother asked. "What's she going on about now?"

"Crazy," I explained. "Jessica is saying this is crazy."

"I'm with her," Mother said. "This is plum crazy. I don't know what your father is going to say."

We untangled Poppy's body and stuffed her in the smaller of the Louis Vuitton (caskets) trunks, and Jess helped Fantasy haul them to the sundeck, a secluded step-down enclosed space on the other side of the pool. It had a gate that locked from the inside and a double sun chair with a retracting canopy. Built for privacy. Which is something you need when you're stashing Louis Vuitton trunks full of dead people.

Jessica helped without complaining. She was too afraid not to and somewhere in the middle of lugging dead bodies, she made the decision to cross over and become a team player. I don't know if it was because she was sick of herself or petrified of us. Whichever; when we explained we'd never get out of 704 if we didn't work together, she went along wholeheartedly.

"Now that we have all our cards on the table, Jessica, I want to ask you a few questions." I opened *The Compass*; Fantasy let out a sigh. "What, Fantasy?"

"Skip the book, Davis. Get to the husband."

The second body in one hour had our tempers taut.

"Hey." Mother stepped in. "Weren't you just now telling Ding Dong," she shook a crooked finger at Jess, "that we have to work together? Cut it out, Fantasy. Let Davis show her the book."

"My name isn't Ding Dong."

"Well." Mother was suddenly very invested in examining her lap. "You're right and I take it back." We could barely hear her. "I apologize."

Words my mother very rarely spoke.

Before they had a chance to hug it out, I gave *The Compass* a spin so it was facing Jess. "Do you know this girl? Do you know who she is?"

"What the hell?" Jessica leaned in and read the fine print. "She is *not* our stateroom attendant! She isn't *anyone's* stateroom attendant!" Jess stabbed *The Compass*. "She's a pilot! A craybitch pilot. She's a *hella*bitch pilot!"

"A what?" Mother asked.

Jess looked up to Mother. "She drives airplanes."

Why in the world would a pilot be listed as our stateroom attendant? "How do you know her, Jess?" I asked.

"She's Max's pilot." Jess turned to me. "Max's craybitch pilot. So, what is going *on*?"

"What in the world does a pilot have to do with anything? We're on a boat." Mother asked. "And who is Max?"

"Jessica is married to Max," Fantasy explained.

"Another hellabitch," Jess said.

"Is Max a woman?" Mother asked. "You're married to a bitch named Max?"

Jess carefully weighed Mother's questions.

"Time out." Fantasy's hands slapped her knees and she spoke to Mother. "Max is a man. He's Jessica's husband. Davis's book says the woman in the picture is our stateroom attendant, but we know she's not. As it turns out, the woman in the book is Max's pilot. Which means somehow, someway, she's in on it." Fantasy took a breath to let Mother catch up. "This means we were set up to be locked in our suite before we ever stepped in the door. Poppy was in on it; she was here to hurt us. Burnsworth wasn't in on it; he was here to keep us safe. Max's pilot is in on it, which means Max is probably behind it."

"Well." Mother crossed her legs. "Somebody could have said so."

Confusion and angst had been Jessica's only two channels since we'd walked in the door of 704 and they crashed into each other right then and there on the white linen sofa as Fantasy's words hit home: Her husband was the reason she was trapped in 704.

"So, what is Max *doing*?" Jess's dark eyes made several rounds against ours, seeking answers none of us had, finally landing on mine. "What is going *on*?"

"That's just it, Jess," I said. "We have to work together to figure out what he's doing and what's going on." I placed the picture of No Hair in front of her. "Do you know this man?"

Her head bobbed. "Mr. Covey."

"Right," I said. "He's our boss."

Jessica's head continued to (spin) bob.

"They have him, Jess. Your husband and his pilot, whatever they're up to, they need you, us, and our boss out of the way."

Jessica picked up the picture of No Hair and examined it. "So, why isn't Mr. Covey locked in here with us? Why is he in the submarine?"

And just like that, we located No Hair.

"So?" Jess shook No Hair's picture. "What is going *on*?"

"Jessica." I took the picture from her. "You're the only one who knows."

"*What*?" Her arms flailed through the air. "I don't know!"

She knew more than she thought she knew. She just told us where No Hair was. "Think, Jessica," I said. "If this is your husband's pilot, and together they've locked us in here, it means Poppy," I pointed to the sun deck, "was working *for* or *with* your husband. Maybe if we can connect her to him, we'll figure it out. Think, Jess. Think."

"Think?" She bounced balled fists off her temples. "I can't."

"Picture Poppy in a different place," Fantasy suggested. "In different clothes, with different color hair. Think about her voice. Have you ever heard it before?"

"She's someone your husband is associated with, Jessica," I said. "Maybe she was one of his clients. Think. Think hard."

"You two hold your horses." We'd forgotten Mother. "She can't *hear* herself think. Give her a minute. And you," she said to Jess, "stop hitting yourself in the head."

Time stopped and the ship stopped.

We stared at each other in disbelief.

The Caribbean Sea calm, *Probability* an engineering masterpiece, the weather fair, it was easy to forget we were in constant motion. Until we weren't. It wasn't a jolt, a halt, or anything discernable. It was utter and complete stillness.

"It's so quiet." Jessica's eyes drooped, her head began wobbling, then boom. Fantasy jumped up and caught her before she face planted into *The Compass*. She eased her back. Jessica's tongue lolled.

We stared.

"If that doesn't beat all."

Mother reached for a fifth of whiskey on the table between us and drank straight from the bottle, then passed it to Fantasy, who tipped it back. I fell against the sofa cushions, giving the babies more room. They took advantage of it and one pushed the other into my ribs. I let out a woof of surprise.

"What's the matter with you, Davis?"

I waved her off. Nothing, Mother. Just your two grandchildren fighting for space in your daughter's body.

The silence and calm were disquieting; the silence and calm were welcome.

We waited patiently on Jessica. She woke abruptly, her legs flying up and out, then she bolted upright. "Poppy works at the bank."

Yes, she did. As soon as the words came out of Jess's mouth, I realized I'd seen Poppy too, and I remembered when and where. An image of her posture, her athletic prowess, her speed, and her blonde ponytail pushed its way from the back to the front of my memory. Six weeks ago, I'd spent that hour with the Knot on Your Life slot machines at the Bellissimo. No Hair and I walked in the front door of the slot staging room, which held wall-to-wall slot machines being programmed by the Cayman bank. I remembered the Pea in a Pod sweater I was wearing that day (I grew out of the next), and a ponytailed flash running across the room and out the back door that had caught my eye. The flash was the broken-neck blonde we just stuffed into the lesser of Bianca's two trunks.

* * *

We tore up Poppy's stateroom. We tossed it like a crime scene. We found a laptop between the mattress and box springs, a Beretta PX4 with LaserMax sights in a lockbox under the bed, and central nervous system depressants in a zipper bag between towels in Poppy's bathroom: Temazepam, Paxil, and Ketamine.

"What is all this?" Mother shook the amber containers.

"Knockout drugs," Fantasy told her.

"Good thing she wasn't making our drinks."

I sat beside Mother on the foot of the bed with the laptop. I cracked it open and pushed the power button. The screen lit up with nothing. The laptop had power, but no operating system. I tried a little of everything.

"What's wrong?" Fantasy asked.

I turned it over. I shook it. I cast a spell on it. (No, I didn't.) "Everyone look for a flash drive."

"Who?" Mother asked.

"This?"

Fantasy held up a ScanDisk Cruzer USB flash drive.

"Where'd you find it?" I held my hand out.

"Inside her pillowcase."

Smooth move. Poppy had separated the hardware from the software on the off chance one of us found her laptop. I popped in sixty-four gigabytes of computing and began what would be a slow crawl to the deep web. Not so I could shop for a kidney or join a crime ring, but so I could hide. If ever there was a time I didn't want anyone tracking my cyber movements, it was right now. I was in a desperate hurry to communicate with anyone in any position of authority, anyone on this ship who could help us, not to mention my husband, but not at any cost. Because the cost would be our lives. I had to work smart and slow, which meant the deep web, off the grid, far below the surface, and don't ever go there. Mother watched me while Fantasy shook out Poppy's *Probability* uniforms. We had Jess pilfering through the closet. "So, what am I looking for?"

"Anything."

"Anyone recognize this?" Fantasy shook a black cord.

"That's my phone plugger," Mother said.

"Look at this." Jess opened a thick red folder she found in the closet. "It's me."

"What about you?" Mother asked.

"Everything." She turned a page. "So, everything. Even about my father."

"Tell me what it says when you get to me." Fantasy was halfway under the bed.

"Don't tell me what it says about me." I was back in the laptop.

Jess turned another page, then spoke to my mother. "So, are you sick?"

I moved as quickly as my bulky body would let me. "Let me have that, Jess."

*   *   *

Mother stirred whole milk with a wooden spoon in a saucepan. She folded in chocolate sauce. She whipped cream. She served it up in a beer mug, and cradling it in both hands, held it out to me. My eyes tingled with nostalgia. "Oh, good grief," she said. "You're crying over cocoa?"

No. And if I actually let go and had a good pregnant cry, it would be for the babies I was sure I'd give birth to in *Probability 704*. It would be for my husband, halfway across the world, who had no idea. It would be for my father, who didn't know my mother was in danger. Or for my mother, standing in front of me. I could have easily cried right then for her, for the thirty-four years we'd wasted sniping at each other, for what she'd been through, for what she might still have to go through. Or for No Hair, speaking of going through, who was somewhere near me and, at the same time, as far away from me as anyone else was and I hadn't found a way to get to him yet. Or maybe I'd cry for Fantasy, throwing in the towel on her marriage, or maybe for the two dead people on the sundeck, or for Jess, who was just as much a victim as the rest of us, or for the naked African children. All brought on by a hot mug of chocolate kindness from my mother. But the truth is, if I did let my guard down and have a good cry in my cocoa, it would be out of weariness. I was worn out. I was exhausted beyond all reason. I was dead on my (fat) feet. Which was preferable to being dead in a Louis Vuitton trunk.

We were fresh out of trunks.

It was eight o'clock and the four of us were lined up in sun chairs as far away from the private sun deck as possible and under blankets and a million stars. I'd never seen so many stars in my life.

Ever. *Probability* remained at a standstill in the middle of the Caribbean Sea and we had no idea why. The chickens were in the refrigerator; even I had no appetite. My three companions were sipping whiskey—bourbon, Scotch, and tequila. I think they'd have been shooting doubles if we didn't have such a long night ahead of us, but seeing as how we did, they were comfort drinking only.

"So?"

"So, what?" Fantasy asked Jess.

"What's next?"

"We have several possibilities." I was at the bottom of my hot chocolate and all over the laptop we'd found in Poppy's room. We had our resources on the tables between the chairs: Mother's useless but charged cell phone, the dead V2s, $50,000 in *Probability* casino chips, and, of course, *The Compass.*

"What are they?" My mother asked.

"I'll crack Poppy's computer in a minute," I said. "And hopefully I'll be able to communicate with someone. If that doesn't work, we wait for the ship to start moving again so we can use your phone to call for help."

"What if the ship doesn't start moving again?"

A terrifying proposition.

"Then we'll wait until after the Tie the Knot wedding when the casino opens and get a flare up the wall." I went in the back door of the laptop's software programming and found *control userpassword2.*

Jess raised a hand. "I volunteer myself as tribute."

"What is she talking about?" Mother asked.

"It's a line from a movie, Mother."

"So, I'll climb that wall."

"Wearing your housecoat?" my mother asked.

"My clothes will fit you, Jess," Fantasy said. "You need to put some clothes on."

If someone had told me this morning that Fantasy would be offering clothes to Jessica tonight, I wouldn't have believed a word of it. Not that I'd have believed at breakfast that Burnsworth and

Poppy would be dead before dinner. What we'd been through in this one day of surviving 704 would make friends of even the worst enemies. Part of it was knowing we had to work together or we'd never get out, but mostly, it was widespread shellshock.

"And because my clothes will fit you," Fantasy said, "you can't climb the wall. You're too tall."

"Earlier today, we actually considered sending Poppy up the wall," I said.

"So, that's not happening."

All four sets of eyes went in the direction of the sundeck past the pool.

"You know what that's for?" Jess asked.

"Sex," my own mother said. "That's where people go to have sex."

"Mother!"

"What, Davis? You think I don't know these things?"

I finally hacked far enough in to change Poppy's password. I hit Enter. "I'm in."

"Hot damn," Fantasy said. "For God's sake, get the police."

"I'm getting in touch with my husband, then the Coast Guard," I said. "Give me two minutes."

Jess leaned in. "You can make phone calls from the computer?"

"Email, Jess. I had to break into Poppy's computer the hard way and now I have to hack into the Bellissimo mainframe so I can send emails from a secure site."

"How do you do that?"

"It's my superpower," I said.

"So cool."

"She's good with the cable television too."

"Thank you, Mother."

The browser on Poppy's computer was Firefox, which saved me a ton of time on the way to the deep web, because if the *Probability* server was watching Poppy's laptop for unusual activity, it might notice her downloading Firefox but it wouldn't notice her *on* Firefox. She could be rolling through her Facebook newsfeed or window shopping at Killers R Us. From her Firefox browser I downloaded and installed TOR Browser Bundle (torproject.org) then filtered through to kpvz7ki2v5agwt35.onion. From there, wiki, index, php, then main page, enter, ta-da! I was deep and dark and had access to (all manner of places I didn't want to go) the Bellissimo hard drive.

Wouldn't you know it. I couldn't get past the encryption software *I'd* installed on the Bellissimo system.

"Mrs. Way?" Jess leaned over me and the irony of it all, then spoke to Mother. "Can I ask you something?"

"Well, I don't know. Can you?"

"If you get it, like, you know that's for sex," Jess pointed to the (morgue) private sundeck, "why don't you talk about being sick or her being pregnant?"

There was no taking it back.

In one breath, Jess managed to ask her everything the rest of us couldn't.

Mother took a breath so deep, it surely filled her toes with oxygen. She addressed her words to the stars. "I don't talk about the cancer," she said, "because it's done. It was caught before it could do me any great harm and it wasn't any bigger than a minute to begin with. To tell you the truth, I wonder if I really *had* cancer. Or if that was just the doctors having fits. But that's done. I'm not sick and I'm going to be fine. So, what's to talk about?"

Not a muscle moved. Not one.

"And I don't go on and on about Davis making me a grandmother because she already has. Davis made me a grandmother forever and a day ago. And when she's ready to talk about the child she already had, then I'll be ready to talk about the two she's going to have."

The dam burst and I broke into wracking raging sobs.

FIFTEEN

Throwing myself overboard would do nothing but punish the sea, so I dragged my sobbing self off the sun chair and blindly batted a path to my stateroom. I didn't want to see anyone ever again. I didn't want to talk to anyone ever again. And to tell the truth, I didn't want to draw another breath. Ever again. I didn't care if I ever got out of 704 or off *Probability*. None of it mattered in the least. And it never would. Ever again.

Ever.

But my babies chose that minute to stir and remind me of their father, and in the depths of my misery, I found a splinter of light and amended the rest of my life to include (breathing) my husband, my babies, and my cat. We'd live on an unmapped island. Or deep in a jungle. Or maybe this damn hostage ship would effectively cut us off from the rest of humanity. I didn't want to see anyone else ever again. Not even my sister, Meredith. Or my niece, Riley. Or No Hair. Or Fantasy, Baylor, Bianca, or Mr. Sanders. Or even Daddy and That Woman he was married to. I *especially* didn't ever want to see That Woman again, or anyone associated with her, any human she'd ever made contact with, anyone who'd ever laid eyes on her, again. Ever again.

Ever.

I made it through the sitting room and stumbled to the bedroom, but my journey and my plan came to an abrupt halt when I accidentally caught a glimpse of myself in the dresser mirror. My knees buckled at my own reflection. Instead of seeing the person I thought I was—Mrs. Bradley Cole, mother of twins, good wife, daughter, sister, friend—I saw the sixteen-year-old unwed mother who gave birth those eighteen years ago. Eighteen years and two months ago. Eighteen years, two months, and five days ago. It was her in the mirror, the scared senseless stupid girl who didn't really know where babies came from until she was carrying one. I wasn't the contributing member of society I passed myself off as; I was the young stupid girl who thought she was doing the right thing. And I did. I did the right thing those eighteen years, two months, and five days ago. For *myself*.

It was all about me then and it was all about me now.

No wonder That Woman hated me so much.

With the hard look at who I really was, I realized my plan would never work. I couldn't reduce my world to my husband, my children, and my cat, because I didn't deserve a husband and children. Or a cat. No part of me deserved Bradley—I'd known it all along—and I certainly didn't deserve his children, and when it got right down to it, I didn't even deserve Anderson Cooper. I made it to the hall leading to the dressing room door with the rest of my life mapped: I would deliver Bradley's babies, pass them to him, then go *away*.

I'd had it with trying to separate right from wrong. I'd had it with trying to live right, do right, *be* right. The wall it had taken me eighteen years and two months and five days to build had just crashed down at my feet. And with its destruction, I knew I'd have to live the rest of my life alone. I'd have to disappear. I'd live alone on the unmapped island, in the jungle, or on this damn hostage ship. All at once, I understood Fantasy wanting to get the hell out of everyone's way. Because she didn't deserve to be in it.

Exactly.

I let out the breath I'd been holding for eighteen years and two months and five days, and it was coming out in miserable wrenching sobs that threatened to make me sick when I finally found the dressing room door, for once so eternally grateful that my cat was stone deaf and couldn't hear my heart breaking wide open.

Closing the door behind me, I stumbled to Hers and my stone

deaf cat wasn't in her bed. I ripped an Alice + Oliva sherelle feather maxi skirt from the hanger, rolled it into a ball, and used it as a pillow on the round ottoman. I'd rest while I waited on my cat. Who was surely up the wall. Then I'd tell her what happened. I'd tell her everything, going back eighteen years, two months, and five days.

Anderson Cooper was a good listener.

* * *

The tapping woke me up. I didn't move, except to spit feathers. More tapping.

"Davis?"

It was Fantasy.

"Davis, let me in."

"No."

"Come on," she said. "It's me."

"No."

"You can't stay in there forever. You don't have food or water. Davis, let me in."

"No." I still had a teeny white feather in my mouth. "Where's That Woman? Wait," I said. "You know what? I don't want to know."

"She feels horrible, Davis. She didn't mean for it to come out that way."

"Oh yes she did."

"No, Davis. She really didn't."

"I don't even care, Fantasy. And I wish you'd go away."

"I can't go away. I love you, Davis."

"Well, stop."

"Is this how it's going to be? A big pity party?"

"Look who's talking."

That shut her down. For about three seconds. "Why didn't you tell me?"

I dragged myself up, unrolled my pillow, spread it across my lap, and picked feathers from it. "I didn't not tell you, Fantasy."

"But you never told me."

One feather, two feathers, three feathers, four.

"Does Bradley know?"

"Of course he knows."

Five feathers, six feathers, seven feathers, more.

"But you never told me?"

"Fantasy." I watched a feather float. "There's no good way to say I got pregnant the summer of tenth grade. By my twenty-one-year-old History teacher. Then had a baby. Then gave her to parents who could give her a life. There's no way to tell that story. There's no way to *start* that story." My heart was in a vise grip. "And why now? Why here? Why would she *do* this to me?"

"It's why she came on the cruise, Davis. She was looking for the right time to tell you the baby you had grew up."

"Like I can't count."

"Davis, the baby you had went to Pine Apple to find her birth mother. She found *your* birth mother."

I was dizzy with motherhood.

An hour or four passed. "When?"

"On her eighteenth birthday."

Two months and five days ago. When Mother was sick. Really, truly, sick.

I found a voice. Not necessarily my voice, because I don't usually sound so strangled. "Why didn't anyone *tell* me?"

"Your parents didn't know if you could handle it."

A valid concern. Considering the shape I was in.

"Davis, your dad set this up. He thought it would be a good idea for you to hear it from your mother."

What? That wasn't what this was about. Daddy asked *me* to help That Woman face the truth. And he sent *her* with truth for me? I'd never speak to either of them again. Ever again.

Ever.

Had I not been sitting I'd have fallen down when That Woman said, "She's going to Oxford, Davis."

Another wave of rage, shame, and the end of my life as I knew it knocked me down all over again at the sound of her grating voice. I opened my mouth to tell her to go straight to hell, but what came out was, "Mississippi? She can't. No one graduates from Ole Miss. She shouldn't go to Oxford."

"Oxford in England," That Woman said. "Not Oxford in Mississippi. She's very smart, Davis, like you. And very beautiful. She looks just like you."

A picture slid under the door. A picture of the daughter I knew I couldn't do right by eighteen years, two months, and five days ago. I reached for it with a shaking hand and laid eyes on my firstborn for the first time since she was an hour old. It looked as if her adoptive parents had done very right by her. And with the small studio portrait of this angel eighteen years of questions were answered. Eighteen years of guilt assuaged. Eighteen years of curiosity satisfied. And eighteen years of love with no visible target found a home.

I touched her face, I kissed her picture, I placed her against my belly button and whispered, "It's your big sister." Maternal love poured over me in buckets and might have drowned me had it not been so rudely interrupted.

"So? Will you let *me* in?"

Are you kidding me? I rolled my eyes all over the crystal chandelier above my head. They were all three sitting in the hall? Then I heard the ungodly sound of an Anderson Cooper caterwaul. Coming from the wrong side of the door. She wasn't up the wall; she'd been in the bedroom. Or the sitting room. The people on the other side of the door had my cat. They were all four sitting in the hall.

"Anderson Cooper wants in, Davis." (Fantasy.)

I wasn't about to open the door. I wasn't ready. I might never be ready. I wanted to be alone. With my picture. And my cat. "Leave Anderson and go away."

Then That Woman tried to bribe me. "I made you a sandwich."

My stomach growled. "Go away. Leave my cat and go away." I wondered what kind of sandwich.

"I sliced the chicken real thin," That Woman said. "It's on French bread with a little dab of mayo and shaved provolone. It won't keep out here forever."

"I'm not hungry." I was famished.

"I brought you a pickle spear."

I love pickle spears. "Leave my cat and leave the sandwich and go away." Chips would be good.

"I brought you chips too."

Dammit. My mouth watered. My babies kicked around.

"Fantasy only," I said.

"Okay, honey."

Honey, my ass.

I used the feather skirt to mop my face, because my eyes were still leaking a little.

"Are they gone?"

"They're gone." Fantasy spoke through food.

"Are you eating my sandwich?"

"She made me one too."

With one last look at the picture That Woman would never get back, I tucked it close to my heart. I unlocked the door, cracked it open, shot out my arm, and said, "Give me my cat." I pulled Anderson in, sat her down, then put my arm out again. "Give me my sandwich." I hoped it was a big sandwich.

"You can't hold it with one hand."

"The sandwich is bigger than Anderson Cooper?"

I repositioned myself, cracked the door a half inch more, and put both hands out. I pulled in a serving platter piled high with chicken sandwiches. I couldn't even count the sandwiches, cut diagonally like That Woman does, and I shouldn't have been trying to count them, because the door slammed open. They flew in on the wings of a cat and chicken sandwiches. That Woman, Jess, and Fantasy marched right past me.

Dammit.

Fantasy had the computer tucked under one arm, *The Compass* under the other, and a bag of Ruffles between her teeth.

That Woman had a stack of dinner napkins and three bar glasses, and Jessica had a bottle of wine and the dead V2s she dragged everywhere. Did they not bring me anything to drink? That Woman pulled a bottle of raspberry lemonade from a pocket and held it out. I'd never forgive her, but I wouldn't die of thirst just because she was mean. And cruel. And had a little bitty black heart. I was ready for them to leave, now that I had my cat, and the sandwiches, and the raspberry lemonade, but when I opened my mouth to kick them out, it stayed open. Because we heard something solid banging and bouncing its way down the bulkhead behind the mirror.

We crept in the direction of the noise.

It was a V2. It fell down the wall and landed in the shreds of Bianca's Monique Lhuillier strapless gown.

That Woman said, "Look what your cat did to that dress."

We had a V2. And it worked. Or it would have worked, if we had the right thumb.

SIXTEEN

The front door of 704 laughed at our V2, flashing red for no instead of green for go. It was surely programmed to open a door somewhere, just not here. We filed back to the dressing room, way slower on the return, and gathered around the chicken sandwiches. Which were delicious. I was on my third. I reached for my fourth. I'd stop after this one. Maybe.

"Did we think it would open the door?" Fantasy asked.

"If the thumb lock was overridden it would," I said.

"Even if it was," Fantasy said, "what did we think we were going to do? March out in the hall?"

"So, yes."

"No, we wouldn't, Jess," I said. "We don't know what's out there. Do you want to walk out the door and get shot? Or locked in the submarine with No Hair?"

"So, no."

"We have a working V2, and I know we can find a way to use it to our advantage, but right now our best options are still the computer, the cell phone, or that." I pointed to the wall.

"I'll do it."

We all looked at That Woman.

"You'll do what?" Fantasy asked.

"I'll climb up the wall," That Woman said. "I used to climb trees, you know."

I turned to my interpreter. Fantasy.

"Tell her I said no."

Fantasy spoke to That Woman. "Davis said no."

"Tell her my father would kill me." Of course, he'd have to get in line behind Bianca. Anderson Cooper destroyed her Monique Lhuillier, which was now designer silk confetti. And I'd pulled half the feathers out of her Alice + Oliva sherelle maxi skirt when I'd used it for a (Kleenex) pillow. And then there was the Louis Vuitton luggage. I should gather the rest of Bianca's luggage, clothes, shoes, and jewelry and throw the lot of it overboard just to make a clean sweep of all things Bianca's.

Fantasy passed on the news. "She says her father would kill her."

"I heard her." That Woman leaned past Fantasy and spoke to me. "I can hear you, Davis."

"Tell her the chances are too great that the minute one of us pokes our head outside of this suite, someone will blow it off. They have our biometrics."

Fantasy opened her mouth to relay the news, but before she could That Woman said, "I don't even know what that is."

"So, when you registered." Jess spoke slowly to That Woman. "Remember when you filled out your paperwork a long time ago and they took your picture with the camera that went around your head?" Jess made a wide circle above her head, demonstrating. "They were recording your face. So, your cheekbones—" Jess traced her own dramatic cheekbones, then she began drawing circles around her dark eyes,"—and your eye sockets. And your chin." She tapped her chin.

"I never had my picture made with a round camera."

"She's right." I dropped my fourth sandwich. "She flew in last minute under the radar." I pointed at That Woman. "She's not in the *Probability* system."

"And she's the only one of us who'll halfway fit up the wall," Fantasy said. "Come on, Davis, you said it was a service area behind a bar. How dangerous is a service area? We'll be able to see her and talk to her the whole time."

"I'm not talking to her," I said.

"Suit yourself, sourpuss," That Woman said.

"That cat of yours has been up and down the wall fifty times and there's not a scratch on it," Fantasy said.

"Her."

"Whatever."

It was ten o'clock. Most, if not all, *Probability* passengers were toasting the bride and groom at Tie the Knot, far from the casino, which wouldn't open for another two hours. If we were going up the wall to find (help) the owner of the V2, now was the time.

"It's too dangerous." I couldn't let anything happen to her. "And that's my final answer."

"Well, you're not the boss of me, Davis Way." That Woman stood. "I'll be right back." She got up and marched out of the dressing room.

"Fantasy, where is she going?"

"How would I know?"

"Well, ask her."

"Mrs. Way, where are you going?"

"I'm putting on my party suit."

Fantasy looked at me. "This I gotta see."

"So, me too."

Fantasy and Jess stood and followed her, leaving me sitting on the ottoman alone. Anderson Cooper and I brought up the rear. I wasn't sure where we were going, but I was going too. I turned back to grab the last sandwich. Just in case. They were so good.

"What are we doing?" Jess asked as we filed through the salon.

"I'm going up that wall to the casino," That Woman said over her shoulder. "And I can tell you this right now." She stopped cold and we ran into each other. Boom boom boom. That Woman turned and spoke to us. "Gambling is a mortal sin. I don't want to have to explain it when I meet my maker. I'm going on a rescue mission. I'm not going to play casino games. Everybody got that?"

We got that.

* * *

The Party Suit was wide-legged black trousers with brass sailorette buttons marching down the long pockets, paired with a red twinset featuring black whales blowing white bubble fountains. It was cuter than it sounds, very sensible, and obviously brand new. I paced and tried not to pay attention.

Jess said, "Your hair. Pull it back in a chignon. So classy."

That Woman sat on a stool at the makeup mirror. "You go ahead. I don't have eyes in the back of my head."

"She's lying." I said it through the last of the chicken.

"Do not talk with your mouth full, Davis Way."

I wished I had another sandwich (in general), so I could talk through every bite of it.

"So, like, your hair didn't fall out," Jess said.

"Child, nowadays they freeze your head. Ice cap. Keeps your hair in."

"Was it cold?"

"It was ice," Mother answered. "On my head. So yes. It was cold."

Fantasy was digging in That Woman's makeup. "Do you own stock in Estée Lauder? I've never seen so much of this in my life."

"Get my rouge out of there, Fantasy," That Woman said. "Give me some spots of color. And get my Youth-Dew."

"Who is Youth-Dew?"

"It's my signature fragrance, Fantasy. Everyone needs a signature fragrance."

Fantasy was deep in That Woman's forty-year-old makeup bag full of fifty-year-old makeup. She pulled out a gold-capped bottle half full of amber liquid with a beat-up gold bow tied around the waistline of the pleated glass, then asked, "How old is this?"

That Woman snatched it, craned her neck, squirt squirt, and filled the room with the scent of my life. "It doesn't go bad, Fantasy." She shot a stream on the inside of her left wrist, then rubbed her wrists together. "It's not eggs."

After what felt like an eternity, That Woman was ready. And barefoot. "Davis, get my high heels."

"You can't wear heels, Mrs. Way," Fantasy said. "You need traction."

I looked in the closet and found what That Woman called heels, and they did, indeed, have a hint of a lift at the back of the shoe. Maybe. They were Naturalizer black patent leather pumps, and I found them on a shoe shelf beside a pair of bright blue Easy Spirit Traveltime Cloggers. I passed the cloggers to Fantasy.

"I'm not wearing those," That Woman said. "They don't match."

"Tell her this isn't a fashion show," I said. "It's a reconnaissance mission. To see what's up there. She doesn't even need to dress up and she sure doesn't need high heels."

Fantasy opened her mouth and That Woman said, "I heard her. And I'm wearing my heels. We don't know what's up there. You don't get a second chance to make a good first impression."

She was right about one thing: We don't know what's up there.

The shoe fight ensued and a compromise was reached. She could fit her high heels in her big pockets and change when she got up the wall. Fantasy talked her into the cloggers for the climb.

We marched back through 704, Anderson and I bringing up the rear again. When we stepped inside my sitting room, I held back and let the others go. I could hear Fantasy and Jess passing out uphill advice. I could hear That Woman assuring them she'd forgotten more about climbing in her sleep last night than the two of them put together ever knew when they were awake. I kept my nose buried in Anderson Cooper, who was resting on my babies. I tried to keep my breathing slow and steady, and I wondered why I was so cold. Maybe I wasn't so cold, but I was shaking, head to toe.

"Davis?" A finger lifted my chin. "Look up here."

I met her dark caramel eyes, the exact color of mine. "Did you tell her about me?"

She tapped my nose. "I told her how much I love you."

My eyes started leaking again. "Mother, please be careful."

* * *

The high heels in her pockets didn't last two minutes. They came banging down the wall, first the right, then the left.

"Dadburn it." She was reporting from somewhere near the middle of the chute behind the mirror. The acoustics were quite good. "My high heels."

"Don't worry about your shoes, Mother. Just don't slip and fall."

"I'm scooting up on my backside," she said. "There's nowhere to fall. Boy, I'll tell you, it's tight in here. Davis, you keep your seat. It'd take the Jaws of Life to get you out of here. Or in, for that matter."

Five excruciatingly long minutes later, and from much farther up the tunnel, she shouted, "I'm almost there."

"Can you see anything, Mrs. Way?"

"So? Can you?"

"Mother, be careful."

Fantasy, Jess, Anderson Cooper, and I had our heads stuffed into the hole in the wall. It was close quarters. Considering how much of me there was. Jaws of Life and all.

"I can see where Davis's cat is getting in and out." From the top, by the time her voice traveled to us, it bounced off the bulkhead and amplified. "It's a—" we waited impatiently to hear what it was, "—a little closet of some sort."

A closet?

"There's something stuck up here. HOLD ON."

"Oh, Lord." I had to back out of the hole in the wall. "I can't stand it."

"I'M GOING TO PUSH IT!"

"We can hear you just fine, Mrs. Way," Fantasy said. "Maybe not so loud."

Next we heard a grunt, then the most godawful noise, most likely Mother's detached head bouncing down the wall. Fantasy and Jess scrambled out of the way, and I had to clap my hand over my mouth to keep the scream in. The noise got louder and louder until it stopped.

"I can't look," I said. "I can't. Is she alive?"

"It's a piece of wood, Davis."

I peeked through two fingers. It was a three-foot by three-foot square of plywood covered on one side with industrial blue carpet. A smooth chunk of the wood had broken away, the edge of the carpet dangling, which was surely Anderson's in and out. The next thing we heard was Mother, from above. "Well, hello there!" Then a blood-curdling scream.

* * *

Her name was Arlinda Smith. She was a *Probability* casino server and her locker in the casino employee service area behind the main casino bar was directly above the middle mirrors of my dressing room.

"No way."

"Arlinda," I said. "I have your V2. I'm not going to send it up. You need to come get it."

Ten minutes earlier, Mother had introduced herself to poor unsuspecting Arlinda, who happened upon a floating head in the floor of her locker as she searched for her missing V2. Mother invited her to join us in 704, Arlinda vehemently declined, then, at my insistence, Mother slid back down the bulkhead so I could conduct negotiations with (our only hope) Arlinda Smith.

Mother squealed "Whee!" twice on the way down and "I hope I'm not picking my pants" three times. Fantasy and I pulled her out. She stood, brushed herself off, then announced, "That was the most fun I've had in a long time." She looked past us and pointed.

We turned to see Sleeping Beauty Jess spread-eagle passed out across the ottoman, her hair hanging off and spilling onto the carpet, Anderson Cooper having her way with Jess's dark locks. "Davis, your cat is going to snatch her bald." I caught Anderson's eye and signed for her to stop. She sat down and pouted.

I got on my back behind the mirror, my head in the hole, babies playing leap frog, looked up the wall, and tried to talk Arlinda down. Now that more light spilled from above, I could see that the path between us was relatively smooth, but it sloped and slanted right and left like a primitive prototype of a waterslide. I really couldn't believe my mother had traveled up and down this wall. I knew for a fact my father wouldn't believe it.

"Please come down and talk to us," I called up.

"I'm getting security," Arlinda called down.

Fantasy and I yelled, "NO!"

"Who are you?" She cast a long shadow down the wall. "Tell me who you are and I might come down there. Maybe."

"I'm Mrs. Sanders."

"Bellissimo Mrs. Sanders? You're her?"

"Yes!" No. "We're locked in our room, Arlinda, and we really need your help."

"Your V2 opens the door," she said.

"Our V2s don't work. We need your help."

"What do you mean your V2s don't work?"

"I don't know how to explain it any other way," I said. "They don't work."

"Well, my V2 works," Arlinda said. "And I need it. Really, Mrs. Sanders, or whoever you are, give me my V2 or I'm going to get security. Right now."

"Arlinda." I had to get through to this girl. "We are trapped in our suite. Four of us. We've been locked up since we walked in. We truly need your help." I let my plea sit there until things were very still between decks seven and eight.

"How do I know you're not lying to me?"

"Why in the world would I lie about something like this?" I asked. "Please, Arlinda. Please come down here." And turn on your phone.

Nothing.

I pulled out the last trick I had up my sleeve. "I have your tips."

I waited. And waited.

"How'd you get my tips?" she asked. "And how'd you get my V2?"

"Your V2 fell and I have your tips because my cat has been climbing the wall."

"You have a *cat* on this ship?"

Well.

"Okay, move," she finally said. "I'm coming down."

It took Fantasy and Mother to haul me up from the floor and out of Arlinda's way. We listened intently as she slid down. A shoe knocked its way down. It was an Alexander Wang bone pump. Four-inch heel. Then the other shoe dropped. Fantasy showed them to Mother. "Now, these are high heels." Finally, we saw one bare foot appear in the hole in the gauntlet gray, then another. Then one long brown leg, then its mate.

"Now what?" Arlinda's voice was much closer. "I'm stuck."

"That last curve is a booger bear," Mother said.

It took ten minutes to figure out how to get Arlinda, several inches taller than Mother, out of the wall she was wedged in. Fantasy pulled her by the ankles until she had room to flip over, then pulled again, Mother directing traffic the whole time, which wasn't helping a bit, and finally Arlinda Smith appeared. The three of us crowded around and got our first good look at her as she dusted herself off. Then she took inventory of our motley crew. She took a step back and bumped into the gauntlet gray wall. Her eyes were darting and wild.

I believe we frightened her.

"Give her some space," I said.

Mother and Fantasy moved in closer.

Arlinda squared her shoulders, took a deep breath, and bravely asked, "Where's my V2?"

I held up a finger to my crew—I got this. "What's directly above us?"

"My changing room and my locker," she said. "Where's my phone? Where are my tips?"

"Why is the ship stopped?"

"Engine trouble. Where's my phone? Where are my tips?" She was considerably taller than me and a lot less, or let's say not at all, pregnant, with china-doll skin, short dark shiny hair, and bright chocolate-brown eyes. She was wearing two ounces of a navy blue sailor suit. It was barely past a bikini. "I'm really confused," she said. "I don't understand what's going on."

Get. In. Line.

"Can I have my V2?" Arlinda's shiny hair bounced as her head jerked around the room. She rocked back and forth on her bare feet. Her voice shook when she said, "I really don't think I should be here."

"It'll be okay, Arlinda," I tried to reassure her.

"Can I have my V2? And my tips? Please?"

"Yes," I said. "You can have them. I'll give everything to you if you'll give us fifteen minutes. Just fifteen minutes."

Her chin trembled.

"Arlinda, I promise you no one here will hurt you. I promise."

Her eyes swept the room again—the remnants of our chicken sandwich picnic; snoring Jess, sprawled out like a drunk prom date in her red undies; Anderson Cooper, ho-hum, grooming her little paws like these were the kinds of escapades she witnessed daily; Mother in her Party Suit and Traveltime Cloggers, animated and energized by her adventure; six feet of Fantasy plus two feet of hair, tapping an impatient foot, hands on hips; and, well, me. Arlinda's eyes stopped at the remnants of Bianca's Monique Lhuillier gown in a pile of silk streamers on the gray shag carpet at her feet. She kept her eyes on it as she asked, her voice hollow and thin, "Who are you people?"

Just then, behind us, Jess woke like we'd dumped a load of ice on her, long bare legs flying through the air, one enormous breast escaping the confines of her red demi bra. She sat straight up on the ottoman. "SO? SO? SO? SO? SO? SO?"

Arlinda didn't take her eyes off mine as she stooped and batted blindly for her Alexander Wangs. "I'm sorry," she said, "but I can't help you." She tucked her shoes under an arm and held out her hand for her V2 and tips. "I promise I'll send help. I promise I will send help in five minutes. But I can't help you."

Fantasy shifted her weight and sighed, then spoke to the chandelier. "Arlinda. That's not an option. You're here and we need you."

"No." Arlinda was on her way through the rabbit hole in the wall. "You can keep my things. I'm sorry."

She was making a run for it.

Fantasy looked at me. "Why is she doing this to me?"

I shrugged.

The top half of Arlinda had disappeared, but the back half of her froze when she heard the unmistakable sound of a 9mm round being racked into the chamber of a handgun. "Arlinda," Fantasy said it on a huge sigh. "Get back here."

And then the hostages in 704 had a hostage of their own.

SEVENTEEN

A door off the foyer led to the dining room, a long skinny room that connected to the kitchen by a large pass-through serving window. I'd poked my head in the dining room last night when I was looking for a way out, but hadn't spent any time there until now. I thought it best to get Arlinda out of my dressing room. Change of scenery and all.

We filed in through the foyer, Fantasy wagging the Hi-Point C-9 behind 704's newest and most petrified guest, and made the dining room Mission Control. Maybe, with the laptop and Arlinda's help, I could assess the danger level outside of 704.

Jess tried to comfort Arlinda. "They're really nice," she told her. "They haven't killed me."

"Really?" Arlinda was barefoot and wearing a scuba blue Givenchy cashmere blazer of Bianca's over her bikini sailor suit. "Good to know."

Mother said, "That ugly statue is gone." A directional light pointed at nothing on a marble display stand in the foyer.

"How about that," said dumbstruck Fantasy. "Wonder what happened to it?"

In keeping with the simple décor throughout 704, the dining room was tastefully underdone, with a long white-oak parson table surrounded by eight white linen armless chairs on wheels. Under all that, a wheat sisal rug. Above all that, two birdcage chandeliers on a dimmer switch. I cranked them up.

We spread our goodies across the table, everything, including Fantasy's gun, with the exception of Arlinda's V2 and tips, which I wasn't about to hand over. Yet. I sat at the head of the table and indicated I'd like Arlinda to sit beside me. She fully complied.

We settled in.

"Would anyone like a cup of coffee?" Mother asked.

"I'd love some coffee," Jess said.

Fantasy seconded that motion.

I looked at Arlinda, who nodded, because she was too afraid not to. I think I could have offered her a cup of battery acid and she'd have gone along with it.

My hands clasped on the table, the laptop and *The Compass* in front of me, I turned to our guest. "I'm not Bianca Sanders."

She whimpered, a short desperate little noise.

"My name is Davis Way Cole and I work for the Bellissimo."

"You're Mr. Cole's wife?"

My head dropped. My eyes landed on my babies. I spoke to them. "Yes." Mr. Cole, my husband, the father of my twins, whom I hadn't spoken to in almost thirty hours.

"I'm her mother." Mother waved.

"I'm her partner." Fantasy waved.

Jess sat there, lounging across the dining room table with her stack of dead V2s, trying to figure out who she was in relation to me. I finally said, "That's Jessica."

Arlinda passed around an unsteady smile.

Mother went to push back from the table without remembering the chair was on wheels. She let out a roller-coaster whoop, laughed at herself, and for a split second the thick tension in the room dissipated. "I'll go see about that coffee."

To our guest, I said, "You are our first contact with anyone outside of this suite since before we left Biloxi. And we need your help."

"You look just like Mrs. Sanders."

She knew who Bradley and Bianca were. "Do you work for the Bellissimo, Arlinda?"

She nodded yes. Then she shook her head no. Which was to say she did, but she didn't plan on ever setting foot in the

Bellissimo again. "I'm a server in high stakes. I'm one of several Bellissimo high-stakes servers on *Probability*."

"Well, you just got a big fat raise, Arlinda."

She wasn't impressed.

"Yes, I look like Mrs. Sanders. I'm who you see at the Bellissimo and in media when you think you're seeing her. I'm her body double."

She was a little impressed.

"Are you?" Her eyes were fixed on my middle. "Are you really expecting or are you being her body double?"

I patted my babies. "All me."

"Do you need a doctor?" Arlinda asked. "Are you having your baby *now*?" She inched away from me as Mother appeared in the doorway with a pot of coffee and four martini glasses.

"She's not ready yet," Mother said. "She looks like she's about to go, but she's carrying twins. They don't know what kind of twins because they're waiting to be surprised. She's carrying low, has been since she started showing, so I think she's having boys." She stopped at Fantasy. "Move that thing." Fantasy picked up the gun and tucked it at her hip. Arlinda let out a barely audible sigh of relief. Mother stopped at Jess. "Get your elbows off the table." Jess's hands slid into her lap. "These will be my first grandsons." Mother poured steaming hot coffee into Arlinda's martini glasses. "She's got another sixteen weeks or so, but you know doubles come early."

Well, look who could write a book.

Arlinda considered the martini glasses curiously and she was the last to pick one up by the stem to take a sip. When she did, she waited to drop dead. When she didn't, she took another sip. She opened her mouth to say something, changed her mind, then tried again.

"Go ahead, Arlinda."

"My V2," she said. "Let me have it. I'll turn it on and you can call the police."

"It's not that simple," I said.

"Why not?"

"The ship is smart," I said. "Very smart."

"Oh, I know." Arlinda nodded.

"If I were holding an entire suite hostage," I said, "the first thing I'd do would be to monitor the electronic activity in it." I didn't bother her with the deadly consequences details in the letter that were directly connected to attempts at communication. "I can see where making a call on your V2 would look like the easiest way out. But we're sitting dead still in the middle of the sea. I can't call the police, the Coast Guard, or anyone else who could get here faster than someone on this ship could get here and do us harm. Not to mention it would jeopardize you. The person or people who locked us in here would know the call came from inside this suite and from your V2."

Mother said, "Davis is a thinker like that. Always has been. She gets that from her daddy."

Arlinda was so pasty pale.

"We need to approach it from a different angle," I said. "Or at least be on the other side of the door before we make a phone call. And if we can get on the other side of the door to call for help, we need to make the call on our way to this man, who's also being held." From my stash, I pushed a picture of No Hair in front of her. She bent over it. "His name is Jeremy Covey. He's our boss." I toggled a finger between myself and Fantasy. "And he's the head of security on *Probability*."

She looked at No Hair's picture at length. "The head of security is locked up?"

"Yes," I said.

Arlinda began to see the gravity of our situation, that the problem might be bigger than four women, a gun, martini glasses, and a cat stealing her tips. "Why is he in the submarine?"

There it was again. "This is why we need you, Arlinda. You're helping already. How do you know he's in the submarine?"

"The round porthole windows," Jess said. "You can see them in the picture. They're only in the submarine."

Well, there you go.

"We need your help getting him *out* of the submarine, Arlinda," I said.

"You're locked in here." Arlinda tapped the table. "How are you going to get your boss out of the submarine if you can't leave your suite?"

"That's where you come in," I said.

She surrendered. Her chair rolled back. She was poised for flight.

"Seriously," she said, "I can't begin to help you. I'm in my last semester of law school at Loyola, I serve cocktails, and I do *not* know why your boss is in the submarine. I have no idea how to get him out. Please just give me my V2, let me go, and I'll send someone who can help."

I patted the table, inviting her back to our inner circle. She stayed right where she was. Fantasy, with an exaggerated sigh, pulled the Hi-Point out and slammed it down. Arlinda reluctantly scooted her chair up a half inch.

"It's okay, Arlinda," I tried to comfort her. "I promise it's okay. Stay with me for a few more minutes."

She swallowed. She tucked her hands under her bare legs. She eyed what was left of her coffee in the martini glass.

"Want me to warm you up?" Mother asked. "It's the Starbucks."

"Arlinda." I continued to speak to her in calming tones and if I kept it up much longer, I'd calm myself to sleep. I was tired, so tired. I wanted a martini glass of coffee too, about as much as I wanted out of 704. I had a daughter to meet, twins to deliver, and a husband I loved on the other side of the world. I guess the image of the people I loved was swimming in my eyes when I said, "Please help us."

She rolled back to the table.

Fantasy tucked her gun.

Mother poured another round of the Starbucks.

"Arlinda, there's one more thing I need to talk to you about."

She drew a deep breath, squeezed her eyes closed, and nodded.

"I need to know everything you know about the banking activities in the casino." I reached for the laptop and woke it up. "I think our detainment has something to do with the casino transactions."

Her chocolate-brown eyes popped open. "I don't know a thing about that either! Seriously, Mrs. Sanders, Mrs. Cole, whoever you are!" She looked around the table for help. "I serve *drinks!*"

"You may know more than you think you do," I said.

"I don't. I have one guest." She held up a single finger. "I know what he drinks. I know what his wife drinks. I know what his bodyguard drinks. That's truly all I know."

She had to know more than that.

"If you'll let me see my V2 I can explain."

I raised one eyebrow at Fantasy. *How much harm could it do?* She tipped her head. *I can shoot it out of her hand if I need to.* I shrugged one shoulder. *True.*

"I get it!" Arlinda said. "If I try to make a call *I'll* be in a lot of trouble. I get it!"

Fantasy stood. "Be right back." She took off at a jog and was back in a flash. She held it out of Arlinda's reach. "Don't get any bright ideas."

There was a little tug of war.

"Fantasy," I said. "Give it to her."

"My guy's name is Fredrick Blackwell." Arlinda swiped her thumb across her V2, poked, then flipped it to show me a headshot of Fredrick Blackwell. He was in his mid-fifties, more salt than pepper hair, wide-set green eyes, bushy gray eyebrows, a thick neck, and he was dead serious about having his picture made.

Jessica leaned in to take a peek. "Space Man."

"Why do you only serve drinks to him, his wife, and his bodyguard?" I asked.

"There are fifty servers and fifty guests," she said. "We're each assigned a guest. Fredrick Blackwell is mine."

I held my hand out and Arlinda reluctantly surrendered her V2.

I poked around and found her handy bio of Mr. Blackwell: Fifty-four years old, Houston resident, one wife, two grown daughters, three poodles.

"He's in outer-space asset management and regulation," she said.

"Come again?" Mother asked.

"He's in charge of space," Arlinda said.

"Well, I never," Mother said. "What in the world?"

"He keeps satellites from crashing into each other," Arlinda said.

"Lands alive," Mother said. "It's the Twilight Zone."

Jess was busy building a V2 house with a flat V2 roof from her stack of dead V2s.

"What does a gig like that pay?" Fantasy asked.

I read from Arlinda's V2, "His net worth is five billion."

"Well, bully for him. Is he single?" Mother pointed to Fantasy. "She's looking."

"No," Fantasy snapped. "I am not."

"What's his game?" I asked.

"He's a slot player. He's playing Knot on Your Life."

"How's he doing?"

Arlinda tucked a thick lock of shiny dark bob behind an ear. "He's even," she said. "He spends more time swiping money in and out than playing. He puts a hundred thousand in, loses ninety-nine of it, then wins a hundred and ten. He deposits the win and starts over. And over. Why?"

Heavy play. Heavy transactions. "How are the other players doing?"

"Same thing," Arlinda said. "Everyone playing is dead even. They win, they lose, they win again. Why?"

"Even Steven," Mother said.

"And they swipe, swipe, swipe?" I asked.

"That's all they do," Arlinda said. "They can only deposit a hundred thousand at a time and they go through it in five minutes. Then they're swiping again."

I'd seen the Knot on Your Life slot machines six weeks ago at the Bellissimo with No Hair. I'd played it in demo-mode—buoys danced, ship wheels twirled, and anchors, even one on the payline, paid $50,000. Two paid $250,000. Three anchors hit the jackpot. It was a game built for billionaires with a mouthwatering payout of $2,500,000 for lining up three anchors, and it was a $10,000 per-spin game. Which meant, with a $100,000 deposit limit, the players were indeed swiping themselves stupid.

Why?

"Has anyone hit the jackpot?" I asked.

"No," Arlinda said. "Noticeably not."

"What do you mean?"

"It's just," Arlinda chose her words carefully, "no one is winning. But no one is losing. They're constantly checking the balances on their V2s and it's the same all the way around. Everyone's even. They're getting bored."

And I was finally getting somewhere. My guess was they weren't even at all. In fact, the billionaires playing Knot on Your Life may very well be going broke. The money trail started at the individual player's personal banks feeding the *Probability* accounts. Wins were supposed to go the opposite direction— through the *Probability* account back to the personal in Denver. Or Dallas. Or Des Moines. But what if they weren't? What if the deposits on the *Probability* end were being diverted? Not going to Des Moines. Someone could be stockpiling the Knot on Your Life deposits and I needed to find that someone fast.

I knew Poppy was someone, but she wasn't the someone I was looking for; I knew what her role was and unfortunately for her, I knew exactly where she was. Everything else pointed to Maximillian DeLuna and his pilot Colby. If I was right and this was about diverting Knot on Your Life wins, they were only half of the story. The other half would be at the Cayman bank doing the collecting. If DeLuna was working this end taking the money, who was working the other end receiving it? I needed to know the names of everyone benefitting from the con on the Caribbean.

Then what? I was locked in 704.

If I could get to the casino when it opened tonight, I'd track down Fredrick Blackwell and advise him to dig a little deeper. There was no doubt his V2 was pulling the money going into the slot machines from his personal bank, but when he won, V2 might not be giving it back. V2 could be sending the wins somewhere else and lying to him. Showing him a balance that wasn't really there. But seeing as how I couldn't get to the casino or Fredrick Blackwell, then talk him into letting me have access to his personal account funding his *Probability* account, I'd need to sneak a peek the hard way. I pulled the laptop closer and wiggled my fingers over the keyboard. To the collection of ladies around the dining room table trapped in 704 with me, I said, "I'm going to need a minute."

Mother poured the Starbucks.

* * *

I couldn't go straight to the bank. The quickest way to open the door to 704 would be to hack into the bank processing the Knot on Your Life transactions. Within minutes, the door could bust open and we'd all be dead. And I couldn't go the deep web route—banks were onto the deep web. So I needed a proxy server, a computer application that acts as an intermediary for users like me who need information from protected computer systems. Like banks. A non-judgmental cyber middleman who wouldn't let anyone know I was asking, didn't care who I was or what I intended to do with the information, but would help me gather it with no one the wiser.

"So, what are you doing?"

I was pretending to be Poppy in Firefox, searching the internet for an open HTTPS transparent proxy so I could bypass filters and censoring, both *Probability's* and Fredrick Blackwell's bank's, which I wasn't about to explain to Jess.

"Jessica," Fantasy said, "leave her alone. She's working."

"I'm waiting," I said.

"On what?"

"I'm waiting on a socket, Jess. And I think I found one."

Arlinda was eyeing her Starbucks martini. "Are there coffee cups?"

"There were," Fantasy said. "We ran out."

"Where *are* all the dishes?" Mother slapped the table.

"Listen up." I looked around. "I found a socket." Garbled code flashed on the screen. "Now I have to build a script to get in. This will take a minute."

"So cool you know how to do this," Jess said.

"She can find recipes on the interweb too," Mother told Jess. "Ask Davis for a pumpkin loaf recipe and she will give you ten."

"Pumpkins? Ten pumpkins?"

I imported the socket, then the thread module, because I needed the proxy's functions. I declared settings, adding a listening port, buffers, maximum connections, translators, and a connection function so I could shut it down fast if there was any indication someone out there didn't think Poppy should be such good friends with a proxy server.

"When you finish, will we be out?"

"No, Jess." I didn't look up. "But I think we'll know who locked us in here. Which will help get us out."

I asked the proxy server to find Fredrick Blackwell's bank. It came back with six hits, Mr. Blackwell spreading the love around central Texas with five different financial institutions, but the last on the list was what I wanted. LTWI Trust Company. In Grand Cayman. I clicked, asking Proxy to sneak me in the bank's back door, then plugged in the eighteen digit *Probability* number from his bio.

"What are you going to do when you find them?"

"Jess," Fantasy said. "When she's on the computer, you have to leave her alone. The answer is when she finds them we're going to kill them."

Arlinda screamed a little.

"I'm just kidding," Fantasy said.

"She's kidding," Mother chimed in. "I think she's kidding."

"So, I think you *should* kill them."

Paydirt. I was in Fredrick Blackwell's *Probability* account. I found the withdrawals Arlinda told us about, a long list of $100,000 debits totaling almost $2,000,000, and that after only one day of playing the Knot on Your Life slot machines. There were no corresponding deposits. Not a one. Not a penny of winnings going back into Fredrick's personal account. I was right and the deposits were going somewhere else. And that was why we were locked in 704.

I took a breather and sat back. I rubbed my eyes. "No one's killing anyone."

Jess's latest V2 house design imploded.

Arlinda was getting edgier by the minute. "Let me ask you something."

"Sure." I sat up and went back to the laptop.

"There are four of you."

I nodded.

"But she has five V2s."

Tap tap on the keyboard. "Uh-huh?" I asked Proxy to follow Fredrick's money. Where were the deposits going? Who was ultimately behind this? Who was DeLuna working with or for? Who was stealing from the billionaires? Boom. Fredrick Blackwell's deposits weren't going into his *Probability* account because they were being diverted to an account at the Banco de la Elima, also in the Caymans. The account was a new one, opened forty-eight hours ago, with a current balance of $120,000,000. In just one day, the players lost that much money off Knot on Your Life. If left unchecked, DeLuna & Co. were looking at a billion-dollar paycheck by the end of the cruise. Give me a name, Proxy. Tell me who (to kill) locked us in here.

"Mrs. Cole." Arlinda Smith gently tapped the table beside the laptop with an open palm, finally getting my attention. "You have five V2s but only four people. Where is your fifth person?"

My fingers slid off the keyboard.

It was as if someone slapped me and Fantasy.

It happens.

"It's not where the fifth person is—" I started the thought.

"—it's where the sixth V2 is," Fantasy finished.

And that's how Super Secret Spies do it.

"There are *six* people in this suite?" Arlinda's head bobbed as she took roll around the table just to make sure. "Where are the other two people?"

Proxy found the account. It flashed green on the screen and I had a target.

I had two targets.

There were two people on the receiving end of the Knot on Your Life scam.

It was a joint account, registered to Bradley W. Cole and Jessica E. DeLuna. The Cayman account holding one hundred and twenty million dollars of skimmed *Probability* casino cash was *Bradley's*. And Jessica's. Who we never should have let sit in an armless chair on wheels.

She must have been counting V2s, which must have the same effect on her as counting sheep. She went nighty-night, tipped over, and the rolling chair shot out from under her. Jess hit the floor and the chair hit the wall, both with a boom. Arlinda Smith clapped her hand over her mouth and screamed into it. Fantasy and I made a run for the sundeck. We'd buried Poppy in a Louis Vuitton trunk with a V2 somewhere on her person. There wasn't a doubt in my mind Poppy's V2 worked just fine. And with her V2, we could waltz right out the door.

EIGHTEEN

It's not like we could waltz right out the door.

It was the same problem we'd have faced if Arlinda's V2 had opened the door: We didn't know what was waiting on the other side. We knew for a fact the cameras would catch us, which might set the deadly consequences clause into motion, so we had to get out the door without the cameras seeing us. The only way we could come up with, over Poppy's dead body, was the lifeboat in the closet behind the closet in Burnsworth's room.

Neither of us was in a very big hurry to revisit Burnsworth's room.

It's not every day you search a dead body. We'd passed exhausted hours earlier, and stripping a corpse to look for electronics had done us in. The dark, cool, absolute quiet of the deck combined with the hypnotic lull of the sea would have been unnerving if either of us had a nerve left. We hid, shoulder to shoulder, sharing a blanket, on the side of a sun chair. Catching our breath. Thinking our next move. Wondering if we even had a next move. Acting too quickly, as in running out the front door, might mean winding up dead. Or in the submarine with No Hair. At least we were relatively safe inside 704. With beds. And a pool. And a computer. But not acting quickly, as in running out the front door so I could, at the very least, talk to my husband, left us in jeopardy. And we were sick to death of jeopardy.

I honestly couldn't believe Knot on Your Life deposits were going into an account in Bradley's name. I couldn't believe Max DeLuna and his pilot were that smart.

"They set Bradley and Jessica up to take the fall for this," I said. "They have slot players believing the balance on their V2s, knowing full well that at some point, one of the players will dig a little deeper, past what the V2 says, all the way to their home bank, at which point the jig will be up."

"Probably why the pilot is in on it," Fantasy said. "Quick getaway."

"While Bradley and Jessica take the fall."

"In the time it takes to clear Bradley and Jess, even if it's only an hour, they'll be long gone with the money."

"And they don't know it yet, but they got a raise," I said.

"They don't have to split anything with Poppy."

If we had it to do over, we wouldn't necessarily put bodies in trunks, then put the trunks in direct sunlight. It didn't feel hot, tropical breeze and all, but we weren't dead and stuffed into Louis Vuitton trunks with the afternoon sun beating down on us for hours. As it turned out, the walk-in refrigerator would have been the better body storage choice. We found Poppy's V2 strapped to her ribcage. And it was disgusting.

"Do you think this is warping my babies?"

"Your baby boys?" she asked.

I'd have laughed at that if I had a laugh left in me.

"Your babies have no idea what's going on."

"Neither do yours," I said.

"What's that supposed to mean?"

"You need to come clean with them, Fantasy. Tell them the truth. You can't let them think the divorce is Reggie's choice or even a mutual decision."

"Maybe I'll worry about that later."

(Later.)

"It's hard to believe I can't call my husband. Just turn on this V2 and dial his number."

"Poppy would never call Bradley," Fantasy said. "We'll get out the door and use Arlinda's phone to call Bradley. I doubt anyone cares who Arlinda calls."

"Right."

"We have to tackle Burnsworth's room first."

"Right."

Neither of us jumped up to tackle Burnsworth's room.

"Your mother." Fantasy said it on the weariest laugh imaginable.

"I know."

There wasn't a sound in the world. Not one.

"What I can't believe is my father."

"He pulled a fast one on you, Davis. I doubt he meant for her to hurt you like that. I don't think *she* meant to hurt you."

"She didn't." Much. "It's been such a hard part of who I am for so long, to tell you the truth, Fantasy, it's a relief."

"What are you going to do?"

"What do you mean?"

"You have a choice, you know." Fantasy was hogging the blanket. "You don't have to act on the information." She leaned in and spoke to the middle of me. "Your mommy's already a mommy."

I took a swat at her. "Leave the boys alone." She sat up and we tipped heads, hers so pillowy, and stayed there three seconds. "I'm barely older than her," I said. "I don't feel old enough to have an eighteen-year-old."

"That happens when you have a baby at sixteen."

"Mother's mother had her when she was fifteen."

"I wonder if it's too late for me and Reggie to have another baby," Fantasy said. "Maybe we'd have a girl. Maybe we could start over."

We were discussing babies—past, present, and future—as if nothing else was happening in our world. I don't know if we were avoiding what might be ahead or sharing what might be our last quiet moments before the deadly consequences. Because we had Poppy's V2 and one way or another, we were on our way out the door. And one way or another, I was calling my husband. And one way or another, we were making a run for the submarine. Just as soon as we worked up the nerve to tackle Burnsworth's room.

Our time in 704 was up.

"Are you going to see her?"

"I can't wait to see her," I said. "If we ever get off this boat."

"Davis!" Fantasy took my half of the blanket when she bent over double laughing.

"What?" I yanked the blanket.

"It's a ship!"

*　*　*

"I'll go in," Fantasy said. "You wait here."

"No. It's just blood." As I said the words I could hear my own blood roaring through my ears. "Let's just do it."

"At least let me throw a blanket over it, Davis." She had her hand on the door that led to Burnsworth's bloody berth.

"His blanket is at the bottom of the sea, Fantasy. Just go." I gave her a little push.

We stepped around it.

I found the half door on the back wall of the small closet. I slid it open. It was barely wide enough to pull the inflatable lifeboat out, and the real treasure was hidden underneath. We found a skinny file with three surveillance shots of Maximillian DeLuna entering Banco de la Elima in Grand Cayman, opening the account in Bradley's and Jessica's names. At noon on Friday. Four hours before I boarded, seven hours before *Probability* left port. And that's where the pilot came in. There's no way he'd have been able to pull off that kind of timeline without a jet. It didn't explain why Colby Mitchell was listed in *The Compass* as our stateroom attendant, but it did explain her role.

Burnsworth knew. Which meant No Hair probably knew. DeLuna ran the clock so tight No Hair didn't have time to act on the information before DeLuna took him out of the equation. And Poppy killed Burnsworth before *he* could do anything, and that meant, like Burnsworth said before he died, it was up to us.

Me, he said. It was up to me.

"Do we know Banco de la Elima?" I studied the photographs for information.

"Elima is Hawaiian."

Which didn't help a bit. Or maybe it did. "Isn't Jess from Hawaii?"

"What does that matter?" Fantasy asked. "DeLuna opened the account in the Caymans."

We closed Burnsworth's door and stepped into the salon where Mother demanded to know where we'd been. "You went out one door and came back in another."

Fantasy looked to me for an explanation. "Old Irish superstition," I said. "Mother thinks you should come and go through the same door."

Fantasy scratched her three feet of hair.

"What is that?" Mother asked.

"It's a lifeboat," Fantasy said.

Arlinda whimpered.

"Let's get ready." I pumped up my words with energy I didn't have.

Jess popped up from a sofa. "For what?"

"We're getting out of here," I said. Arlinda collapsed with relief. "After we lock up Jessica's husband."

Jess looked like someone had slapped her. "Not *here*. Don't bring him here."

"How are we going to get him? Are we going to clobber him?" Mother threw an air punch.

"Arlinda's going to do it," I said.

"Clobber him?" Mother asked.

"What?" Arlinda cried. "*What*? How?"

"You're going to tell him the truth, Arlinda. The truth."

* * *

I could have stayed in the shower forever. I could have slept standing up in the shower. And as soon as I could talk to my husband and rescue No Hair, I would sleep. I might climb in my *Probability* bed and sleep until the babies were born. When I finally turned off the hot water, I'd been in the shower so long Fantasy had showered, dressed, and corralled her hair, and Mother had cleared the dressing room of the chicken picnic. She'd rifled through Hers and chosen clothes for me, and they were laid out on the ottoman between Jess and Arlinda, whose shoes were resting on her bouncing knees. Ready to go. My hair was pulled back in a wet Bianca blonde ponytail and I'd taken two seconds to swipe on mascara and lip gloss. No Hair had been through enough. I didn't want to rescue him and simultaneously scare him to death.

Mother chose a sleeveless Elizabeth and James ivory tunic and paired it with skinny black pants, skinny being relative, and when I dropped my towel to climb into them, Arlinda got her first peek at a Destination Maternity bra. The poor girl would be scarred for life from the events of the past hour and my pregnancy in her face might be the worst of it. Mother and Fantasy helped me dress and the question on everyone's mind was, just how much bigger is she going to get?

Maybe it wasn't the exact question on everyone's mind, but seeing myself in four huge mirrors, trust me, it flew through mine.

"So," Jessica said from the ottoman. "You need pearls."

Her husband had imprisoned her and implicated her in the heist he had going on above our heads, it would surely take a strong team of lawyers to untangle herself from this debacle, and in spite of it, she was accessorizing me.

It could be, as my husband believed, there was a lot more to Jessica DeLuna than met the eye.

Or maybe she just didn't get it.

Dressed and ready, I spoke to Arlinda. "It's eleven thirty. There's a ninety-nine-point-nine percent chance Mr. DeLuna is in the casino waiting for it to open. It's where he's stealing his fortune. He'll be there. Go back up the wall, find Mr. DeLuna, and tell him exactly what happened."

"Which is?" she asked.

"Your V2 fell through the bottom of your locker and in the process of looking for it, you found people trapped on the floor below. Including his wife."

"Then what?" she asked.

"He'll want to see for himself."

"You're sure?"

"I'm positive."

"Then what?"

"You take him to your changing room."

"What do I do then?" she asked.

"The locker is in the back of the changing room, right?"

"Right," she said.

"He'll want to see for himself. Let him get all the way to the locker. When he does, close the door to your changing room, zap it with your V2, and walk away. He'll be locked in. His V2 won't open the door to your changing room."

NINETEEN

Arts and Crafts were only mildly successful. We were working against the clock so it was a hack job. Because we only had two minutes. Then we had to rescue No Hair before DeLuna was out of the changing room and hot on our trail. My best guess was we'd have a half hour. If Arlinda managed to trap him.

If.

"Strips, you think?" Fantasy stood in the middle of the salon twirling one of the long-lost carving knives. "Like a turban?"

"Hoods." Mother had a butcher knife. "And then we'll cut eye holes."

"I don't care," I said, "as long as we don't suffocate."

We wouldn't let Jess have a knife for fear she'd fall (asleep) on her own sword, so she and I stood back as Mother and Fantasy hacked through the lifeboat, leaving deep slices and slashes in the salon's silver rug. Jess and I watched from the safe distance of a white linen sofa, where I was deep in *The Compass*. The ten-man raft being destroyed was made of a PVC-based synthetic rubber fabric encapsulated in polyurethane with a reflective Mylar coating. The Mylar coating would blind the cameras. We were fashioning hats from the lifeboat so the surveillance cameras would see a bright orb of unidentifiable light instead of people. With the exception of Mother, who the *Probability* system didn't know, there wasn't a doubt in my mind that bells, whistles, and sirens would sound the minute we stepped out of 704 and we'd never get to No Hair. Unless the cameras couldn't see us.

"It's actually a life raft," I said. "Not a lifeboat."

Mother wielded her butcher knife. "What's the difference?" She passed me a short cape of silver and white plastic. "Try this on."

I dropped it over my head. It wasn't as large as a bath towel, but it weighed five times as much.

"Bind your die moles, Dapith."

"WHAT?" I couldn't hear her through the Mylar. But I could sure hear myself.

"EYE HOLES!" she said. "FIND YOUR EYE HOLES!"

We donned our hoods and felt our way to the door, Mother in the lead, because (she was the only one with all her faculties) we were incapacitated under our raft smokescreens. It didn't help that I had a cat with me under mine. I expected Anderson Cooper to shriek in protest as soon as I put it on, and because there was no way for the sound to escape, we'd both be deaf.

We came out from under the Mylar to reconsider. Getting out of 704 might be the hardest thing I've ever done in my life.

"Davis, leave your cat," Fantasy said. "DeLuna can't get in here. We have the only V2 that opens the door."

"We don't know that," I said. "He could have ten V2s that open the door. And how do we know he won't come down the bulkhead? Mother and Arlinda got down it."

"He's too big," Mother said.

"So, you know Max?" Jessica asked her.

"No, but if he's man-sized at all, he can't get down the wall."

"He's a slimy little bastard," she said.

"I'll be dog," Mother said. "Why in the world did you marry him?"

Jess opened her mouth to answer, I interrupted. "Could we possibly talk about this later? Can we focus? Please? We're on a rescue mission and Anderson Cooper goes where we go." If something happened and we couldn't get back in, I didn't want my cat locked in 704 alone. "And we need to get going."

"Where *are* we going?" Fantasy was dabbing at her eyes with her sweater. "With Anderson Cooper."

"To the data center."

"Who?" Mother asked.

"I'll explain on the way. Put your hats on." The Mylar headgear might or might not keep us alive. I couldn't breathe, see, hear, or navigate again as soon as I flipped it over my (cat) head.

"This present dong fork!"

I think the words came from Fantasy. I couldn't really tell, because just then, I bumped into the foyer wall. "WHAT?" I blasted my own eardrums to bits.

Fantasy pulled off her hat. "THIS ISN'T GOING TO WORK, DAVIS!"

"Dough boy," I barely heard Mother say.

I heard a loud thump and tossed back my hood to see Jess sliding down the foyer wall.

"It's too dark under there for her," Mother said. "Put her out like a light. And where are her *clothes?* Are we really going to let her walk around in her red underpants? I swear she had clothes on yesterday."

I was too tired to think.

Mother wasn't. "My sun hats." She shuffled off in her Traveltime Cloggers. When she returned, we (woke up Jessica) draped our camo hoods over Mother's big sun hats, which gave us air, audio, and much less limited vision. We stood at the door.

"Go ahead," Fantasy said.

I pointed Poppy's V2 at the door. I pushed the power button.

It asked for Poppy's thumbprint.

"What?" Fantasy asked. "Go ahead. Open the door."

I looked at her from under my life-raft spy-hood sun hat. "I can't. We have to have Poppy's thumbprint."

In the end, it was Mother. She said, "Oh, good grief, you big babies. Where's the butcher knife?"

We were all going to hell. Me, Mother, Fantasy, and Jess. Straight to hell.

As we ran toward the elevator bank I put the V2 in phone mode and dialed Bradley Cole's cellphone from the safety of outside 704.

Nothing. It didn't even ring.

In the elevator, I read the last message Poppy sent from her V2:

Babe, we're covered on this end. Everything is good here, except I'm going crazy. These people are so stupid I don't know how they sit up and feed themselves. I'm going dark now. See you in George Town.

I wondered if Jessica knew, or cared, about Poppy and Max, and I decided I wouldn't waste one more second feeling bad for Poppy. Or her thumb.

* * *

Designed by a team of geniuses at Tufts University near Boston, *Probability*'s computer system was unmanned. An interdisciplinary squad of big brains designed, built, and installed the autonomous system that ran itself and *Probability*. In ten years, all computer systems will be run by computers instead of humans, and on this ship, the future was now. Somewhere—Boise or Bakersfield or Baton Rouge—a human sat at a desk insuring everything digital hummed along as it should aboard *Probability*, but the onsite system was not operated by nor did it recognize humans.

The good news: It was almost midnight. When we made it to the Orlon Deck, the lowest level on the ship, storage and maintenance, where both the submarine holding No Hair and the unmanned computer system were housed, it was deserted. We didn't have to go to the trouble of incapacitating anyone. We arrived, via a freight elevator, without incident. Lots of commentary and complaining, but no incidents.

The bad news: Hacking a system like *Probability*'s would be about as easy as catching a shooting star, and Computer Services was fore, at the front of the ship, while the submarine, and No Hair, were aft. The back. A football field away. *The Compass*, for all the information it had, didn't specify what lay between Computer Services and the submarine. It was either no man's land or so boring the editors of *The Compass* didn't think anyone needed or wanted to know.

"Is this it?" Fantasy's whispered words bounced off spooky dark walls.

"It must be." We were somewhere under the world, standing at dark glass double doors. Behind them, I could see multicolored lights racing up, down, and all over nine-foot-tall metal server cabinets. The cabinets went on forever. And ever.

"Davis, we're burning daylight," Mother said.

"My feet are so cold."

Mother turned to Jess. "Whose fault is that? You need shoes, clothes, a hairbrush—"

I put my hand on the door. "We need in and out of here as quickly as possible. Of the million things I'd like to do, we only have time for one." Nods all around. "Everyone ready?" I pushed through.

Probability's computer system surely ran the world. For as far as we could see it was servers and routers and switches topped off with an intricate acrylic pipe cooling system. Computer Services was, like the rest of *Probability*, so far ahead of its time.

"Keyboard, keyboard!" I called out. "A monitor, a station, a keyboard! Find me a keyboard!"

We shot off in four different directions. Jess won. "So, over here!"

We raced.

I passed Anderson Cooper to Fantasy. Fantasy held Anderson at arm's length like she was covered in spiders.

The operating system was Linux. I went to the default Grub boot menu by holding down the shift key, then patched directly to a boot shell prompt from there. I was in. The time it took to pull up the facial recognition software from the system menu, because it was so extensive, was excruciating, made even more so because everyone was breathing down my neck. The surveillance software was digiCam, easy to navigate, and two minutes after I pulled it up I had myself, Fantasy, and Jess deleted from the system. Poof. We were gone. We had a way in and out of 704, we had guns and ammo, we had a phone, and now we had anonymous mobility all over the ship. To celebrate, I sailed my life-raft hat through the air.

"Hey!" Mother snapped. "That's my new sun hat."

"Are we done here?" Fantasy was ready to give Anderson back.

"Not just yet." I was still over the keyboard. I found Max DeLuna's profile. I asked digiCam to find him to see how close he was. There wasn't a doubt in my mind he was looking for us, but he wouldn't find us in the system because I'd just wiped us from it and he'd never think to look for us on the Orlon Deck. But if he'd made it to 704, we wouldn't be able to go back. We'd be sleeping between server cabinets in Computer Services. The system pinged his V2, found him, and my mouth dropped open. I couldn't believe it. "Look at this."

"What?" (All three of them.)

I checked the time. "He's still locked in Arlinda's changing room."

Jess squealed with delight.

"How is he still in her changing room?" I wondered aloud. He'd had all the time in the world to escape. "Why hasn't he called anyone to let him out?"

"The pilot," Fantasy said. "Why hasn't he called her yet?"

A very good question. I asked digiCam to locate Colby Mitchell. Her profile popped up.

"She's such a craybitch," Jess said.

"Who?" Mother asked. "What?"

"Crazy bitch," Fantasy interpreted.

"Craybitch." Mother tried it on for size. "I know a few of those."

I asked digiCam to find her. It couldn't. Colby Mitchell was either in her stateroom, which I doubted, not on *Probability*, which I also doubted, or somewhere completely out of DeLuna's V2 reach, which I suspected. Otherwise he wouldn't still be locked in Arlinda's changing room. It made no sense she wasn't here. I asked digiCam if Colby Mitchell had *ever* set foot on this ship. Yes, she had. Boy, had she. The system couldn't pinpoint her exact location just then, but the evidence of her boarding a week ago with the ship's crew piled up on the screen. So much footage, it would have taken the rest of the night to watch it. Colby Mitchell and the late Poppy Campbell, dressed in stateroom attendant uniforms, starred in scene after scene moving in and out of 704, the submarine, and the casino, setting *Probability* traps. I froze the screen on a surveillance shot of them clinking glasses at a bar table Friday night, the night before we sailed. They were laughing. At us.

"Let's go," I said.

My posse followed me out. One of them barefoot.

*　*　*

Prospect 1000 didn't look like a submarine at all. It had submarine features, primarily its underwater operation capabilities, but it looked like a mini *Probability*. Diesel powered, max submersive speed of five knots, *Prospect* held a crew of six, had seating for thirty-two day passengers, and five-star overnight accommodations for six. With an operating depth of a thousand feet, *Prospect* was built for *Probability* passengers who wanted to explore the deep silent subsea in complete luxury. It was sixty-five feet long, twelve feet wide, weighed seventy-two tons, and had one airlocked door. *Prospect* was bulletproof, bombproof, and a perfect prison.

Storage and supplies—crates of romaine lettuce and baby carrots inside walk-in coolers, wrapped pallets of a thousand folded *Probability* pool towels, hundreds of sealed cases of liquor—marked our path from Computer Services to *Prospect*. The ceiling was dark and low, the floor cold and slick, and eerie florescent drop lights swayed above us, casting odd shadows. Jessica DeLuna's grip on my arm got tighter and tighter with our every echoed step, and she would surely rip it off before we reached the submarine. We passed a section of replacement deck furniture, the large cage of a workshop, complete with electric drills and power saws, and at the end of the path we stood in from of an eight-foot-long glass aquarium. Inside the aquarium, a thousand live lobsters tried to climb and claw the glass walls, and behind the aquarium was a dark blue industrial rolling steel garage door.

The entire time, maybe fifteen minutes that felt more like fifteen hours, we didn't see a soul. In a way, it would have been less terrifying to have happened on someone we had to explain our (predicament) (Anderson Cooper) (Jess in her undies) presence to. It would have been less frightening to have been challenged, detained, forced to pull a gun on someone. As it was, while we made our way to *Prospect 1000* at the other end of the ship, we felt like the only people in the world. By the time we made it around the lobsters to the rolling garage door, we'd moved in on one another so tight we were traveling as a huddled unit. I didn't realize it until we stopped, but Mother, on my right, had wrapped a protective arm around my babies and was holding on with all her might.

We couldn't open the garage door.

We didn't have the right V2.

We slid down the blue garage door and sat on the cold floor.

I waited for Jess to start screaming "So? So? So?" but the second she sat down, she conked out.

"He has the V2 to open the garage," Fantasy said. "DeLuna has it." DeLuna's wife's head fell on her shoulder.

"I wish I could sleep like her." I didn't realize Mother and I were holding hands, but we were. "I could use forty winks."

"What does that even mean?" Fantasy asked. "I know it means take a nap, but if you're winking forty times during your nap are you getting any rest?"

We sat against the garage door silently. Except for Jess snoring. Anderson Cooper purred on the babies.

Fantasy said, "I guess everyone's in the casino."

"Yep." I tried to keep my eyes open. "Did either of you see a cart anywhere?"

"In those coolers," Mother said. "I saw a cart with milk bottles."

"Bottles?" Fantasy asked.

"I hope it's on wheels," I said.

"Are we going to roll Jess?" Fantasy asked.

"No," I said. "Let's take tools back to our suite."

"What kind of tools?" Mother asked.

"The kind to patch the hole in the wall so DeLuna can't come down it."

"If we have access to tools—" Fantasy repositioned Jess's dark snoring head, "—let's break into this garage and get No Hair out."

"It's electric," I said. "The only thing we can do is electrocute ourselves or tear up the door. We have to have the right V2 to open it." We needed DeLuna's V2. I'd taken my one and only shot at the *Probability* system twenty minutes ago when I deleted our faces from digiCam so we could move around. By now, the system knew it had been breached and was certainly locked down. If I could get back in, I'd reroute his V2 functions to Poppy's phone. I'd transfer his phone brain to hers so we could get to No Hair, just behind the garage door, so close. The best I could hope for now was an hour's sleep and enough brain function to hack into *Probability*'s system through Poppy's laptop and gain access to his V2 that way. And turn ours on while I was at it.

Mother's head snapped up when her chin accidentally hit her chest. "Oops-a-daisy," she said. "The sandman hit me."

"Time to wake her up?" Fantasy squirmed under the weight of Jess.

"Yes," I said. "Let's go."

I placed an open palm on the garage door before I walked away. My promise to No Hair I'd get him out. One way or another, I'd free him.

* * *

We made it back to 704.

From the relative safety of the public elevators and companionways, I made four more attempts to reach Bradley with Poppy's V2. None of the calls made it through. *Probability* was still dead in the water, so calling anyone in any position of authority still wasn't an option.

We couldn't find the energy to patch the hole in the dressing room wall.

"We'll sleep in shifts." Fantasy pulled up a gun and a chair. "You go first, Davis."

And that's the last I remember of Sunday.

The next thing I knew, we were up, down, across, curled, spooned, and tangled in my bed when the dawn of Monday morning reached Anderson Cooper's little eyes. She made several rounds with her pokey little paws until she was sure everyone was awake.

It took me a minute to process that we'd lived through the night. And at some point while we slept, the *Probability* engines started up and we were moving again.

Jess sat up first. "So, how did we get back here? So, what happened?"

Mother's bed head popped up. "I could eat a horse."

Fantasy's pushed Anderson to me. "Take your alarm clock."

I saw legs I knew, but didn't know. I lifted blankets and followed the legs to their owner. "Ar*linda*?"

TWENTY

By silent agreement, we moved to my stateroom. Safety in numbers.

It looked—the sitting room full of everyone's everything, the bedroom a study in pillows and blankets, the dressing room sprinkled with power tools and scattered *Probability* server bikinis, the gold bathroom countertops brimming—as if 704 had flipped, shaken, then righted itself.

We gathered around the kitchen table at nine thirty, two and a half hours until noon, when ninety-nine-point-nine percent of *Probability* passengers and security would be in the casino, providing enough cover for us to attempt another No Hair rescue. Two and a half hours to figure out *how* to attempt another No Hair rescue. Two and a half hours and a computer to somehow contact my husband, Mr. Sanders at the Bellissimo, my father, the Coast Guard, Pizza Hut, 911, the Red Cross, GEICO Roadside Assistance, Hawaii Five-O, Aquaman—anyone or anything that could or would help us.

Mother, freshly showered and dressed in a nautical jogging suit featuring anchors and buoys connected by loopy boat lines, fed us sausage biscuits, a cinnamon pull-apart cake, and cantaloupe. She wedged the food onto the white kitchen table between the laptop, *The Compass*, her (no signal whatsoever) portable phone, and the V2 we took off a corpse. Then she came at us with two coffeepots. She poured steaming hot coffee into English pub beer glasses for herself, Fantasy, Jess, and Arlinda, and when she got to me, she poured from the second pot. "This is a little bit of the regular Starbucks, Davis, and a whole lot of the Starbucks decaffeinated."

Why hadn't I thought of this?

Mother stood there in her sailor suit with the two coffeepots and launched into one of her favorite speeches: "The Good Old Days." The television had three channels, kids played outside, mothers didn't work, nice young men wearing snappy uniforms pumped gas, empty soda bottles somehow turned into Saturday matinee tickets, and pregnant women drank coffee.

"So, when was this?" Jess had showered and changed into a clean pool towel, her long dark hair still dripping. "Are you talking about Dr. Phil?"

I stared at the coffee trying to figure out how to get through the blue garage door. Mother stared at me as I stared at the coffee trying to figure out how to get through the blue garage door. Which brought on another of her favorites: "Keep Your Chin Up." Don't meet trouble halfway, every cloud has a silver lining, tough times call for tougher women, paddle the canoe you find yourself in, and the darkest hour is just before the dawn.

"We have a canoe?" Jess asked.

My babies rolled and tumbled.

Arlinda reached for more cinnamon cake.

"This is delicious."

*   *   *

The primary bar servicing *Probability* casino patrons was located directly above 704. Five small satellite bars were strategically scattered elsewhere in the casino for alcohol emergencies, but ninety percent of the cocktails and one hundred percent of the wine came from the main bar. Behind it, the fifty (supermodels) servers, all female, had their own changing rooms and lockers. The changing rooms were cozy personal cubbies with full-length mirrors, lighted makeup mirrors, rolling wardrobes, and shoe racks. Against the back wall the servers had a locker for personal items and valuables. The changing rooms and lockers were V2 access only.

For the week-long cruise, the servers had a total of twenty-one skimpy uniforms. Three wardrobe changes a day. Their V2s alerted them when it was time to change, and they were allowed eight minutes to put down their trays, hustle to their changing rooms, strip out of one nautical bikini, and tuck themselves into the next, then be back on the casino floor passing out Red Bull and vodka. Between uniform changes the servers weren't allowed to leave the casino floor.

When the casino opened at the stroke of midnight after the billionaire married the nanny, no one entered the changing rooms again until the next uniform change at two a.m. So no one knew Max DeLuna was trapped until the V2 alert went out to remind the servers a uniform change was approaching. At eight minutes 'til. Max DeLuna had been trapped in Arlinda Smith's changing room for two solid hours. He couldn't break down the door, because one thing *Probability* did very well was doors, and he couldn't fit down the passageway in the floor of her locker, had he even wanted to fit down the passageway, which he probably didn't, because he believed his wife to be at the end of the tunnel. And it was a very safe bet he didn't want to see her.

What we hadn't taken time to anticipate last night when we sent her up the wall to trap him in her changing room was Arlinda's exit strategy when Max DeLuna escaped. Arlinda had gone straight to work on the casino floor and tried not to *think* about Max DeLuna locked in her changing room again until she received the second V2 warning to prepare for a wardrobe change. Only then did it occur to her she would have to deal with the aftermath of locking him up. Because she realized, as she passed the main bar, that had he managed to escape, she'd know about it already. He'd have tracked her down first. And throttled her.

Her pace slowed as she approached the changing rooms, her sister servers flying past, and she was the last one to set foot in the common area. She found a small crowd at the door of her changing room, most in various stages of nakedness climbing in and out of bikinis. One said, "Arlinda, there's a man in your changing room."

She died a little.

"You need to let him out."

He would surely kill her the rest of the way when she opened the door. So she waited until more servers stopped to gawk, several already in bright yellow push-up bras with matching boy shorts sporting embroidered captain's wheels on the butts, because the more witnesses the merrier.

"You need to let him out, Arlinda."

"Yes, Arlinda." A man's voice from inside her changing room. "Let him out."

She had no choice but to scan the door with her V2.

Max DeLuna stepped out, straightened his tie, and found Arlinda in the server crowd. He held out his hand. "Give me my V2."

"I don't have your V2, Mr. DeLuna."

"Yes, you do. Give it to me."

"No, I don't." Her knees wobbled. "I don't."

This went on until server V2s all around sounded the third and final warning and servers began scattering. It got down to the two of them.

DeLuna said, "Get your things and come with me."

"Mr. DeLuna," Arlinda said. "It was an accident."

"Don't insult me. Get your things."

Arlinda went to get her things. But the second she stepped into her changing room she kicked the door closed and scanned it locked. She began sailing her personal belongings down the chute that led to 704 and slid down behind them. She found a pillow and a blanket, then crawled into bed with us.

Sometime during the night, the path from 704 to the floor of her locker had been permanently sealed, blocking any future 704 exit by bulkhead. But that was okay. Because I'd wiped our faces off the Probability grid and we had Poppy's V2 to get in and out the door. Max DeLuna thought he'd solved his 704 problem.

I intended to let him keep thinking it.

It was ten thirty and I'd finished my third English pub glass of the Starbucks (so good) before Arlinda finished the story. I tried her V2 again. Nothing. DeLuna knew where she was, he knew her V2 had come down the wall with her, and it was just as operable as ours were, which is to say not at all. "Where *is* Mr. DeLuna's V2, Arlinda?"

She shifted in her white seat. "I don't have it and I don't know where it is. He pulled it out of his front pocket and passed it to me when he bent over to look in the locker."

"You should have given him a little push when he bent over to look in the locker," Fantasy said.

"Then he'd be here." Jess tapped the table. "I'd hate that so hard."

I'd hate that so hard too. Because we didn't have another trunk. "And then what?"

Arlinda demonstrated. "I had my V2 in this hand. I had his in this one. I had to get out fast. I didn't want to get the V2s mixed up so I sat his down."

"Where?"

"I can't even remember. My shoe rack, I think."

"He was in there two hours," I said. "Alone in a closet for two hours. How'd he miss it?"

It was a think tank all around the white table, except for Jess, who asked, "So?" Then every chair scraped back except hers and we made a run for the dressing room, Jess trailing behind, holding up her towel, yelling, "So? So? So?"

We sidestepped the power tools to get to Arlinda's scattered shoes. Mother found it inside a red leather Fendi ankle boot.

We had Max DeLuna's V2.

TWENTY-ONE

DeLuna's V2 had been cleared of personal information, but not deleted from the system. Which meant he had no idea we had it. He might not know where it was, but he didn't suspect we had it or it would've been completely scrubbed. As it was, factory settings and all, the home screen apps were available and the passenger identification information transferred to a different V2. The V2 we found in the Fendi ankle boot wasn't assigned to anyone. Or anyone's thumb. I pushed the power button; it lit up. Behind a number pad was the phone application. Behind a question mark was the V2 help desk. Behind a black bow tie, we could make restaurant reservations, beside it a mailbox, then a full moon, which turned out to be an app for shipboard stargazing. Behind a rolled newspaper was the day's itinerary, and behind a wind rose was our exact location with a countdown clock showing we would arrive in the Caymans in 9:24:02. (9:23:59) (9:23:56) (And so forth and so on.) My favorite was the padlock icon. What was left of his V2 should still open and close the doors it was programmed for.

"If that's a phone, I don't understand why you can't call your father, Davis."

"For the same reason we can't use Poppy's phone, Mrs. Way," Fantasy said. "We don't *want* DeLuna to know we have a way to call out. We don't want to tip our hand. If we make a call from inside this room, he'll know we have a V2."

"Well." Mother blew a raspberry. "Fiddlesticks."

Arlinda held her hand up, third-grade style. "Who is Poppy?"

"She's a crazed bitch," Mother said.

(OMG.)

"So, a *cray*bitch."

"Right."

Mother mouthed it silently several times so she wouldn't forget again.

"Poppy was our stateroom attendant, Arlinda," I said.

"Was?" she asked. "Where is she? What happened to her?"

"She—" Jessica was about to tell the tale of the trunks.

"Jess?" When we need her asleep she's awake. When we need her awake she's asleep. "Let's stay on track."

"I'm so confused," Arlinda said.

"So, me too," Jess said.

I looked at my watch. I stood.

"We don't have time to be confused."

* * *

The casino opened at noon. I planned on having No Hair out of the submarine at noon-oh-five. What I couldn't count on was the Orlon Deck being deserted at midday like it was at midnight, so Fantasy and I had to get clever. She was cleverly stuffed into one of Poppy's uniforms: khaki shorts and a *Probability* staff T-shirt. The only problem being Poppy was (very past tense) half Fantasy's size. I couldn't fit anything of Poppy's past my elbow, so I had to suck it up and go back to Burnsworth's room. I borrowed a starched white short-sleeve cotton uniform shirt with navy blue shoulder boards that extended a good eight inches past my shoulders. I was wearing the uniform tent over my Mommy 2B white stretch pants, and I looked like I was on my way to knock on *Probability* doors and say, "Trick or treat."

Fantasy pulled the Berretta PX4 we found in a lockbox in Poppy's room from somewhere behind her. It couldn't have been the waistband of the khaki shorts, because there wasn't room to fit an idea in the waistband of those shorts. She placed it in front of Mother. Who stared at it.

"Don't let anyone in except us, Mother. Anyone. And shoot to kill."

"You got it, Davis."

Then, at long last we caught a break.

Fantasy and I walked out of 704 at eleven forty-five using Poppy's V2 to open the door. We traveled the companionway without seeing anyone. We took the service elevator alone to the Orlon Deck, where we found plenty of traffic. We got a few looks because I was so pregnant and Fantasy was so busting out of her t-shirt, but for the most part we blended in. We could have been the butler and stateroom attendant in any of the fifty suites, albeit a very pregnant butler and a six-foot-tall stateroom attendant in Daisy Dukes.

I snagged a wide service cart stacked high with dishes (we could use in 704) so large and heavy it took both of us to roll it. We hid behind the dishes and made our way down the wide path we'd traveled last night without incident. A few close calls with the dish cart today, but again, no incidents. That it was lunch helped. An hour earlier or later might have meant more traffic. As it was, we looked like we were doing our jobs and everyone we passed looked like they were doing theirs. We made it to the lobster tank. We stepped behind it and stood in front of the blue garage door. I aimed Max DeLuna's V2, and with everything I had, prayed the door would open. The lock slid and the blue door raised and rolled. Fantasy ran through first, then helped me cross the gap between metal floor and submarine dock. I aimed the V2 again and closed the garage door behind us, then we took exactly one second to orient ourselves to the massive dimly lit space with a submarine close enough to reach out and touch.

"Where's the door?"

Fantasy's breath was coming in gasps.

Mine too. "Look for a hatch. Find the hatch. There!" I saw a set of dock steps. We ran, we climbed, yelling "No Hair!" the whole way. I aimed, I pushed the padlock, and nothing. The V2 wouldn't open the hatch. I tried it ten more times and as hard as I was trying to get V2 to open the hatch, I was trying harder not to have a full-blown panic attack.

"You're going to have to climb, Fantasy."

"Climb *what*?"

"The submarine. To the escape hatch." I sat down hard on a dock step. "There are four exterior ladders. Find one. Climb to the top. You'll find a round hatch on top of the submarine right in the middle." My heart was beating out of Burnsworth's shirt.

She took off and I dropped down to a sitting position on the dock step in front of the hatch. The air in the submarine chamber was dead, there wasn't a ray of natural light, and *Prospect 1000* was floating in water with wide docks built around it. My eyes adjusted more and I found another blue garage door against the hull of the ship, this one wide enough for *Prospect* to clear.

I listened as Fantasy thumped down the dock in one direction, then the other. She found a ladder. I couldn't see her climbing, but I could hear her.

"I got it, Davis!" Her voice echoed off the chamber walls. I heard the slam of the escape hatch opening. "I'm going in!"

The longest seventeen minutes of my life ensued, during which I wandered up and down the wide dock worrying the hem of Burnsworth's shirt until I had it twisted into knots. I couldn't hear anything from inside *Prospect*; the only thing I could hear was my own pulse slamming my temples and the water gently slapping the submarine chamber walls. It raced through my mind that this level of stress couldn't possibly be good for my babies and if I *ever* got off this ship, I would sit my butt in a chair and stay in it, without moving one single muscle, until the day these babies were born. My thoughts raced past Mother, Daddy, my sister Meredith, my niece Riley, and the daughter I had yet to meet, then they all landed on Bradley. I'd never wanted or needed him more, and alone in the submarine chamber I was on the edge of turning a dark corner of despair—something must have happened to Fantasy inside *Prospect*—certain I'd never see Bradley or anyone else again, when I finally heard Fantasy.

"DAVIS!" She was climbing out from the escape hatch. "*Davis! Davis! Davis!*"

The sheer panic she painted on my name as she called it out paralyzed me.

"*Davis!*"

I took off, running for her, and the next thing I saw, clearing the shadowy corner, was No Hair. The relief of seeing him would have knocked me down had he not started yelling my name too. "*DAVIS!*" Urgency propelled his stiff muscles down the dock. "The pilot!" The two words bounced off the metal walls. "Davis! The pilot! DeLuna's pilot! She's on *Bellissimo One*! She's flying Bradley's plane!"

I passed out.

TWENTY-TWO

There was an underwater quality to my world, as if the ship were sinking. Maybe I'd been tossed overboard. Maybe I fell overboard. Maybe I'd jumped.

Everything in my limited field of vision was floating. No Hair was there, but I didn't remember swimming with him or even swimming at all from *Prospect 1000* to 704. I must have, though, because everything was soaking white linen and my limbs were dead from swimming. I could feel their lifeless weight sinking into the white, with the only active part of my body the wide and spherical middle. Something in the middle of me moved with vibrant energy, and that must be how I was breathing underwater. I was floating on my back and the image of my mother's head zoomed in and out above me, and someone, Fantasy I think, kept putting something to my lips and telling me to drink. I didn't think I should be swallowing, I'd drown for sure, so I refused. It was when No Hair demanded—his voice coming in loud rippling soundwaves, demanding, insisting, breaking through the high-pitched ringing in my ears—that I let my lips part. My mouth filled with sweet, stinging ocean water. It bit my tongue and froze my throat. Above all this, a liquid slideshow played in the air, near the light, near the air, near the surface I couldn't reach. Through the water I saw us in our first apartment: we were at the stove, Bradley was stirring, offering me a taste. Bradley and me in the park, playing with someone's dogs, telling me we needed puppies of our own. Bradley in his office, a woman standing beside him holding three sharp pencils, sharp enough to draw blood, and I tried to take the woman's pencils so she wouldn't stab my husband. The aquatic movie played on and on, and I couldn't understand why No Hair wouldn't pull me up for air. Then everything went dark again. Merciful sleep.

*　*　*

The first coherent words I processed between receiving the news about Bradley on the deck of *Prospect 1000* and waking fully in 704 were No Hair's. "She brought her cat?"

Fantasy dropped Anderson Cooper on my babies. "Here she comes."

I lifted my head and buried my face into the warmth, the scent, the music of my cat. I held her with one arm and reached out with the other to touch my mother, No Hair, and Fantasy, all within reach, all with end-of-the-world faces. Arlinda was across from me, sitting beside Jess, whose head was hanging off the white linen sofa, her dark hair covering her face as she napped. "Is he alive?" The words clawed their way out of my throat. My follow up was, "I need the computer." No one would know if Bradley and Baylor were alive on the Gulfstream. I would have to answer my own question.

Fantasy shot off in the direction of the dressing room.

"Of course he's alive, Davis," No Hair said. "This is a con. There's no money in a kamikaze mission."

He was right. Of course. Yes. Hope. Blessed hope.

Mother moved to sit on the arm of the white linen sofa, at my side. "Davis? Do you want more Coca-Cola?"

"No."

I pushed my hair out of my face. I stirred my sleeping babies, they pushed back reassuringly, then I set to work to find their father.

"I'm going to make you the Starbucks, Davis."

"Thank you, Mother."

She stood, always happy to have kitchen work in times of trouble, and kissed the top of my head.

"I have a pot roast in the slow cooker."

(Slow cooker?)

No Hair and I looked at each other, long and hard.

"He locked us in here."

"I know," he said.

"I had a baby when I was sixteen."

"I know, Davis."

"Fantasy is leaving Reggie. Not the other way around."

A tendon in his neck jumped, the news catching him off guard.

"It's the game, No Hair. Knot on Your Life. DeLuna is diverting the deposits to an account set up in Bradley and Jessica's names. The players don't know because their V2s are showing a balance that isn't there. He'll have two hundred million in a Cayman account before the casino closes today."

"I know," No Hair said. "Fantasy told me."

"Did she tell you about Burnsworth?"

He inhaled sharply. She'd told him. Then she returned, sat beside me on the sofa, and passed me the laptop.

I went straight to (my husband) the deep web, then opened a browser window. I pulled up FlightView and my shaking fingers typed GPT, the airport code for Gulfport-Biloxi International Airport, where *Bellissimo One* was hangared and scheduled to depart from Friday when this nightmare started. The chances of the flight being tracked were so very slim—Colby Mitchell the Skyjacking Pilot would have flown dark, without registering—and plugged in the Gulfstream's tail numbers. Nothing. No flight records. Of course not.

Mother placed a champagne flute of hot coffee in front of me.

No Hair scratched his ear, but didn't ask.

I spent the next five minutes in the airport's Human Resources department, hiring myself. Air Traffic Controller, no dependents, yes 401K, just give me my password. I had to stop, open a second screen, and create a Firefox email account to receive the password. The only person in the room I knew for sure was breathing while I worked my way into the airport's radar archives was Jess, because she was snoring. It felt like hours, but it was just minutes and a champagne flute of hot mostly decaf coffee later when I was able to log into Friday's records and find the one afternoon flight departing GPT without a flight plan.

"Nome," I told my quiet audience. "She flew the plane to Nome."

"Al*aska*?" Fantasy asked.

"The edge of the world," No Hair said.

"Nome." I couldn't stop saying it. "Nome."

*   *   *

The International Airport Transport Association airport code for Nome was OME. And I cyber-hired myself as an Air Traffic Controller for the second time in twenty minutes at the Nome Airport. Having just been through the FAA application and screening, I got the job in two minutes instead of the three it took me to hire myself in Gulfport.

"It was a direct flight from Gulfport to Nome." I didn't look up from the computer. "Five souls onboard. Four thousand miles."

Jessica did the math. "They landed in Alaska at ten on Friday night."

I clicked through Nome departures, a very short list, and found the one unregistered flight between two Bering Air flights. "The plane has been sitting on the tarmac this whole time." *Bellissimo One* slept ten and had every creature comfort known to man, but still, this long? "Until an hour ago." I glanced at the computer clock. "It took off an hour ago."

"For where?" Everyone in the room asked the question.

"South. The plane is traveling south. It's over the Bering Sea right now."

"We need that plane traveling east," No Hair said. "Where in the hell is it going?"

I looked up from the laptop. "Hawaii."

"Of course," Fantasy said. "The bank."

"So, Elima?"

Fantasy and I stared at Jess.

"What?" she asked.

"Yes," I said. "Elima. Banco de la Elima."

"I'm not following," No Hair said.

"They're making a run for it, No Hair," I said. "They're cashing out. Colby Mitchell is flying Bradley to Hawaii to have him withdraw the money. The account is in his name. She's going to walk him to a teller window and have him empty it." I flew all over the keyboard calculating the flight, distance, and speed. They'd land in Hawaii an hour before we docked in the Caymans, exactly when the casino closed for the passengers to disembark. "The Knot on Your Life deposits are being diverted to a Cayman bank," I looked up, "that has a branch in Hawaii."

Jess waved. "Hello! You can't get that much cash and it's not a branch."

Fantasy and I had developed Jessica immunities, knowing we only had to halfway listen to every fifth or sixth thought, but No Hair hadn't been here long enough.

"Excuse me?" he said.

Jessica splayed a hand across her red bra. "Me?"

He was looking right at her. We all were.

"Yes," No Hair said. "You. What did you say?"

"Banks require a fourteen-day notice for large withdrawals."

"Make a lot of large withdrawals, Jessica?" No Hair asked her.

She looked at him curiously. "So, what?"

My husband's very life was at stake. No Hair could interrogate Jess about her banking habits later. I agreed it was well worth looking into, but not here and not now. "Can we talk about this later?" I asked. "This deal is going down *tonight*."

"They can get a cashier's check." Jessica whispered, mostly to herself. "But they can't get that kind of cash. Unless they called ahead."

If I knew the magic words, I'd say them and put her to sleep. I wasn't the least bit concerned with bank rules and regulations and very concerned with what Colby Mitchell had planned for Bradley and Baylor after she got her money. Or her cashier's check. I didn't care. What I did care about was this: When Bradley finished banking for her, what would happen to him? To Baylor?

No Hair got it. "The only way to stop the withdrawal is to stop the plane," he said. "They can't land that plane in Hawaii."

"How do we stop a plane from landing?" My hands hurt. Because my nails were digging into them between laptop operations. "If Bradley or Baylor had control over the pilot or the plane they wouldn't even be on their *way* to Hawaii. They *can't* take control of the plane, No Hair, because they're not *pilots*. And how is it you suggest *we* keep the plane from landing?" Now my hands hurt and my face was wet. I swiped at my wet face with my hurt hands.

My questions filled the salon and no one had answers.

Mother began saying the Lord's Prayer under her breath.

Arlinda stood. "Mr. Blackwell. My player." She pointed up. To the casino. "He was a pilot in the Navy. He was with NASA. He parks satellites. Surely to God he can do something."

Of course he could. Of course. The question was, would he? How in the world could I convince Fredrick Blackwell to disrupt the flight of a jet in the sky? By speaking every billionaire's favorite language on the ground, or in this case, at sea—money.

Money talks.

* * *

From the ottoman in my dressing room, surrounded by *Probability* server bikinis and an odd collection of power tools, I launched a cyber-attack against the thieves who'd locked us in 704, taken No Hair hostage, and now had my husband and Baylor in their grips. I didn't go deep or dark web because I no longer cared and I didn't have time.

I isolated the eighteen-digit Knot on Your Life numbers assigned to the fifty players and cracked into the Cayman bank. I left the withdrawals alone, so funds would still be pulled from the personal accounts, but I stopped the funnel of cash to Max DeLuna. When I plugged in the final eighteen-digit number and hit enter, the flow of player money to con man stopped, and for the first time since the switch was flipped, the Knot on Your Life wins went to the right place—the player accounts.

Max DeLuna still had plenty, the money he'd already stolen, and I took care of it next. I had no idea how to allocate it, which left one option: trigger the jackpots. On all fifty machines. Give them two and a half million each from DeLuna's account and call it a day.

There was no way in the Bellissimo system backdoor, so I went in the front: my name, my password. I wiggled my way into the mainframe and went into the Knot on Your Life software and changed the payout on all fifty machines. Instead of the machines giving and taking, Even Steven, as my mother said, I set them to give. I cranked up the payout code from fifty to one hundred percent.

It's better to give than to receive, Max DeLuna. Everyone knows that.

Clock ticking, I made it to the final screen, my very last cyber chore before we sent Arlinda to the casino to recruit Fredrick Blackwell. I entered the new payout codes into the fifty slot machines, and there, I hit a wall. The Knot on Your Life software wouldn't take the new payout codes. The machine payout percentages couldn't be changed remotely, a safeguard, so clever hackers couldn't bring down the house from the comfort of their cruise ship dressing room ottomans. A security feature of land-based casino slot machines I was well aware of, but I had no idea it would apply to the Knot on Your Life machines in the *Probability* casino. The final step had to be completed manually on the ship just like it had to be completed manually on the casino floor. A gaming regulation I never dreamed would apply to a bank of machines with a one-week shelf life operating on international waters.

One of us had to do it. Live and in person.

Not only would it return the money to the rightful owners, all fifty jackpots hitting at once might be the fastest way to convince Fredrick Blackwell to help, in addition to sending DeLuna into a tailspin and providing the cover we needed to reroute *Bellissimo One*. The Knot on Your Life machines were about to hit the motherlode, and it would have to be my mother who hit the load. The software would have to be installed live, directly into the lead slot machine's brain, the one slot machine that told the other forty-nine what to do, and my mother was the only candidate. She was the only face Max DeLuna didn't know.

My mother was our only hope.

We had one flash drive in all of 704 and it was busy running the laptop. With the Knot on Your Life hack, we'd lose the laptop, because we'd lose the flash drive. But it was our only chance of keeping Bradley and Baylor from landing in Hawaii. A very easy choice.

Mother came out of the gold bathroom and modeled for me. She struck several poses in her red and white striped skirt and her navy twin set buttoned up to her chin. On her feet, her high heels.

"Mother, you look precious."

"If your daddy could see me now."

I patted the ottoman. She scooted in beside a nail gun.

I gave her step-by-step instructions: which end of the flash drive was up, what a USB port looked like, how and where on the machine to find and insert it.

She reminded me she taught me how to walk.

I studied the dressing room floor. I took my mother's hands in mine and we studied the gray carpet together. "I don't think you'll be in any danger, Mother, because we're only up against three people. One is on our deck in a trunk, we know where the pilot is, and DeLuna is in the casino. He doesn't know who you are, he won't be the least bit interested in what you're doing, so I believe with all my heart you'll be safe."

Mother's hands showed her years more than her face, her body, or as I'd learned during our time together on *Probability*, her spirit. They were rough from a lifetime of potato peeling and gardening, they were thick with ropey veins ravaged by the recent barrage of hypodermic needles, and her wedding rings were so loose on her spindly fingers the weight of the stones flipped them under. I could only see the backs of the two worn gold bands representing my parents' lives together. Of which I wanted there to be more. I rolled the rings around for her. We stared at the diamonds.

"Why are you telling me all this, Davis?"

We were closer than we'd been in decades. Three-point-four of them, to be exact. "I need you to know I'd never let you do this if I thought I was putting you in the line of fire. Daddy would never forgive me. I'd never forgive myself."

"Well, let me tell you something, Davis." She cupped my face in her hands. "It's my turn and I'm ready."

"Oh, Mother." My face dropped out of her hands.

"Davis, I get tired of being on the sidelines. You and your daddy always saving the world and me at home ironing. I'm tired of ironing. I'm ready to live it up a little. Everyone knows you and your daddy are made of the strong stuff, but the truth is I'm made of strong stuff too."

I knew. Deep down, I knew.

"But there's one thing I have to say to you before I go, and I want you to listen carefully."

I prayed she wouldn't tell me what she wanted me to do with her salt and pepper shaker collection should she not make it back to 704. If for no other reason, I didn't want to be charged with telling someone Mother left them two hundred salt and pepper shakers.

"Look up here at me, Davis." She scoped the dressing room to make sure we were alone. "Don't you breathe a word of me playing a gambling game to anyone. I mean it. If it ever got back to my Sunday School class, I'd be done for. Out on my rear. This is our secret."

"You got it, Mother."

* * *

Arlinda was dressed in today's uniform, Set Sail: navy and white striped high-waist hipsters, a bright red triangle halter top, white sailor hat. Jessica was wearing Friday's uniform, Walk the Plank, a one-piece rhinestone anchor with six-inch silver heels. In a way, seeing Jess in a different outfit was a breath of fresh air. In a couple of other very noticeable ways, it wasn't. Jess was more Fantasy's size, less Arlinda's. So her choice from the stash Arlinda threw down the wall to wear under her fresh *Probability* robe wasn't built for her.

We walked Mother and Arlinda to the door of 704, we, minus Jess. Guess what she was doing in her rhinestone anchor suit and six-inch silver heels. Just guess.

"Mother, you have Poppy's V2, our only way in and out."

She patted her left pocket.

"And please don't use the gun unless you have to."

She patted her right hip. "I don't plan on shooting anyone while I'm gone and don't make me shoot anyone when I get back."

I had no idea what she was talking about.

She cleared her throat. "In one hour, exactly one hour, cut my pot roast off. Just turn it off. By the knob." She demonstrated. "On. Off." She toggled her closed fist on and off a few more times. "Do *not* lift the lid. Do you hear me, Davis?"

"I hear you."

"It needs to sit for another three hours without anyone lifting the lid. It will keep on cooking and it will make its own thick gravy if you don't lift that lid. You've all seen pot roast before and you can wait to see mine until I get back and serve it. I've got tinfoil under that lid and I'll know if you picked it up. I'll be able to see the marks in the tinfoil. Do not pick the lid up."

"I won't pick up the lid, Mother."

"And that goes for you too." She aimed at No Hair and Fantasy. They surrendered. "And when So and So wakes up, you tell her too."

"We will, Mother."

I turned to Arlinda. "You understand the risk you're taking? Stepping out the door?"

"I do," she said.

"Way more than Mother," I said. "He doesn't know Mother. No one on the ship knows Mother. He knows you, surveillance knows you, and security knows you."

"I understand." She patted her sailor hat, tipped forward on her head, obstructing as much of her face as possible.

"Number one, Arlinda, is my mother."

She nodded.

"Oh, poo," Mother said. "I can take care of myself."

"Get in and out of the casino with Mother and Mr. Blackwell as fast as you can."

She nodded.

"Good luck."

And they were off.

TWENTY-THREE

"It was a simple plan." No Hair broke the silence that settled over the salon after the door closed to 704. "Lock us up, steal the money."

"Did you hear that?" I asked my babies in a shaky voice. "A simple plan." A simple plan that had their father forty thousand feet over an ocean at the mercy of a felon pilot. I was so glad the babies didn't know, couldn't know, I hoped they'd never know.

"It's only been," No Hair looked at his watch, "forty-eight hours."

"It feels like forty-eight years." But he was right. It was only two little days ago, almost to the hour, when I walked through the door of 704, No Hair was captured, and the cabin door on *Bellissimo One* closed with Bradley and Baylor inside. It was a simple trap, was what it was, and we fell right in it.

"What do we think happened on the plane?" No Hair asked gently, quietly.

"Just like in the movies," Fantasy said. "She incapacitated the pilots."

"How'd she get on the plane in the first place?"

"Impersonated a crewmember?" No Hair said. "Caught the flight attendant before wheels-up, took her out, then took her place?"

The three of us had years of speculative conversations about perps behind us—their motivations, their methods, their maneuvers—but never with stakes as high as these.

"I wonder *how* she incapacitated the pilots," Fantasy said.

"There were two of them and one of her. Plus Bradley and Baylor."

"She held them at gunpoint," No Hair said. "She had to have." His voice trailed off in time with the last drops of blood draining from my face. "Davis." He leaned my way. "You said it yourself. Brad isn't in a position to overpower her. He can't fly a plane. What you have to focus on is the fact that she has nothing to gain by harming him. She has to have Brad to get the money. He's in one piece, Davis. She needs him."

No Hair was right. There was no better way to walk away with two hundred million dollars than to have it handed to you by the man in charge of the money.

No Hair took a steadying breath of non-submarine air. "How's this going to happen, Davis, with the plane?"

A welcome shift from problem to solution.

I explained if all went according to plan, which was entirely dependent on Arlinda recruiting Fredrick Blackwell, the plane would change courses. "One phone call to the FAA and the plane will be located. Blackwell will ask ground control to activate the automatic flight mode, let him at the controls, then divert it. Colby Mitchell won't be able to override him, at which point Bradley and Baylor can subdue her, and the plane won't land in Hawaii."

Any number of things could go wrong. The thought of which was making me woozy. The odds weren't necessarily in our favor.

The mission could be easily accomplished, the Gulfstream 650 equipped with automated flight plan and landing aid systems. But not by me, because I didn't have the credentials to divert a paper airplane. Fredrick Blackwell did. And Arlinda Smith was directly above us trying to convince him to put those credentials to good use, as in save the day. Interrupting an aircraft in flight is serious business—the business of terrorists, and Arlinda might not be able to convince Blackwell to *listen* to her, much less risk his career by taking part. Chances were he'd never heard a story in his life like the one he was hearing now. She had one shot at recruiting him— his wallet. In the least amount of time possible, she had to tell him he'd been swindled and prove it with fifty jackpots. Maybe, just maybe, he'd help. If not, Mother and Arlinda would be back soon. My husband would land in Hawaii. We'd have pot roast. We'd dock in the Caymans, DeLuna would walk off with the money, and that would leave Bradley and Baylor—where? I could barely breathe and apparently Fantasy couldn't either. She leaned in to say something, but before she could get it out her short shorts surrendered with a loud rip. She held up an excuse-me finger, banged into furniture backing out of the salon, and No Hair came very close to cracking a smile.

In her wake, Jess sleeping it off, No Hair and I talked about what had transpired from our different perspectives in the two short days. He stepped into a Zoom at three o'clock on Saturday afternoon and woke up in the submarine with a note on his chest, his luggage, and a hardback copy of *The Old Man and the Sea*.

I asked if he'd read it.

No.

He had luxury accommodations, provisions, and no way out except for portholes he could barely fit an arm through. The hatch was secured from the outside and the escape hatch Fantasy had gone through to get to him had been disabled from inside. He said it would have taken dynamite to open it. I asked about the panoramic viewing windows I'd seen in *The Compass* and he pointed out he could have knocked them out all day, then electrocuted and drowned. The viewing windows were below the waterline, which made sense, because I hadn't seen them at all, and, his note had warned, wired with live electrical. His note said attempts at escape would be met with deadly consequences, his own, in fact, and besides, he said, he was waiting on me to save him. I told him I'd been waiting on the same thing: *him* to save *me*. I told him they'd thought of everything here too, except Burnsworth. They hadn't planned on Burnsworth. No Hair studied his lap at the mention of his name and Jess jumped into the conversation for the first time with, "So, gross."

Look who was up.

Twenty minutes had ticked away since Arlinda and Mother

left. We had no computer and no way in or out. We still had DeLuna's V2, but that was it. To keep from losing my mind, I poked behind the black bow tie to look at tonight's menus. It would seem we had the only pot roast on all of *Probability*.

No Hair asked me how Mother had been holding up.

Like a champ, I told him.

"She's so retro," Jess said.

No Hair studied her. "This whole time, you had no idea?"

"I have ideas," she defended herself.

"Let's hear your ideas," he said. "What's your story, Jessica?"

"My story? I'm a narc?"

No Hair's head jerked.

I tore myself away from the V2, where I was behind the full moon reading about the Tropic of Cancer, 23.5 degrees south latitude, and said, "Jessica has narcolepsy, No Hair."

We gave it two minutes.

"You fall asleep at the drop of a hat and you're married to a crook," No Hair said to Jess.

"Right," she said. "He's a bastard dirtbag."

"How long?" No Hair asked.

"All day long."

"What?"

"He's a bastard all day long."

"How long have you been married to the bastard?"

"A year." She smoothed the rhinestones across her flat stomach. "But I'm so done with him."

Understandable. I clicked the wind rose app on the V2 to see that we were less than four hours from the Caymans. I couldn't wait to see dry land.

"How did you two meet?" No Hair asked.

"Who two?"

"You and your husband."

"That was a bad day."

"Where was this bad day?" No Hair asked.

"The bank."

I listened to the exchange and it occurred to me that in all this time we hadn't bothered to scratch below the surface with Jessica, to ask her these questions. In our defense, we'd been busy. Jessica told No Hair she was an only child raised by a single father. Which explained a lot.

"Let's back up, Jessica," No Hair said. "Where did you meet him?"

"My father?"

No Hair cleared his throat. "Your husband."

"So, the *bank*." Jess looked at me curiously, as if to say *this one's a little slow.*

"The *bank*?" No Hair gave me the *same* curious look about her, the difference being he hid it.

She leaned in, spoke slowly, and raised the volume. "Max. Worked. At. The. Bank."

"Why didn't you say so?" No Hair asked.

She turned to me. "Is he making fun of me?"

"No, Jess."

"What did your husband do at the bank?" No Hair asked.

"Portfolios," she said. "He came up through the ranks of investments, assets, loans, credit, debt, and collections. He landed in portfolios."

My head snapped up.

"Hybrid and speculative," Jess explained.

She spoke with the poise and authority of a guest on the evening news. My mouth dropped open. Had we stumbled upon a subject Jess was knowledgeable in and comfortable talking about? And that subject was *banking*? How could being married to a banker for a year make her that fluent? Maybe I should have seen this coming?

"Which bank?" No Hair asked.

"So?" She didn't understand the question.

(Welcome back, Jess.)

"You said you met your husband at a bank."

"Right."

"Which bank?" No Hair asked.

"My father's."

"Which bank is your father's bank?"

No Hair was truly struggling through the conversation, much as I had struggled with Jess before I spent two days locked up with her.

"*The* bank," she said.

No Hair gave up.

"What's *the* bank, Jessica?" I stepped in.

She threw her hands in the air. "Elima. Bank Elima."

Just like that. As if we knew, should have known, or should have figured out by now that with Max the DeLuna half of DeLuna-Elima Securities, she was the Elima half.

Hers was never a marriage; it was always a merger.

"Jessica?" I was on the edge of my sofa. "Did you not think to mention that your father owns Bank Elima?"

"No." She ran her hands down her long brown legs. "Because he doesn't."

"You just said he did, Jess."

"So." She picked at white linen. "My father died."

"I'm sorry," I said.

She found a white linen thread and pulled it.

"Jessica, who owns the bank now?" No Hair asked.

She looked up. "Me."

Just like that. And that's why she was with us. She owned the bank.

Jessica the Bank Owner hit the hay. Or the white linen, as it was.

No Hair scratched his bald head.

My eyes dropped to my lap, where, in the shuffle and shock of Jessica's news, I'd accidently opened the mailbox on Max (dirtbag) DeLuna's V2. My mail was sitting in my lap. My *Probability* email had been forwarded to DeLuna's V2 and it was front and center on the small screen.

* * *

Thirty excruciatingly slow minutes had passed since Mother and Arlinda left 704 for the casino when I found my email. Fantasy returned wearing clothes that fit. "What'd I miss?"

"Jess owns the bank and I found my email."

"Jess owns a bank?" She looked at Sleeping Beauty. "That's hilarious."

"For real," I said. "Jessica owns the bank in Hawaii."

"I'll be damned. That solves the mystery of why we have custody of her." She sat beside me and leaned in to peek at the V2 screen. "Look at that. Davis, it's your email."

"I know. I have mail." I shook the V2. "This is how he was taking care of correspondence for me. On his own V2." I scrolled to find four. I skipped the three from Bianca to read the one from Bradley that hit my inbox at four thirty on Saturday. We'd barely said goodbye, he'd just boarded the plane, and we'd just lost our V2s.

Davis,
I think we forgot something. I think we missed something.
Stay safe for me and I'll stay safe for you. I love you.

He knew as soon as *Bellissimo One* took off.

I traced the words with my finger, back and forth, then forced myself to move on. I clicked open the first email from Bianca. It arrived Saturday evening at seven when I should have been prancing around in her Vera Wang jumpsuit at the Welcome Aboard party. "Listen to this." I read it aloud to No Hair and Fantasy. And Jess, who owns a bank, but she wasn't listening because she was asleep.

David, you have ABANDONED in my hour of need. I have dialed your number no less than two hundred times. You're fired. Don't even waste your breath trying to save your or your husband's jobs. Which is not to say I don't fully expect you to fulfill your obligations between now and your certain UNEMPLOYMENT. The photographs of me had better be Life Magazine cover caliber, every single shot, or not only will you be unemployed, you'll find yourself in the middle of a breach of contract lawsuit YOU WON'T WIN.

In the meantime, I insist that you contact Dr. Durrance on my behalf. I am too ill in general, and especially with her, to attempt civil conversation. She claims I am not progressing toward dilation or effacement. Whatever in the world that means. Dr. Durrance also claims Ondine is floating. Whatever in the world she means by that. You refusing my telephone calls leaves me with no one to run INTERFERENCE for me in these, the final hours of my gestation. You have FORSAKEN me. I am left without a soul on this planet who has MY BEST INTEREST at heart.

There's Richard, of course, but my marriage is none of your business.

Not that I've seen a TRACE of him because he is too busy doing YOUR HUSBAND'S JOB. Which is YOUR FAULT.

I need you to call Dr. Durrance immediately. She is demanding I have an ultrasound. Something about covering all the bases and by that, I'm certain she means covering HER OWN bases, which aren't my concern. I researched this MYSELF, as you are NOT TAKING MY CALLS, rather, I assigned the task to this slovenly nurse you saddled me with, you know the one, the unibrowed holistic healer Buddhist tofu person with the thick calves and bulbous earlobes, and she concurs that medical imaging is NOT NECESSARY as all my vital statistics, as well as Ondine's, are PERFECT and there's no need for alarm or RIDICULOUS IMAGING PROCEDURES. David, you know I won't let myself be subjected to ULTRASONIC VIBRATIONS unless LIVES ARE AT STAKE, and although you've chosen to ignore me, for which you will pay dearly, I INSIST you contact Dr. Durrance and explain this. You know barbaric and unnecessary imaging leaves me with blurred vision and a metal taste in my mouth for

days. I refuse to put myself through it this close to Ondine's birth. I simply don't have the energy and my nerves can't take it.
I mean every word of this, David.

No headlines here. Bianca fired me. Again. This time with a twist—she'd fired Bradley too. She was furious at me for not being at her beck and call when *she* was the one who'd sent me on this prison cruise. And ultrasounds, of which I'm well into the double digits on at twenty-four weeks, because watching twins grow is a big job, I knew for a fact didn't hurt a bit or blur anything. Bianca's another story—good grief, don't get me going—and ultrasounds were just one procedure on a long list she refused to participate in. Her prenatal team strongly advised her to have an amniocentesis when she was sixteen weeks along. Because of her age. She wouldn't even hear of it, Mr. Sanders couldn't even talk her into it, and three doctors were fired over it. She'd had two face lifts, two breast augmentations, liposuction on her ankles, several eyelash transplants, butt implants, practically injected her own face with Botox as part of her morning beauty routine, but refused to have ultrasounds.

"What is *wrong* with her?" Fantasy asked.

"Not my problem anymore," I said. "She fired me."

"Why won't she have an ultrasound?" she asked.

"You heard it." I shook the V2. "It rattles her teeth. She had one early on, was sick for two days, blamed it on the ultrasound, and has refused them since."

The second email from Bianca hit my inbox Saturday night, just before midnight.

David,
I need you back here immediately. Something has happened to your husband and Richard was forced to LEAVE ME to replace him halfway across the world. I don't know if your husband has fallen ill or the plane crashed, and frankly, I don't care. What I do know and care about is the fact that I HAVE BEEN DESERTED.

Both by you, and now because of you, by MY OWN HUSBAND.
I will NOT be left alone at a time like this. It's INHUMANE.
Pack my bags in a hurry. And don't you dare pack haphazardly and damage my Louis luggage. May I remind you that each of those pieces was COMMISSIONED, and in addition to my wardrobe you are traveling with, you have my new luggage I HAVEN'T EVEN LAID EYES ON? Do you understand, David? You are using my new luggage BEFORE I AM?

Now, David, I have unsettling news. <u>Brace yourself</u>. Unless there is notable progress very soon, I will be preparing myself to undergo a Cesarean section to bring Ondine into this world. <u>SURGERY, David</u>.

In addition to the TRAUMA you have landed in my LAP impeding my very ability to DELIVER MY DAUGHTER INTO THIS WORLD IN THE WAY GOD AND I INTENDED, according to Dr. Durrance, my BLOOD PRESSURE has SKYROCKETED. As you can well imagine, I'm devastated and your vacation is over. Be at the ship's helicopter pad at seven Sunday morning to be transported to the plane I'm sending. I need you here immediately, and be careful with my Louis. Not a scratch on the trunks, David. Do you hear me? Not one scratch. I will see you mid-morning Monday. –B

I'd missed the helicopter ride by a country mile.

Then I opened the third email sent two hours ago.

Well, David, I hope you're happy. If Ondine or I don't make it through this, our blood will be on your hands. Be ready. Have my wardrobe, my photography, and my luggage ready.

I dropped the V2 like it was on fire.

"What's that supposed to mean?" Fantasy asked. "What's she saying?"

"I hope it doesn't mean what I think it means," No Hair said.

"What do you think it means?" Fantasy asked him.

"She's on her way," he said. "She called a jet, she's out of that bed, and she's on her way to pick up David."

Fantasy turned to me. "David?"

"Surely not," I said. "She wouldn't *travel*. She hasn't been out of her bedroom in six months!"

"Davis," No Hair said, "Richard isn't there to stop her. You aren't there to stop her." He looked at his watch. "It's less than an hour in a jet between here and there and I bet you money she's either on her way or already on this ship."

"She can't," I said. "If she sets foot on *Probability*, DeLuna will think she's *me*."

We sat quietly, contemplating what Bianca would and wouldn't do (the woman had no boundaries whatsoever) when DeLuna caught on.

At some point, he had to catch on.

I'd say we reached that point.

I'd say fifty jackpots hitting sent him over the edge.

(She did it! Mother did it!)

I'd say he blamed 704.

He cut the power at eight minutes after four on Sunday afternoon—lights, air, appliances—everything electrical ground to a lifeless stop. It was the loudest quiet any of us had ever heard. The quiet was so profound it woke Jess. "SO? SO? SO?"

The good news was Mother's pot roast. We hadn't even thought about turning it off and we'd have never remembered. The bad news was DeLuna's V2 went down with the power, leaving us with no contact whatsoever with the world outside of 704. The worst news was Mother and Arlinda were on one side of 704 and we were on the other.

Where was Mother? Where was Arlinda? Where were Bradley and Baylor? The most immediate where of them all—where was very pregnant Bianca Sanders? The most terrifying—where was Max DeLuna?

TWENTY-FOUR

What now?

Since the minute I stepped aboard *Probability*, it'd been an ongoing question of what now.

Anderson Cooper, the air around her having changed, wandered out of my stateroom and onto my lap. She opened her little mouth and let out a wail of protest at this newest development. We clapped our hands over our ears as it echoed around the salon.

"Oh, dear God, Davis, your cat."

"We have more to worry about than my cat, Fantasy."

"She's got something stuck on her fur." No Hair pointed.

It was a chip of gray gauntlet paint. Which is when I remembered. "The tools!"

I tried to get up.

"The tools!" Fantasy shot off, No Hair on her heels, and Jess hauled me up.

"What happened in here?" No Hair looked around the dark dressing room. "Did someone forget to tell me about the bomb?"

It was a little messy.

He dangled the bottom half of Arlinda's Skipper uniform by a finger. "What have you ladies been up to?"

I grabbed the bikini from him.

"What the hell happened to the wall?"

"About that." I took a deep breath.

"Don't." He stopped me. "Tell me later. Or never tell me. Just find the tools." He took two steps forward, bent over, and raised up with something sinister. "What did you think you were going to do with this, Davis?"

It was large, a little oily, and had a Frisbee-sized brown middle. "I'm not sure what it is."

"It's a floor sander. And you see this?" He dangled a thick yellow cord with a three-prong plug. "Even if we wanted to sand through a lead door, we have no *power*."

"So, does anyone smell something? It smells like a Christmas tree. Or church. Or rainbows." She tipped her head back and sniffed. "So, it smells like rainbows on a Christmas tree at church."

"It's pot roast, Jess," I said.

"It smells so delicious."

"Don't look at it." Fantasy was holding a nail gun.

"Why? Will it hurt my eyes?"

Maybe DeLuna had his wife locked in 704 because she owned the bank processing his illegally obtained millions. Or maybe he wanted her out of his hair and in ours.

"Jess?" I asked.

Her head spun around. "So?"

"Who regulates banks?"

"The Federal Deposit Insurance Corporation, the Federal Reserve System, and the Office of the Comptroller of Currency."

Fantasy's jaw dropped.

I said, "The pot roast won't hurt your eyes."

"But don't look at it," No Hair said.

She scratched a rhinestone shoulder strap. "So."

"Davis?" No Hair opened a box of something and pulled out a silver disk with sharp teeth. "These are miter saw blades. I don't see a miter saw."

"No Hair." I fell down on the ottoman. Something cold rolled to my thigh. "We were exhausted. We were in a hurry. We just grabbed. Sorry if we grabbed the wrong tools."

"Give me that." He pointed. I passed him the something at my thigh. "Now this," No Hair said, "we can use."

We were running through the salon to blaze through the front door of 704 with a blowtorch when we saw it—dry land. No Hair came to a sudden halt, Fantasy ran into him, Jess ran into her, Anderson Cooper and I landed on top. I could barely hear No Hair from the bottom of the heap. He said, "You ladies get off of me. I'm going back to the submarine."

* * *

Probability slowed as we approached the Cayman Islands.

"What is that?" Fantasy asked.

"It's West Bay. The tip of Grand Cayman." We were miles from shore. "We won't go much farther."

"So, what does that mean?"

"The ship will drop anchor soon, Jess," I said.

It was almost five o'clock and *Probability* was arriving in the Caymans as scheduled. Cool trade winds blew across the deck, the late afternoon sun hit me with warmth and promise, and I could see tourmaline water lapping sugar sand beaches at the shore. The sky was stellar, a color that went so far past blue Crayola didn't even know the name of it, and I felt a trickle of calm at the sight of dry land. Consular agencies. Telephones. Dishwashers. Telephones! Mother's portable phone! I'd forgotten all about it!

The doorbell rang and I forgot about it all over again.

We didn't know 704 had a doorbell.

There was electricity on the other side of the door.

It rang four more times before we made our way inside, through the salon, and into the foyer that led to the door. I was first in line. "Mother!" I rattled the knob and beat on the door with my fists. "Mother!"

"She can't hear you." No Hair brought up the rear, having stopped to retrieve the blowtorch.

"How do we know it's your mother?" Fantasy asked. "It could be anyone. It could be DeLuna."

"So. No."

The doorbell rang again.

"Give me the gun." No Hair held out a hand. Fantasy pulled the Hi-Point 9mm from her hip and passed it to him. He popped out the magazine, checked it, slammed it back in, clicked off the safety, tucked it, then said, "Stand back."

We shuffled in reverse.

"This is a tabletop blowtorch." Show and Tell. "It runs on butane or propane and I don't know how much juice it has. For all we know, it's empty."

The doorbell rang again.

"The door is strongest along the perimeter." He said it more to himself than us as he knocked all over the door with his knuckles. "I think getting through the doorknob and keypad is out of the question."

"Burn a smaller door," Fantasy said. "Just..." She traced a frame through the air with her hands. "You know. A smaller door. Like a doggie door."

"That's not a good idea," I said. "If we burn an opening large enough for us to get out it will be large enough for someone else to get in."

Think, think, think, Davis.

I turned to Jess. "Can you get into a bank vault with a blowtorch?"

"No." She tapped her chin. "You'd need a thermal lance. Just know it will reduce anything in the vault to ash. You'll get in, but you'll lose everything: currency, stock certificates, deeds."

Fantasy's jaw dropped. Again.

"How would you break into a vault if you only had a blowtorch?" I asked Jess.

"You'd burn a small circle halfway through, then knock it out."

"So you could reach in?" I asked.

"Yes," Jess said.

"I'm not even believing this," Fantasy mumbled.

"So, what?" Jess asked her.

No Hair was already burning a circle in the middle of the door.

"I need a mirror and something to knock this out with."

Fantasy took off and was right back with her Ming Dynasty antennas and a Bobbi Brown brightening brick in Coral.

"What the hell is this?" No Hair looked at the black square in his hand.

The doorbell rang.

She dropped what used to be a priceless piece of art to the floor and opened the compact for No Hair, the mirror catching the lone ray of sun streaming in from the salon, then bouncing off a crystal in the foyer chandelier and sending a starburst to the ceiling.

"So, wow." Jess's head tipped back.

"What the hell is *that*?" No Hair asked.

"Something to knock a hole in the door with." Fantasy picked up her antennas. "Move," she said.

"Wait!" No Hair motioned Jess and me against the wall.

Fantasy aimed her Ming Dynasty art in the center of the circle, then put all her weight behind it and knocked a saucer-sized hole in the door. No Hair pushed her out of the way and immediately filled the hole with the business end of a semi-automatic pistol.

"Whoa! Whoa!" The voice on the other side of the door was a man's. "Don't shoot! I'm here about a pot roast! Don't shoot!"

"Who are you?" No Hair asked, trying to angle the mirror with his free hand so he could see for himself.

"It's Fredrick Blackwell, No Hair!" It had to be. I jumped to the other side of the hole in the door. "Mr. Blackwell." I stayed away from the hole. Just in case. "Where's my husband?"

"Is your husband on the Gulfstream?"

"Yes!" I had my hands on the babies waiting for news about their father. "Yes!"

"He's on the way," Blackwell said. "A little under two hours out."

"Where's he landing?"

"George Town Municipal."

"Have you talked to him?"

"No, the onboard communication system has been disabled."

Which meant we still didn't know what was going on inside the Gulfstream. Nor did we know exactly who was or wasn't on *Bellissimo One*.

"Where's my mother?"

"Mrs. Way?"

"Yes!" I inched closer to the peephole.

"I'm not sure," Fredrick Blackwell said. "There was an enormous amount of activity in the casino, and last time I saw her she was in the middle of it."

"With Arlinda?" I asked.

"Arlinda is with my wife in our suite. She couldn't get in this room."

No. No, no, no. How did Mother and Arlinda get separated?

"How long has it been since you saw my mother?" I stuck my face in the peephole, and got my first look at Fredrick Blackwell. Who also got his first look at me. And it was a look I knew all too well.

"Oh, holy crap," I said through the big peephole. "You've seen me."

He took a step back, nodding.

"And I'm pregnant?"

"Very," Fredrick Blackwell said.

"Oh, shit." (Fantasy.)

"SO?"

"Bianca Sanders is here, Jess. On the ship."

Fantasy didn't have to explain it to Jess, but she did have to catch her on her way down.

* * *

We interrogated the poor man. Or maybe that was just me. In the end, I asked for one more favor: turn on our electricity.

He looked at his watch. He glanced up and down the passageway. He was on his way to the Jing Ping ferry boats to meet two Federal Aviation Administration supervisors from Fort Worth, Texas, at George Town Municipal Airport for *Bellissimo One's* arrival. The FAA reps told Blackwell he could be there of his own free will or they were coming to get him.

He'd ruffled a few feathers.

Bellissimo One was coming in with military escorts.

This might get ugly.

"How am I supposed to turn on your electricity?" He scratched his neck; he looked up and down the passageway; he inched away.

"Mr. Blackwell, you turned an airplane around. Surely you can turn on our electricity."

He sighed heavily.

"And just one more really small thing," I said.

He rolled his eyes.

"Would you unlock your V2 and let us have it?"

"What do you mean unlock it?"

"Override the thumb swipe."

"Or give us your thumb." (Fantasy.)

Thirty minutes later, we had power. We had Fredrick Blackwell's V2 so we could move around *Probability*, but still no way to get out of our own door.

"Fantasy," No Hair said. "Go get me a miter blade."

"What?"

"The silver Frisbee saw thing," I said.

She took off.

No Hair, in a move I'd give anything to have on video so I could send it to MacGyver, heated a strip of metal teeth with a hiss of orange from the blowtorch, held the saw blade as close to the panel above the doorknob as he could, then tipped it up and tapped once against the sensors. He shot a jolt of heat through so quickly it temporarily short-circuited the keypad. The door popped open.

(Could we have done this two days ago? Seriously? Could we have?)

One thing we couldn't do was wake up Jess, so we piled her on the tool cart and rolled her. It's not like we could leave her in 704 for her outlaw husband to find, because there wasn't a doubt in anyone's mind he was looking for us. We closed the door behind us and heard the gears click into place.

We were now officially locked out of 704. Which felt so different than being locked in.

The first thing that happened was the elevator doors closed and caught a corner of Jess's *Probability* robe. The elevator ate the robe, which left us pushing her around in her rhinestone anchor suit and six-inch silver heels.

* * *

Probability was all but deserted. Scattered staff in spots, but no passengers. The fifty zillionaires and their guests were either in their staterooms, at the garages on the Transportation Deck in line for a Jing Ping ferry, or on the ferries to George Town. We didn't pass anyone who wasn't talking about (Jess on a cart) the Knot on Your Life jackpots. The casino, we overheard, was closed until further notice.

I guess so.

First, we used Fredrick Blackwell's V2 to call Arlinda.

"Davis, I'm sorry," she said. "Have you tried to talk your mother into anything? She absolutely would not leave the casino with me. I *had* to go with Mr. Blackwell. I couldn't be in two places at one time. I had to make a decision between your mother and your husband."

Oh.

"The last time you saw Mother was in the casino?" I asked.

"With Mrs. Sanders," she said.

"Do you have any idea where they went? Did Mother say anything?"

"SO!" Jess's dark hair flew as she tried to figure out (a) where she was, and (b) who we were, and (c) what had happened to her *Probability* robe.

"She said something about the pot roast."

Mother and Bianca Sanders were on their way to 704.

"Let's go." I twirled a finger through the air for No Hair and Fantasy to turn the cart around. "Mother and Bianca are in our room."

"So, where's my shoe?"

I aimed Fredrick Blackwell's V2 at the elevator panel and asked it to take us back to 704.

"So, my shoe?"

"Since she's awake shouldn't we have taken the Zoom?" Fantasy asked.

"Who has my shoe?"

"Where's DeLuna?" No Hair asked.

"Where's anyone?" The mirrored elevator wall held me up. "Where's everyone?"

No Hair put a big arm around me. I dove in. He smelled like rainbow Christmas church trees. "It'll be okay," he said. "We're going to get through this."

The elevator doors parted on Deck Seven. Fantasy pushed the tool cart out, Jess hobbled out, dark hair flying, looking here and there for her other silver shoe. No Hair and I silently brought up the rear, his arm still around my shoulders.

I spotted her from a mile away, standing at the door of 704. There was no missing Bianca Sanders, not even at midnight wearing solid black in the recesses of a cave. There was certainly no mistaking exceptionally pregnant Bianca Sanders dressed in head-to-toe snow white at the end of a brightly lit passageway. She looked like a white teepee or a short white triangle, wearing a blizzard white flowing cape secured at her neck and blooming around her. Her blonde hair was stuffed in a white pill box hat. She was barefoot (and pregnant) holding her white heels with one hand and her other hand was working the doorbell. Before I could get her name out she stepped into 704. With everything I had, I hoped and prayed it wasn't Max DeLuna opening the door.

My prayers were answered.

There's no mistaking the pump of a bolt-action rifle.

"Well, hello, hello."

Max DeLuna.

*   *   *

Instinct dictates a scream-and-run reaction to a gun at your back.

No Hair, Fantasy, and I knew better.

Jess didn't know better; she was so far ahead of us she didn't even hear it and if she had, we might have all died right then and there in the passageway on the seventh deck of *Probability*. She undoubtedly would have had a fit, charged him, and gotten us all killed.

Keep looking for your shoe, Cinderella.

"What do we have here?" DeLuna was smug, confident, and why wouldn't he be. "Hands on your heads."

What do you do when someone has a gun on you? Whatever they say.

Rule number one: Calm. Don't scream, don't run, don't anything. Rule number two: Follow instructions. Rule number three: Don't make any sudden movements. No Hair broke rule number three in the process of following rule number two. He picked me an inch off the floor and planted me down directly in front of him as he moved his arms to place his hands on his head. It was slick and swift and he made himself a human shield for my babies. Fantasy was directly in front of me, which put us in a straight line.

Jess was still wandering the hall in a zigzag path, now much farther ahead, looking for her shoe.

DeLuna had leveraged control over us by virtue of the fact he had a firearm on us, so we had to take psychological control. First, by making him look at us.

"Can we turn around?" No Hair wasn't asking for permission; he was telling us to turn around. Which we did. Hands on heads. Now I was behind No Hair instead of in front of him.

DeLuna was still firmly in control, but now he was

uncomfortable, because it's a lot harder to shoot someone you're looking at. Then, it occurred to him he couldn't shoot three people at once. He assessed his situation, glancing at his gun, trading his cocky posture for defensive, probably realizing it would take a rocket launcher to shoot through us while we were lined up three deep. "Move where I can see you."

Together, we took a step to the right.

"Move apart."

We took a step to the left.

He rolled his eyes. "You, here. You, there." Fantasy and I split. He used the barrel of the gun as a pointer. "You stay right where you are." DeLuna tapped No Hair's heart with the gun.

"Do you want to do this?"

No Hair kept his voice low, his tone nonthreatening, everything about him tranquil and soothing as he used his elbows to point out the light fixtures above our heads hiding surveillance cameras, drawing DeLuna's attention to the fact he'd never get away with it.

DeLuna blinked. And with the blink, he reconsidered killing us.

Our next move was to show DeLuna ways out of the predicament he found himself in that, clearly, he hadn't thought all the way through. We'd present him with alternatives to (our sudden deaths) violence, remind him this was about money, something we could possibly help him with, but we never got the chance. Jess finally realized we weren't with her and turned around. I don't know if she could see her husband, but it was obvious he saw her. And there went our dialogue with the gunman.

It happened so fast. DeLuna forgot all about us as he leveled the gun on his wife.

Rule number four: When all else fails, surprise the gunslinger. I yelled, "We have Poppy!"

In the split second DeLuna stopped to hear Poppy's name, No Hair dropped into a barrel roll and took him down. I got myself and my babies out of the way as Fantasy rushed past with the cart and pinned him to the wall. No Hair disarmed DeLuna and turned the gun on him so fast it was nothing but a flash of cold steel.

We had him.

It was over.

We had DeLuna.

"*Hey!*"

No Hair didn't take his eyes off DeLuna, but Fantasy and I turned to the sound of my mother's voice, our eyes passing over a sleeping stack of Jessica on the floor.

"Get in here!" Mother yelled down the passageway. "Her water broke!"

TWENTY-FIVE

I'd been an officer on the Pine Apple Police Force (of two) for about ten (minutes) months when the phone rattled on the desk and woke me up from a great nap on a steaming hot Friday night in July. Without lifting my head, I batted for the receiver, thinking it would be my father telling me I could lock up and go home early. It wasn't. It was Hanny Conklin, who lived in a trailer park off Freedom Farm Road with his wife Effie and their seven children. He called to say number eight was on the way with a bullet.

"What, Hanny? *What?*"

"Effie's dropping the baby."

Who has a bullet? Who dropped a baby?

I shook myself awake and we started over. Hanny was calling for police escort to the Women's Health Clinic in Luverne, Alabama.

"Hanny." It was almost midnight. "There are ten hospitals between here and Luverne. It's on the other side of the interstate."

"I know where it is, Davis. We go there ever nine months."

You'd think, the Conklins being frequent flyers and all, that someone at the Women's Health Clinic would sit them down for a family planning chat.

"She's about to spit it out. We gotta go, Davis."

"If she's about to spit out a baby, Hanny, why are you still at home talking to me?"

"I'm not home. I'm at Bubba Phil's using the phone."

Oh, good grief. Bubba Phil Wilson lived twenty trailers away. Everyone in Shady Acres Mobile Home Estates had a television the size of a barn door and forty-inch tires on their trucks, but only one or two had phones. "Get her loaded, Hanny, head this way. I'll be ready. But we're not going to Luverne," I said. "We're going to Kizzy."

"Oh, *hell* no. I'll let Kizzy touch my wife when *pigs* fly."

We had one doctor in Pine Apple. Three hundred and ninety-nine of four hundred residents wouldn't go to Dr. Kizzy for a Band-Aid, much less procreation.

"Then we're going to Stabler Memorial in Greenville," I said. "They deliver babies all day, Hanny. We can get there in fifteen minutes."

"We're in*dig*nant care, Davis." He was getting short with me. Very short. As if I was part of the indignant problem. "It's Luverne or the side of the road."

As it turned out, it was the side of the road. Effie delivered her fifth daughter in the back of my patrol car on the corner of West 3rd and Montgomery Highway, and I did the honors.

My mother knew this. And she ratted me out.

We stood outside Mother's stateroom, Bianca inside, but we had to wait to discuss it until the howling on the other side of the door tapered off enough for us to hear each other.

"I am *not* going in there," Fantasy whispered.

I whispered back, "You big chicken."

"Hey." Fantasy shook her finger at Mother's door. "That's your problem."

"She's *not* my problem," I loud whispered. "She *fired* me."

"I don't work for her in the first place, Davis. I work for *you.*"

"Well, you're fired if you don't go in there with me."

"Fine by me." Fantasy crossed her arms. "Burger King, here I come."

Mother was between us. I wasn't getting anywhere with Fantasy so I tried her. "What happened? She was standing in the casino an hour ago and now she's having a baby?"

Mother shrugged. "Tale as old as time. Her water broke. She's in labor."

"What happened in between the casino and her water breaking?"

"She marched into that casino like she owned the place."

Not the least bit surprising.

"Which was a good thing," Mother said. "Because that craydirt man was gunning for *me* 'til he saw *her*."

"Slow down, Mother. What happened? Is this when the slot machines hit?"

"Boy howdy, did they ever." She had the jackpot look, a look I knew well, but never dreamed I'd see on Mother. "I did just what you told me. Popped that thing in there." She demonstrated. "Those gambling machines, every one of them, had conniption fits. First a gold anchor showed up, and it went DING DING." Mother did a little ding-ding dance. "Then another gold anchor, ding-ding, then another gold anchor, ding-ding, then BOOM!"

I rolled my hands, hurrying Mother along.

"Oh, Davis, everyone was so happy." Mother clapped her hands. "Then here comes craybitch, poking through the crowd looking for *me* until he saw *her*." Mother pointed at the door. "I grabbed her and said, 'Come on, Stuck Up.'"

"You called her Stuck Up?" Fantasy asked.

"I couldn't remember her name right off the bat," Mother explained. "There was a lot going on with those anchors." Mother did her jackpot dance. "Ding ding. And she is stuck up."

"You did the right thing, Mother."

"Well, except for I let the cat out of the bag."

"What cat?" Fantasy checked our immediate area for Anderson Cooper.

"She asked about her suitcases and I told her most of them were gone."

There's another problem solved. We had DeLuna and the Louis Vuitton news had been broken to Bianca. Now, if I could find my husband and get off this damn ship, maybe I could live the rest of my life.

"Then, Mother?" How long was this story?

"I told her to wait at the elevator and I'd see about the suitcases," Mother said, "but that was a lie. I really wanted to check on my pot ro—"

Mother stopped mid-roast. Or, rather, Bianca stopped her mid-roast. We'd been discussing how this nightmare transpired and who was going in for just about two minutes when from the other side of the door, Bianca began working up a shriek. I clocked her. After forty-five seconds she hit the top and began squealing her way down.

"What is she saying?" Fantasy asked.

"It sounds like she's saying giddy up." Mother cocked an ear. "Giddy *up*! Giddy *up*!"

"Oh, holy crap." I stared at my watch. "Her contractions are two minutes apart and they're lasting a minute. She's going to have that baby."

"There's a helicopter."

I looked at Mother, trying to figure out what a helicopter had to do with anything.

"She got here in a helicopter," Mother said.

"Let's get her back to the helicopter." Fantasy liked the idea.

"And let her have her baby in a helicopter?" I looked at my watch again. "I don't think you two get it. Her contractions are right on top of each other. She's having this baby. I don't think we can move her an inch."

"Well, you'd know," Mother said.

There was way too much going on for me to know exactly what Mother was talking about. I'd know because I'm pregnant? Because I had a baby eighteen years, two months, and six days ago? Because I'd taken a ten-minute first aid and CPR course a million years ago in Officer Basic Course Training?

"Remember Effie Conklin?" Mother asked. "You delivered her baby."

Fantasy poked my arm.

"Gotcha! Go for it, Dr. Davis."

I couldn't wait to see Fantasy in a Burger King uniform.

Bianca, from the other side of the door, said, "Chugga, chugga, chugga, CHUGGAAAAAA!"

"Oh, boy," Mother said. "You better get in there."

I put my hand on the doorknob, squared my shoulders, looked them both in the eye, and told them they were going to be sorry.

I cracked the door. "Bianca?"

"DAVID!"

* * *

Mother ran her legs off gathering childbirthing this and that—ice cubes, pool towels, boiling water. ("Why are you boiling water, Mother?" "Well, because." "Mother, we don't need boiling water unless someone wants pasta." "We're having pot roast, Davis.") And she fed me information through the crack in the door. No Hair had DeLuna secured on the sunporch. Fantasy was on one of our V2 phones with George Town Municipal Airport waiting for news on Bradley and Baylor and at the same time, running all over Probability looking for a doctor. That left Mother to assist the midwife.

And by midwife, I mean me.

"Mother, go to my room—"

"WOULD YOU LOWER YOUR VOICE, DAVID? I CAN NOT HEAR MYSELF DYING!"

Bianca's white pill box hat had slipped from the top of her head and was clapped over her left ear. I don't know how she could hear me whispering to Mother.

"IF YOU'RE GOING TO TALK TO ANYONE IT HAD BETTER BE MY HUUUUUUUSSSSBAAAAAND!"

Then Bianca did a full-on back bend in the bed, soundtrack Poltergeist.

I spoke through the crack. "Mother, where's your portable phone?"

"In my pocketbook."

"Bring it to me." You bet I'd get her huuuuuuusssssbaaaand on the phone. "And dig through my clothes for something I can change her into."

Mother shuffled off. When she returned I had to get Bianca out of her ten miles of chiffon dress so I could get her into my maternity sleepshirt. It took four contractions to get her out of the white cape and into the t-shirt because I had to stop for her to yell, "GLUGGA! GLUGGA! GLUUUUGGA!" and "SWROUP! SWROUP! SWROOOOUP!" I worked fast before another one hit, shaking out the t-shirt and pulling it over her head, and when I did, I knew this would be my last day on earth after all. Printed across the front in big purple letters were the words I ATE THE WORM.

Then the miracle of childbirth was put on hold while I enjoyed the miracle of communication with a human not on *Probability*. I flipped open Mother's old phone, dialed Richard Sanders's number, and I almost fell to the floor when he answered.

I paced back and forth at the foot of the bed with Mother's impossible phone. The first thing I intended to do if I ever got off this ship was buy her a new one and donate the old one to a history museum.

"I'd have never left if I had any idea she would go into labor, Davis."

"I know, Mr. Sanders. I'm sure she knows that too."

"RICHARD, I AM *LEAVING* YOU! DO YOU HEAR ME? I WANT A *DIVORCE*! AND *DRUGS*! DAVID, GET ME NARCOTICS!"

"Bianca?" I pulled the phone away from my head. "You need to calm down. For Ondine's sake."

"What *happened*?" Mr. Sanders asked. "The last person I talked to before I left was Dr. Durrance. She assured me at the rate Bianca was going there might not be a baby in a *month*."

"Because she's been so sedentary, Mr. Sanders. I guess the minute she got out of bed and started moving she went into labor."

"KOOVA! KOOVA! KOOOOOOVVVVVA!"

I needed out of the room to talk to Mr. Sanders, to ask what he knew about her blood pressure, her gestational diabetes, and the apparent loss of all her mental faculties, but Bianca wouldn't let me out of her sight.

When we'd talked for two minutes, Mr. Sanders assuring me he'd get here as fast as God and Gulfstream would let him, but considering the fact he was still in China, it wouldn't be anytime soon. Then he asked to speak to his wife.

"Bianca?"

"WHAAAAAT?"

I turned my head for one minute, then looked back to find Bianca backwards, facing the headboard, riding the bed like a pony, spread eagle with one foot off one side of the bed, one foot off the other. I cocked my head one way, then the other, trying to figure out how she'd assumed that pose.

"Mr. Sanders wants to speak to you."

Blond hair flew. "YOU TELL HIM TO KISS MY ASS! PARUNKK! PARUNKK! PAR*UUUUUNK*!"

Oh, someone save me.

"Mr. Sanders," I said, "she can't talk right now."

"I heard."

He asked to speak to No Hair, so I stuck my head out the door and watched for Mother to waddle down the hall. Anything to keep from watching Bianca buck on the bed. No Mother. I held the phone behind me and yelled, "Mother!"

"I'm coming!"

She peeked in the door. "Heavens to Betsy. What in the world is she doing?"

"GUANTAAA! GUANTAAA! GU*AAAANNNNN*TAAA!"

Mother shuffled off with the phone just as Fantasy rounded the corner in a dead heat. She bent over, head hanging, hands to knees with the news. "There isn't a doctor on this boat. Not one."

"ZUZZZA! ZUZZZA! ZU*UUUZZZZZ*A!"

"God almighty." Fantasy raised up, got a peek at Bianca, then crossed herself. We watched Bianca's head spin for a minute, I crossed myself too, I'm not even Catholic.

"Have you gone down there yet?" Fantasy whispered.

"What?"

"You know."

"No, I don't know."

"Have you looked?" she asked.

"At what?"

"You know."

"No, Fantasy, I don't know."

"Yes, you do."

What? *No!* "NO!" I smacked her. "Sick!"

"You have to take a peek, Davis."

"Oh, hell no, I don't!"

Mother turned the corner at a full gallop. "We have a problem."

Exactly what we needed.

"I gave Big Guy No Hair my portable phone." Mother was patting her chest and panting. "And the next thing I knew, So and So was in my pocketbook. She got the gun. Davis, she's going to kill that little weasel crayman."

"Mother, listen to me." I grabbed her forearms. "Go to the kitchen, close the door, and stay there until one of us tells you it's clear to come out. Do you understand?"

She understood. I turned around to find Bianca on her back, her head hanging off the foot of the bed. We looked at each other upside down. "David." She wasn't screaming. In fact, I could barely hear her. "Please don't leave me."

"I won't, Bianca."

TWENTY-SIX

No Hair had secured DeLuna to a sun chair and the chair to the iron bistro table, the same table we sat around two (years) days ago when our V2s went down. DeLuna's hands were cuffed behind the chair, his feet strapped to the frame. He wasn't going anywhere, and if he did it would be over the deck railing with a chair and a table to splat on the deck below. He was bound, gagged, and out of the way until Jess, just up from a nap, stared at the butt of the Hi-Point 9mm peeking out of Mother's pocketbook too long. No Hair stepped out of the salon to talk to Mr. Sanders, leaving Jess staring at Mother's pocketbook so long she came up with a bright idea. And now she had her bright idea pressed against her husband's left temple.

Bianca was in the middle of the bed on all fours, soundtrack, *The Blair Witch Project*.

I looked at the second hand on my watch, knowing another contraction would hit her in twenty seconds, long enough for me to step out on Mother's balcony and access the situation on the sun deck. I slid open the doors, keeping one foot in the bedroom with Bianca, the other firmly planted on the deck. A welcome gust of Caribbean breeze blew through me and hit Bianca in the face.

"Oh, thank you, David."

Words I'd never heard pass the woman's lips.

The next words from her lips were, "MY LOINS HAVE IGNITED! IGNITED! I'M ON FIRE! HIT ME WITH A HOSE, DAVID! PUT OUT THE FIRE! THE *FIRE*!"

"Bianca?" I waited for the storm to subside before I spoke.

"You need to rest between contractions. And *please* try to pipe down." Because you have no idea what's going on right outside this door, one of your outbursts might trigger more bloodshed, and you're totally out of trunks.

I stuck my head out the door.

"Young lady, you don't want to do this."

No Hair was negotiating with Jessica.

"I do. I want to so hard."

I couldn't see or hear DeLuna.

"Have you ever shot a gun?" No Hair asked her.

"No."

"It's messy, Jessica. It's ugly," No Hair told her. "You'll be covered in his blood."

Jess looked down at her rhinestone anchor.

"Let me have the gun." No Hair extended an open palm. "Give it to me."

My heart jumped in my throat when Jess turned to answer No Hair and the gun went with her, the death end flailing in No Hair's general vicinity.

"JESS!" I drew her attention and the gun away.

"So, Davis?" I could see the sun glinting off the gun. A flash of it hit me in the eyes. "I'm going to kill him!"

"JOOOOBAA! JOOOOBAA! *JOOOO*OBAAAAAA!"

Someone help me.

"Jess?" Fantasy stepped onto the sun deck from my stateroom. Now we had her surrounded. "Let's rest a minute. Close our eyes and think about it. Maybe sit down, relax, and talk about it."

I smelled a lullaby on the way.

"*HEEY*A HEEYA HEEYA HEEYA!"

(Squatting. She was up on her haunches. I cut my eyes to see Bianca squatting in the middle of the bed, rocking on her feet, side to side, chanting to the childbirth spirits.)

Nothing was working. No Hair couldn't talk the gun away from her and Fantasy couldn't put her to sleep.

It was up to me.

"JESS! 2008! The financial crisis! What happened in 2008?" I shouted over "HEEYA HEEYA," the wind, and the deck.

Her dark hair whipped around her head, the 9mm finding everyone when she used her gun hand to push it out of her face. Fantasy gasped and No Hair dove out of the line of fire.

"*The collapse!*" Jess waved the gun through the air. "*The bailout!*"

And with that, Jess's anger was temporarily redirected.

"WHY?" I asked, *The Exorcist* playing out behind me.

"Banks didn't support transparency for hedge funds! Mortgage bankers didn't obtain financial statements! Subprime loans were out of control!" No Hair took a tentative step toward Jess. "Mark to market accounting rules weren't followed! And there was no regulation of credit default swaps!" No Hair and Fantasy closed in on her as Jessica got the last of the Banking Collapse of 2008 off her chest. "Anti-predatory state laws were *overridden!*" Jessica DeLuna, dark hair flying, wearing a rhinestone anchor and one silver shoe, wielding a gun, screaming at the top of her lungs for all of the Caribbean to hear, unleashed the financial devastation anger she'd held for years.

"But what was the *real* problem, Jess? Whose fault was it? What went *wrong?*"

I don't remember moving, but I was all the way out of Mother's room at the edge of the balcony. "Where was the *failure*, Jess?"

"Leadership!" Jess waved the gun through the air to make her point. "Total and complete lack of *leadership!*"

"POOOKALOO! POOOKALOO! POOOOKALOOOOO!"

"You're the leader, Jess! *You* have to lead! Put that gun down and take back your bank!"

"My bank! My bank! *My* bank!"

Just then, Max DeLuna weighed in. He couldn't have managed words, and if he did say something through the gag she understood, I didn't hear it. He must have sneered—at her, at the idea. It was just a flash, but the end result destroyed our collective attempts at defusing the situation, and the barrel of the gun was making an impression on Max DeLuna again. Right between his eyes.

"You *bastard*," she said.

Now that I heard.

"Jess!"

She wouldn't look at me.

"If you shoot him—" I gave every word the time and attention it deserved, "—he won't go to prison for what he's done. *You* will."

In the end, it wasn't the prospect of her life over just for the satisfaction of ending his, or the idea of returning to Hawaii and taking her rightful place at her father's bank that loosened Jessica's grip on the gun. It was Anderson Cooper. My cat launched through the air like a missile to catch Jess's soaring hair. Jess screamed, Anderson screamed, and the gun hit the deck to skid and spin to a stop at Fantasy's feet.

The reading chair on Mother's balcony caught me when I stumbled back. My head was thick with the close call, my heart hammering, and it was with glazed eyes I watched No Hair and Fantasy scramble to lock everything and everyone down.

"Davis?"

Then I began hallucinating.

"Davis, honey?"

It was my husband.

✳ ✳ ✳

I thought she might be singing a Christmas carol.

The lyrics to Bianca's song sounded like, "*On Dasher, on Dancer!*"

She was actually belting out the word *Ondine*, opera style, hitting a very impressive range.

We were as far from Bianca's birth plan as could be imagined in any of her wildest dreams or my worst nightmares and there was no going back. Bianca was bringing her baby into the world aboard *Probability*.

After the kiss to surpass all other kisses in the history of kisses, Bradley Cole, my husband, the father of my twins, told Bianca he liked her t-shirt on his way to Mother's powder room, where he rolled up his blue oxford sleeves and scrubbed.

My legs were too weak to hold me up, so I sat on the bed beside Bianca and found her hand. She asked me why I was crying—I didn't know I was—her breath ragged, her blond hair plastered to her face, her icy green eyes seeking mine. After her next contraction, during which she fractured all the bones in my hand, she told me to stop crying, because she might reconsider my employment at some point in the future.

"What, Bianca?"

She started to repeat it, but said, "UUUUGAAAKK! UUUGAAAAKK! *UUUUGAAAAAAKKKK!*" instead.

Bradley lifted a chair over our heads, placed it at the foot of the bed, grabbed Bianca by the ankles and pulled.

She let out a woof.

"Let's do this, Bianca."

At the door, Baylor, a head taller than the rest of the spectators seeing way more of Bianca than they wanted to, said, "Dude." Then introduced himself to Arlinda.

(Really? Right now?)

Bradly asked for volunteers from the audience. "Caroline? Fantasy?"

Mother and Fantasy climbed on the bed with us. Each took a Bianca knee.

I held my breath until Bradley came up for air. "She's crowning. This baby's coming. Help her, Davis. Get behind her." His incredible blue eyes met mine.

Which was when Bianca started singing Christmas carols.

I held my breath, Bianca belted out opera, until my husband made the announcement.

"It's a...boy?"

Bianca fell back and collapsed into my arms. I pushed her hair from her face.

"It's a *boy*," he said. Mother helped Bradley wrap the beautiful little life in a *Probability* towel. "Bianca, you have a baby boy."

Richard and Bianca Sanders named their son David.

* * *

Emmeline. My daughter's name was Emmeline.

Having said goodbye to her when she was an hour old at the UAB Women and Infants Center in Birmingham, Alabama, I said hello to her again eighteen years, two months, and thirteen days later at my childhood home in Pine Apple, Alabama. It was forever, holding on for dear life, lest the connection that had escaped us once slip away again, before either of us spoke. And when we did, they weren't exactly words. It would be four hours later when Emi and I finally stepped out of my high-school bedroom. We let Mother in and out with cookies, the Starbucks, and random pieces of life to share with Emi. "This—" she landed a stack of photographs of my ex-ex-husband Eddie Crawford on Emi's lap, "—is who would've raised you."

"*Mother!*" I grabbed them. "Are you trying to scare her to death?"

Between us, my beautiful firstborn, who I'd already told about my misguided attempt to keep her by marrying the village idiot, tried to hide her amusement, her caramel eyes dancing between me and my wildly inappropriate mother.

"Well, Davis, she needs to know what you saved her from."

And who would ever save *me* from *her*?

Which is when I realized, the three of us on the pink eyelet bedspread Mother had tucked me under as a child, I never needed to be saved from my mother. In fact, the only path to being the mother I wanted to be, both from this point forward with Emi and with the twins I would soon deliver, was *through* my own mother.

I wasn't the only one acknowledging Mother's maternal gifts. In the hours after young David Sanders's birth, while the rest of us were busy with the U.S. Consulate in George Town as they took

Max DeLuna and Colby Mitchell into custody to await extradition, Mother stayed with Bianca. And from that moment 'til this one Bianca has called every ten minutes. To speak to my mother. "I'm sorry, David. She knows more than you." To which Mother says, "It's what's been wrong with her all along, Davis. She never had a mother who mothered her, so she's doesn't know *how*."

The mothering came full circle three months later on a Thursday morning.

I woke up in labor, slow and steady, at the beginning of my thirty-eighth week. It would be hours before my contractions were strong enough to leave for the hospital.

Bradley, in a flurry of last-minute overseeing operations of a $700 million corporation, told us he'd be right back. "Reggie and Fantasy will be here in a minute, girls, and Pine Apple, Alabama, all of Pine Apple, is on the way." He sat on the edge of our bed and laced his fingers in mine. "Promise me you won't have our babies until I get back." He kissed my forehead.

"I promise."

Emi took his place beside me with a watch in one hand, to time my contractions, and *The Compass* in the other. I didn't even know I brought it home, the big blue leather-bound component of our escape. Emi opened it to find the only physical evidence of our time on *Probability*. She showed it to me. We smiled at the picture of Mother in her Party Suit.

Emi flipped through. "This is so cool." Her voice a whisper. "The dishwasher."

"What?"

"Where they put the dishwasher," she said.

"Let me see that, Emi."

The white stone waterfall-edge countertop to the right of the sink disappeared with the push of a button. And there was the dishwasher.

Gretchen Archer

Gretchen Archer is a Tennessee housewife who began writing when her daughters, seeking higher educations, ran off and left her. She lives on Lookout Mountain with her husband, son, and a Yorkie named Bently. *Double Whammy*, her first Davis Way Crime Caper, was a Daphne du Maurier Award finalist and hit the USA TODAY Bestsellers List. *Double Knot* is the fifth Davis Way crime caper. You can visit her at www.gretchenarcher.com.

The Davis Way Crime Caper Series
By Gretchen Archer

DOUBLE WHAMMY (#1)
DOUBLE DIP (#2)
DOUBLE STRIKE (#3)
DOUBLE MINT (#4)
DOUBLE KNOT (#5)

Available at booksellers nationwide and online

Visit www.henerypress.com for details

Henery Press Mystery Books

And finally, before you go...
Here are a few other mysteries
you might enjoy:

BOARD STIFF

Kendel Lynn

An Elliott Lisbon Mystery (#1)

As director of the Ballantyne Foundation on Sea Pine Island, SC, Elliott Lisbon scratches her detective itch by performing discreet inquiries for Foundation donors. Usually nothing more serious than retrieving a pilfered Pomeranian. Until Jane Hatting, Ballantyne board chair, is accused of murder. The Ballantyne's reputation tanks, Jane's headed to a jail cell, and Elliott's sexy ex is the new lieutenant in town.

Armed with moxie and her Mini Coop, Elliott uncovers a trail of blackmail schemes, gambling debts, illicit affairs, and investment scams. But the deeper she digs to clear Jane's name, the guiltier Jane looks. The closer she gets to the truth, the more treacherous her investigation becomes. With victims piling up faster than shells at a clambake, Elliott realizes she's next on the killer's list.

Available at booksellers nationwide and online

Visit www.henerypress.com for details

PILLOW STALK

Diane Vallere

A Madison Night Mystery (#1)

Interior Decorator Madison Night might look like a throwback to the sixties, but as business owner and landlord, she proves that independent women can have it all. But when a killer targets women dressed in her signature style—estate sale vintage to play up her resemblance to fave actress Doris Day—what makes her unique might make her dead.

The local detective connects the new crime to a twenty-year old cold case, and Madison's long-trusted contractor emerges as the leading suspect. As the body count piles up, Madison uncovers a Soviet spy, a campaign to destroy all Doris Day movies, and six minutes of film that will change her life forever.

Available at booksellers nationwide and online

Visit www.henerypress.com for details

LOWCOUNTRY BOIL

Susan M. Boyer

A Liz Talbot Mystery (#1)

Private Investigator Liz Talbot is a modern Southern belle: she blesses hearts and takes names. She carries her Sig 9 in her Kate Spade handbag, and her golden retriever, Rhett, rides shotgun in her hybrid Escape. When her grandmother is murdered, Liz hightails it back to her South Carolina island home to find the killer.

She's fit to be tied when her police-chief brother shuts her out of the investigation, so she opens her own. Then her long-dead best friend pops in and things really get complicated. When more folks start turning up dead in this small seaside town, Liz must use more than just her wits and charm to keep her family safe, chase down clues from the hereafter, and catch a psychopath before he catches her.

Available at booksellers nationwide and online

Visit www.henerypress.com for details

THE DEEP END

Julie Mulhern

The Country Club Murders (#1)

Swimming into the lifeless body of her husband's mistress tends to ruin a woman's day, but becoming a murder suspect can ruin her whole life.

It's 1974 and Ellison Russell's life revolves around her daughter and her art. She's long since stopped caring about her cheating husband, Henry, and the women with whom he entertains himself. That is, until she becomes a suspect in Madeline Harper's death. The murder forces Ellison to confront her husband's proclivities and his crimes—kinky sex, petty cruelties and blackmail.

As the body count approaches par on the seventh hole, Ellison knows she has to catch a killer. But with an interfering mother, an adoring father, a teenage daughter, and a cadre of well-meaning friends demanding her attention, can Ellison find the killer before he finds her?

Available at booksellers nationwide and online

Visit www.henerypress.com for details

FIXIN' TO DIE

Tonya Kappes

A Kenni Lowry Mystery (#1)

Kenni Lowry likes to think the zero crime rate in Cottonwood, Kentucky is due to her being sheriff, but she quickly discovers the ghost of her grandfather, the town's previous sheriff, has been scaring off any would-be criminals since she was elected. When the town's most beloved doctor is found murdered on the very same day as a jewelry store robbery, and a mysterious symbol ties the crime scenes together, Kenni must satisfy her hankerin' for justice by nabbing the culprits.

With the help of her Poppa, a lone deputy, and an annoyingly cute, too-big-for-his-britches State Reserve officer, Kenni must solve both cases and prove to the whole town, and herself, that she's worth her salt before time runs out.

Available at booksellers nationwide and online

Visit www.henerypress.com for details

CPSIA information can be obtained
at www.ICGtesting.com
Printed in the USA
LVOW13s1524150617

538255LV00009B/552/P